CRITICAL ACCL

JACOB THE LIAR

"Challenged by the author's gift for storytelling, the reader will be grateful for Becker's courage to reenter a past that refuses to be sealed."
—Elie Wiesel

"Moving . . . almost hallucinatory . . . gives voice to a grief beyond words."
—*Publishers Weekly*

"Harrowing and hilarious . . . provokes a powerful emotional resonance."
—*The Boston Globe*

"Moving, funny, terrifying, and true in tone and heart . . . The greatest Jewish novel written in postwar Germany is finally available in a translation to match its brilliance and spirit."
—Sander L. Gilman, former president of the Modern Language Association and author of *Jewish Self-Hatred*, and Henry R. Luce, professor of Liberal Arts, University of Chicago

"One of the neglected masterpieces of Holocaust literature."
—Lothar Kahn, author of *Between Two Worlds: A History of German Jewish Literature*

JUREK BECKER is one of Germany's most renowned postwar writers. He was a Holocaust survivor, and is the author of the novels *Sleepless Days* and *Bronstein's Children*.

Jacob the Liar

Jurek Becker

Translated from the German by Leila Vennewitz

A PLUME BOOK

PLUME
Published by the Penguin Group
Penguin Putnam Inc., 375 Hudson Street, New York, New York 10014, U.S.A.
Penguin Books Ltd, 27 Wrights Lane, London W8 5TZ, England
Penguin Books Australia Ltd, Ringwood, Victoria, Australia
Penguin Books Canada Ltd, 10 Alcorn Avenue, Toronto, Ontario, Canada M4V 3B2
Penguin Books (N.Z.) Ltd, 182–190 Wairau Road, Auckland 10, New Zealand

Penguin Books Ltd, Registered Offices: Harmondsworth, Middlesex, England

Published by Plume, a member of Penguin Putnam Inc.

This is an authorized reprint of a hardcover edition published by Arcade Publishing, Inc.
For information address Arcade Publishing, Inc., 141 Fifth Avenue, New York, New York 10010.

First Plume Printing, September, 1999

10 9 8 7 6 5 4 3 2 1

℗ REGISTERED TRADEMARK—MARCA REGISTRADA

LIBRARY OF CONGRESS CATALOGING-IN-PUBLICATION DATA
Becker, Jurek.
  [Jakob der Lügner. English]
  Jacob the liar / Jurek Becker ; translated from the German by Leila Vennewitz.
      p.   cm.
  ISBN: 0-452-28170-9
    1. Holocaust, Jewish (1939-1945)—Fiction.   2. World War, 1939-1945—Germany—
  Fiction.   3. Jews—Germany—Fiction.   I. Vennewitz, Leila.   II. Title.
  PT2662.E294J313   1997
  833'.914—dc21   97-23038
                                                                                    CIP

Printed in the United States of America

PUBLISHER'S NOTE
This novel is a work of fiction. Names, characters, places, and incidents either are the prod-
ucts of the author's imagination or are used fictitiously, and any resemblance to actual persons, living or dead, business establishments, events, or locales is entirely coincidental.

Translator's Acknowledgment

My husband William has contributed his knowledge and patience unstintingly to the work of this translation, and for this I warmly thank him.

JACOB THE LIAR

I can already hear everyone saying, A tree? So what's a tree — a trunk, leaves, roots, some beetles in the bark, and a shapely crown at best; so? I can hear them saying, Don't you have anything better to think about to give you that rapturous look like a hungry goat being shown a nice juicy bunch of grass? Or maybe you mean one tree in particular, a special one that for all I know gave its name to a battle, the Battle of the Black Pine, say, do you mean one like that? Or was someone special hanged from it? No, not even that? Oh, all right, it seems pretty inane, but if you get such a kick out of it, we can go on playing this silly game for a while, it's up to you. Maybe you mean that soft sound people call rustling, when the wind has found your tree and improvises a tune on it? Or do you mean the number of board feet your tree yields? Or the well-known shade it casts? It's a funny thing, but at the very mention of shade everyone thinks of trees, although buildings or blast furnaces cast much more shade. Do you mean the shade?

No, all wrong, I say then, you can stop guessing, you'll never get it. I don't mean any of that, although its heating potential is not to be sneezed at. Quite simply, I mean a tree. I have my reasons. First of all, trees have played a certain role in my life, a role I may be overestimating, but that's how it appears to me. When I was nine I fell out of a tree, an apple tree incidentally, and broke my left hand. It healed up fairly well, though there are a few intricate movements I can no longer perform with my left hand. I mention this merely because it had always been taken for granted that I would one day be a violinist, but that's really not important. First my mother had the idea, then my father wanted it too, and finally all three of us wanted it. So, not a violinist.

A few years later, I must have been about seventeen, I lay for the first time in my life with a girl, under a tree. This time it was a beech tree, a good fifty feet tall. The girl's name was Esther — no, Moira, I think — at any rate it was a beech tree, and a wild boar disturbed us. Could have been more than one, we didn't have time to look back. Then a few years later my wife, Hannah, was executed under a tree. I can't say what kind of tree that one was, I wasn't there, I was just told about it, and I forgot to ask about the tree.

And now the second reason why I get that rapturous look when I think about that tree — probably or even certainly the more important reason of the two. It so happens that trees are not allowed in this ghetto (Ordinance 31: "It is strictly prohibited to maintain any kind of ornamental or edible plants within the confines of the ghetto. The same applies to *trees*. Should any wild plants have been overlooked during the establishment of the ghetto, these are to be removed immediately. Offenders will be . . .").

Hardtloff dreamed this up, God knows why, perhaps because of the birds. Countless other things are prohibited too, of course — rings and other valuable objects, keeping pets, being out on the street after eight at night — there's no sense in listing them all. I try to picture what would happen to a person who, wearing a ring, is found with a dog on the street after eight P.M. Actually no, I don't try to picture that at all. I don't even think about rings or dogs or the time of day. I think only of this tree, and my eyes get that rapturous look. I can see their point of view, I mean, theoretically I can understand it: You are Jews, you are less than dirt, why do you need rings, why do you have to hang about on the street after eight P.M.? We have such and such plans for you and intend to carry them out in such and such a way. I can see their point of view; I weep over it, I would kill them all if I could, I would wring Hardtloff's neck with this left hand of mine whose fingers can no longer perform intricate movements; still, I can see the logic of it. But why do they forbid us to have trees?

I've tried hundreds of times to unload this blasted story, without success. Either I tried it with the wrong people, or I made some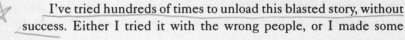

mistake or other. I mixed up a lot of things, I got names wrong, or, as I said, they were the wrong people. Every time I have a few drinks, it comes up again; I can't help myself. I mustn't drink so much. Every time I think these must be the right people, and I think I've got it all nicely together, nothing can go wrong when I tell it.

Yet Jacob, to look at him, isn't the least bit like a tree. There are men, after all, whom one might describe as "sturdy as an oak," tall, strong, a bit awe inspiring, men one would like to lean against every day for a few minutes. Jacob is much shorter; he'd hardly reach the shoulder of any sturdy oak of a fellow. He is scared like all the rest of us, he is really no different from Kirschbaum or Frankfurter or me or Kowalski. The only thing that distinguishes him from the rest of us is that without him, this whole damn story could never have happened. But even there one can be of two minds.

So it is evening. Don't ask the exact time, only the Germans know that; we have no clocks or watches. It's been dark for some time now, a few windows show light: that's all I can tell you. Jacob is hurrying, there's not much time left, it's been dark for quite a while. Then suddenly there's no time at all, not even half a second, for there he is, bathed in light. This happens right in the middle of the street, the Kurländischer Damm, close to the ghetto boundary where most of the tailors used to be located. There stands the sentry, fifteen feet above Jacob, on a wooden tower behind the barbed wire stretched clear across the street. At first the sentry says nothing, just holds Jacob in the beam of his searchlight, right there in the middle of the street, waiting. To the left, on the corner, is what used to be the store belonging to Mariutan, an immigrant Romanian who has meanwhile returned to Romania to safeguard the interests of his country at the front. And on the right is the business that used to belong to Tintenfass, a local Jew now living in Brooklyn, New York, who continues to make high-class ladies' dresses. And between them, standing on the cobblestones and alone with his fear, is Jacob Heym, really too old for such a test of nerves. He snatches off his cap, can't make out a thing in the light; all he knows is that somewhere behind this dazzle are

two soldier's eyes that have found him. Jacob mentally runs through
all the obvious transgressions and can't think of any he has committed. He has his identity card on him, he hasn't been absent from
work, the yellow star on his chest is on exactly the prescribed spot —
he glances down at it again — and he sewed on the one for his back
only two days ago. If the man doesn't shoot right away, Jacob can
answer all his questions satisfactorily: just let him ask.

"Am I mistaken, or is it forbidden to be on the street after eight
o'clock?" the soldier says at last. One of the easygoing kind, his voice
doesn't even sound angry, quite mild in fact. One might feel like
having a chat; a touch of humor might not be out of place.

"It is forbidden," says Jacob.

"And what time is it now?"

"I don't know."

"But you ought to know," the soldier says.

Jacob might now say, That's true, or he could ask, How could I?
or, What time is it, then? Or he could say nothing and wait, which is
what he does, as that seems the most advisable course.

"Do you at least know what that building is over there?" asks the
soldier, having realized, no doubt, that this partner is not the kind of
person to keep a conversation going. Jacob knows. He hasn't seen in
which direction the soldier has nodded or pointed; he sees only the
blinding searchlight, and beyond it are quite a few buildings, but, the
way things are at the moment, only one can be meant.

"The military office," Jacob says.

"What you do now is go in there and report to the duty officer.
You tell him that you were out on the street after eight o'clock, and
you ask him for a well-deserved punishment."

The military office. Jacob doesn't know much about this building; he knows that it houses some sort of German administration —
at least that's what people say. As to what is being administered
there, nobody knows. He knows that the tax department used to be
there; he knows there are two exits, one in the front and one leading
out of the ghetto. But above all he knows that the chances of

a Jew leaving this building alive are very poor. To this day, no such case has ever been heard of.

"Anything the matter?" asks the soldier.

"No."

Jacob turns and walks away. The searchlight follows him, draws his attention to uneven spots in the paving, makes his shadow grow longer and longer, makes his shadow climb up the heavy steel door with its round peephole when Jacob still has many steps to go.

"And what do you ask for?" says the soldier.

Jacob stops, turns around patiently, and replies, "For a well-deserved punishment."

He does not shout — only people lacking in self-control or respect shout — but neither does he say it too softly, so as to be sure the man in the light can hear him clearly across the distance. He takes pains to find exactly the right tone; it should indicate that he knows what he is to ask for, all he needs is to be asked.

Jacob opens the door, quickly shuts it again between himself and the searchlight, and looks down the long empty corridor. He has been here often; there used to be a small table just inside the entrance on the left, with a minor official seated behind it. As long as Jacob can remember, it was always Mr. Kominek who used to ask each visitor, "What can we do for you?" "I've come to pay my semiannual taxes, Mr. Kominek," Jacob would reply. But Kominek would behave as if he had never seen Jacob before, although from October to the end of April he had been in Jacob's little shop almost every week and eaten potato pancakes there. "Occupation?" Kominek would ask. "Tradesman," Jacob would answer. He never showed his annoyance, not even a trace; Kominek invariably managed four pancakes, and sometimes he would bring his wife along too. "Name?" Kominek would ask next. "Heym, Jacob Heym." "Letters F to K, room 16." Yet whenever Kominek came to his shop he had never bothered to order pancakes; he would simply say, "The usual." For he was a regular.

Where the table once stood there is now no longer a table, but the floor still shows the four marks where its legs used to be, whereas the chair has left no trace, probably because it never stood as consistently on the self-same spot as the table had. Jacob leans against the door to catch his breath. The last few minutes have not been easy, but what does that matter now? The smell in this building has changed, somehow for the better. The acrid odor of ammonia that at one time pervaded the corridor has gone; instead there is, inexplicably, a more civilian smell. There is a hint of leather in the air, female sweat, coffee, and a trace of perfume. At the far end of the corridor a door opens, a woman in a green dress comes out, walks a few steps; she has nice straight legs, she goes into another room, two doors are left open, he hears her laugh, she comes out of the room again, walks back, the doors are closed again, the corridor is empty once more. Jacob is still leaning against the steel door. He wants to go outside again, maybe the searchlight is no longer waiting for him, maybe it has sought out something new, but maybe it is still waiting; it seems rather unlikely that it is not waiting; the soldier's last question had sounded so final.

Jacob walks along the corridor. There is nothing on the doors to indicate who is behind them, only numbers. Perhaps the duty officer has the room formerly occupied by the bureau chief, but one can't be sure and it is not advisable to knock at the wrong door. What do you want, some information? Did you hear that? He wants information! We have such and such plans for him, and he comes wandering in here and wants information!

Behind number 15, formerly TRADESMEN A–E, Jacob can hear sounds. He puts his ear to the door, tries to listen, can't understand anything, only single words that make no sense; but even if the wood were thinner, it wouldn't help much, for no one is likely to address another person as "Duty Officer." Suddenly the door opens — what else but number 15! — but fortunately the doors here open outward so that the person coming out doesn't see Jacob, who is hidden by the door. Fortunately, too, the person leaves the door open; he'll be back in a moment — when people think there's no one else around they leave doors open — and Jacob is concealed. Inside the room a radio is turned on; it crackles a bit, one of their "people's radios" no doubt, but there is no music. Since being in the ghetto Jacob has never heard any music, none of us has, except when someone happened to be singing. An announcer is reporting trivialities from some head-quarters, someone has been posthumously promoted to lieutenant colonel, next comes a bit about ensured supplies for the population, and then the announcer reads a bulletin that has just come in: "In a fierce defensive battle our heroically fighting troops succeeded in halting the Bolshevist attack twelve miles from Bezanika. In the course of the action our side . . ."

Then the fellow is back in his room; he closes the door, and the wood is too thick. Jacob doesn't move. He has heard a great deal: Bezanika is not that far away, more than a stone's throw but certainly not an enormous distance. He has never been there, but he has heard of Bezanika, a very small town; if you travel southeast by train via Mieloworno and the district town of Pry, where his maternal grand-father once had a pharmacy, and you then change trains for Kostawka, you eventually arrive in Bezanika. It may be all of two hundred and fifty miles, maybe even three hundred, not more, he hopes, and that's where they are now. A dead man has heard some good news and he is happy, he would like to go on being happy, but in his situation — the duty officer is waiting for him and Jacob must move on.

The next step is the hardest; Jacob tries to take it but is stymied. His sleeve is caught in the door. The fellow who came back to the room has pinned him there without the slightest malicious aforethought; he simply closed the door behind him, and Jacob was caught. He gives a cautious tug. The door is well made, it fits perfectly, no superfluous gaps; you couldn't slip a sheet of paper through. Jacob would like to cut off that piece of sleeve, but his knife is at home, and using his teeth, of which half are missing, would be a waste of time.

It occurs to him to take off his jacket, simply take it off and leave it stuck in the door — what does he need a jacket for now anyway?

He has already slipped out of one sleeve when he remembers that he does still need the jacket. Not for the approaching winter — when you're in the ghetto the oncoming cold doesn't scare you — but for the duty officer, if Jacob ever finds him. The duty officer doubtless could stand the sight of a Jew without a jacket — Jacob's shirt is clean and only slightly mended — but hardly the sight of a Jew without a yellow star on his chest and back (Ordinance 1). Last summer the stars were on the shirt, you can still see the stitch marks, but not anymore; the stars are now on the jacket. So he puts it on again, sticks with his stars, tugs more firmly, gains a few millimeters, but not enough. The situation is, one might say, desperate; he tugs with all his might, something rips, making a sound, and the door opens. Jacob falls into the corridor, a man in civilian clothes stands over him, looking very surprised; the man laughs, then turns serious again. What does Jacob think he is doing here? Jacob gets up and chooses his words very carefully. Not that he's been out on the street after eight. No, the sentry who stopped him had told him it was eight o'clock and he was to report here to the duty officer.

"And then you decided to eavesdrop at this door?"

"I wasn't eavesdropping. I've never been here before and didn't know what room to go to. So I was just about to knock here."

The man asks no more questions and nods his head toward the end of the corridor. Jacob walks ahead of him until the man says, "Right here"; it is not the bureau chief's room. Jacob looks at the man, then knocks. The man walks away, but there is no answer from inside.

"Go in," the man tells him, and disappears behind his own door after Jacob has pressed down the latch.

Jacob in the duty officer's room: he stays by the door, he hasn't put his cap back on since he got caught in the searchlight. The duty officer is quite a young man, thirty at most. His hair is dark brown, almost black, slightly wavy. His rank is not apparent as he is in shirtsleeves; his jacket is hanging from a hook on the wall in such a way that the shoulder boards cannot be seen. Hanging over the jacket is his leather belt with his revolver. Somehow this seems illogical; it should really be hanging under the jacket. Surely a man first takes off his belt and then the jacket, but the belt is hanging over the jacket.

The duty officer is lying on a black leather sofa, asleep. Jacob believes he is fast asleep; Jacob has heard many people sleeping, he has an ear for it. The man isn't snoring, but he is breathing deeply and regularly; somehow Jacob must make his presence known. Normally he would clear his throat, but that won't do here, that's something you do when visiting good friends. Although actually, when visiting a very good friend you don't clear your throat; you say, Wake up, Salomon, I'm here, or you simply tap him on the shoulder. But, even so, throat clearing won't do, that's somewhere between here and Salomon. Jacob is about to knock on the inside of the door but drops his hand when he sees a clock on the desk, its back to him. He has to know what time it is; there is nothing he has to know more urgently right now than this. The clock says 7:36. Jacob walks softly back to the door. They've been having you on, or not *they*, just that one fellow behind the searchlight, he's been having you on, and you fell for it.

Jacob still has twenty-four minutes left; if they are fair, he actually has twenty-four minutes plus the time his stay here has already cost him. He still doesn't knock. He recognizes the black leather sofa the duty officer is lying on; he has sat on it himself. It used to belong to Rettig, Rettig the broker, one of the richest men in the town. In the fall of 1935 Jacob borrowed some money from him, at 20 percent interest. The whole summer had been so cool that he could hardly sell any ice cream at all. Business had never been so slow; not even his famous raspberry ice cream had sold well. Jacob had needed to start selling potato pancakes as early as August but hadn't yet made enough money for the potatoes, so he had to borrow. And he had sat on the sofa in February 1936 when he returned the money to Rettig. It had stood in the outer office; Jacob had sat on it for an hour, waiting for Rettig. He remembered how surprised he was at the extravagance; there was easily enough leather for two overcoats or three jackets — and in the outer office!

The duty officer turns on his side, sighs, smacks his lips a few times; a cigarette lighter slips out of his trouser pocket and drops on the floor. Jacob simply must wake him up now; it would be a bad thing for him to wake up without Jacob rousing him. He knocks on the inside of the door, the duty officer says, "Yes?" moves, and goes on sleeping. Jacob knocks again — how can anyone be that fast asleep? — he knocks louder, the duty officer sits up before being properly awake, rubs his eyes, and asks, "What time is it?"

"Just past seven-thirty," says Jacob.

The duty officer has stopped rubbing his eyes, sees Jacob, rubs his eyes again, doesn't know whether to be angry or to laugh: it's quite incredible, no one's going to believe him. He stands up, takes his belt from the hook, then the jacket, puts them on, buckles his belt. He sits down behind the desk, leans back, stretches both arms wide apart.

"To what do I owe this honor?"

Jacob tries to answer, but he can't, his mouth is too dry: so that's what the duty officer looks like.

"No false modesty, now," says the duty officer. "Out with it! What's the problem?"

A bit of saliva has collected in his mouth. This seems to be a friendly fellow; maybe he's new here, maybe he isn't even aware of this building's terrible reputation. For a moment it occurs to Jacob that possibly he miscalculated the distance, maybe Bezanika isn't that far, maybe barely two hundred miles, or even a good deal less; maybe the man facing him is scared, and the smart thing is to be prepared; there must be a natural explanation for everything. But then he remembers that the report has only just reached the announcer; the duty officer has been asleep and can't have heard it yet. Then again it might be just as well if he hasn't heard it. The report mentioned that the Russians had been halted, you Germans have succeeded in stopping the advance, you've had a success, but maybe this fellow thinks that the Russians are still advancing. Jacob has been speculating too long; that's not smart, the duty officer is getting impatient; he's beginning to frown.

"Don't you speak to Germans?"

Of course Jacob speaks to Germans, why wouldn't he speak to Germans, that's the last impression he wants to give, for God's sake, we're all sensible people after all, of course we can speak to each other.

"The sentry on the tower on the Kurländischer Damm told me to report to you. He said I was out on the street after eight o'clock."

The duty officer looks at the clock in front of him on the desk, then pushes back his sleeve and looks at his watch.

"And that's all he said?"

"He also told me I was to ask for a well-deserved punishment."

That answer can't do any harm, Jacob thinks; it sounds obedient, disarmingly honest. Someone who carries his frankness to such an extreme might be entitled to fair treatment, especially when the offense of which he is accused was never committed: any clock can bear witness to that.

"What's your name?"

"Heym, Jacob Heym."

The duty officer takes paper and pencil, writes down something, not only the name, goes on writing; he looks at the clock again, it's getting later and later, he goes on writing, almost half a page, then puts the paper aside. He opens a little box, takes out a cigarette, and gropes in his trouser pocket. Jacob walks to the black leather sofa, bends down, picks up the lighter from the floor, and puts it on the table in front of the duty officer.

"Thanks."

Jacob goes and stands by the door again; a glance at the clock on the desk has shown him that it's already past 7:45. The duty officer lights his cigarette, takes a puff; his fingers fiddle with the lighter. He flicks it on a few times, then snaps it shut again; the flame is already quite small.

"Do you live far from here?" he asks.

"Less than ten minutes."

"Go on home."

Should he believe it? How many people had the duty officer said that to without their ever getting out of here? What will he do with his revolver when Jacob turns his back? What's out there in the corridor? How will the sentry react when he sees that Jacob has eluded his well-deserved punishment? Why should Jacob Heym of all people, that insignificant, trembling little Jacob Heym with the tears in his eyes, be the first Jew to describe what the inside of the military office looks like? It would take another six days of the Creation, as the saying goes; the world has grown even more chaotic than it was then.

"Come on now, beat it!" says the duty officer.

The corridor is empty again, which was almost to be expected; it's one of the minor sources of danger. But then the door to the outside: had it made any noise when he opened it before, did it open without a sound, or did it squeak or creak or grate? Go ahead, just try to take in every detail, quite impossible — if only he'd known in advance that it would really matter! Matter? In practical terms it makes absolutely no difference whether it can be moved quietly or not. If it doesn't squeak, Jacob will open it; and if it does squeak, is Jacob supposed to stay where he is? At ten minutes to eight?

Gently he presses down the latch. Too bad there's no other word for gently — maybe *very gently* or *infinitely gently*, all equally far from what is meant. One might say, Open the door quietly; if he hears you, it could cost you your life, the life that has suddenly acquired meaning. So he opens the door. And then Jacob is standing outside: how cold it has suddenly become. The wide square lies before him, a joy to step into it. The searchlight has grown tired of waiting; it's having fun somewhere else, it's at a standstill, perhaps it's resting up for new adventures. Keep close to the wall, Jacob, that's it; once you've reached the corner of the building, grit your teeth for the twenty yards across the square. If he does notice anything, he'll first have to swing the beam around and search, but here's the corner already, only a measly twenty yards to go.

It is almost exactly twenty yards, I've measured the distance: to be precise, fifty-nine feet six and a half inches. I've been there, the building is still standing, completely undamaged, only the watchtower is gone. But I had someone show me the exact spot, right in the middle of the Kurländischer Damm, and then I paced off the distance — I have a pretty good feeling for a yard. But it wasn't accurate enough for me so I bought a tape measure, then went back and measured it again. The children looked on and took me for an important person, and the grown-ups watched in amazement and took me for a madman. Even a policeman turned up, asked me for my identity card, and wanted to know what I was measuring. In any case it's exactly fifty-nine feet six and a half inches, no doubt about that.

The building has come to an end; Jacob gets ready to take off. Almost twenty yards have to be covered a few minutes before eight; it's a safe bet, and yet. A mouse is what one ought to be. A mouse is so insignificant, so small and quiet. And you? Officially you are a louse, a bedbug, we are all bedbugs, by a whim of our Creator absurdly overgrown bedbugs, and when was the last time a bedbug wanted to trade places with a mouse? Jacob decides not to run, he'd rather creep, it's easier to control the sounds that way. If the searchlight starts moving, he can still speed up. Halfway across he hears the sentry's voice — don't panic, it's not directed at him — the sentry says, "Yessir!" Again he says, "Yessir," and again. There's only one explanation: he's on the phone. Maybe it's a call from another sentry who is also bored. But he wouldn't keep saying, "Yessir," to him, of course he wouldn't. So it's the sentry's superior giving him some sort of orders? Actually quite irrelevant, but, assuming the best, it's the duty officer on the line: What the hell are you thinking of? Have you gone crazy, giving poor innocent Jews a scare like that? ("Yessir.") Couldn't you see the man was half out of his mind — his legs were trembling with fear! Don't ever let me catch you at it again, is that

clear? ("Yessir.") At the fourth "Yessir," Jacob has reached the opposite corner; let the fellow go on talking till he's blue in the face. Then,
in less than ten minutes, Jacob is home.

Jacob shares a room with Josef Piwowa and Nathan Rosenblatt.
They met for the first time here, in this room. None of them likes
the others much; cramped quarters and hunger make for discord, but
in all fairness it must be said that even the very first meeting was
quite stiff.

Rosenblatt died well over a year before Jacob's safe return. He
had eaten a cat that was careless enough to ignore the warning notices
along the barbed wire, and one day there it lay in the yard, dead of
starvation. Rosenblatt was the first to find it, and as I was saying, he
ate it, and that's what he died of. Piwowa has only been dead for three
months. His passing was accompanied by certain mysterious circumstances; all that is known is that he was shot to death by a foreman in
the shoe factory where he worked. He became insolent one day,
uttered words that even in normal times are better left unspoken to a
foreman, and predictably the enraged man shot him. Some said that
Piwowa could never control his temper; he had always been subject
to sudden rages and was bound to come to such an end. Others,
however, maintained that a violent temper and emotions were no
explanation here; they said it was a case of a perfectly ordinary
though very skillfully provoked suicide. One way or the other,
Piwowa has been dead for three months, Rosenblatt for well over a
year. His bed went up the chimney last winter, while Piwowa's bed,
chopped into neat lengths, is still in Jacob's basement waiting for the
cold times ahead. So far no replacements for his roommates have
appeared; the supply has been used up, damned or blessed be all cats
and guards — in any case they hadn't liked each other. At least
Rosenblatt is silent when he is at home, sitting with closed eyes on
his bed and praying; he is the last to go to bed and the first to get up

because his debates with God consume all his time. Even after his death he didn't give up this habit, but at least he is silent, sitting silently with closed eyes and only an occasional furtive glance.

Piwowa is quarrelsome. The last to move in, he behaves as if he were the first: he changes everything around, has to sleep with his feet toward the window; our bread rations have to be hidden from him. To be frank, Piwowa used to work in the woods, as a poacher. His father before him had been a poacher, but he himself was an even better one; he has no children.

So Jacob comes home. The day has been a great strain: many things experienced, endured, suffered, heard, with much trembling. Rejoice, brothers, go wild with joy, the Russians are twelve miles from Bezanika, if that means anything to you! Open your eyes, Nathan Rosenblatt; stop quarreling, Piwowa. The Russians are on their way, don't you understand? Twelve miles from Bezanika! But Rosenblatt goes on praying; Piwowa goes on lying with his feet toward the window. Let them lie there and quarrel and pray and be dead. Jacob is home, and the Russians had better hurry.

We're going to have a little chat now.

We're going to have a little chat, as befits any self-respecting story. Grant me my little pleasure; without a little chat everything is so sad and gloomy. Just a few words about doubtful memories, a few words about the carefree life; we're going to whip up a cake with modest ingredients, eat only a mouthful of it, and push the plate to one side before we lose our appetite for anything else.

I am alive, there can be no doubt about that. I am alive, and no one can force me to have a drink and remember trees and remember Jacob and everything to do with his story. On the contrary, I am offered some choices. They tell me to enjoy myself a bit: we only live once, my friend. Wherever I look, I see diversion: new cheerful worries interspersed with a little unhappiness; women, that's not over

yet; reforested woods; well-tended graves that at the least excuse
receive such quantities of fresh flowers as to look almost overdone. I
don't want to be demanding. Piwowa, whom I never saw, was demanding: game and bread had to be hidden from him; but I am not
Piwowa.

Hannah, my quarrelsome wife, once told me, "You're wrong" —
that's how she began almost everything she said to me — "a person
is only undemanding when he is content with what he's entitled to.
Not with less."

Seen like that, I must be very content. Sometimes I even feel
privileged: people are kind, obliging, make every effort to look patient. I can't complain.

Sometimes I say, "That was the whole story, thank you for
listening, you don't have to prove anything to me."

"That's not my intention. But you must realize that I was
born in '29 —"

"You don't have to prove a thing to me!" I say again.

"I know. But when the war was over I was just —"

"Kiss my ass," I say as I get up and leave. After five steps I could
kick myself for being so rude, so needlessly insulting, and it hadn't
meant a thing to him. But I don't turn around, I walk on. I pay the
waiter and, as I go out, look back over my shoulder toward the table
and see him sitting there with a baffled expression — What's got into
him? — and I shut the door behind me and refuse to explain.

Or I'm lying in bed with Elvira. To make this clear: I am forty-
six, born in 1921. I am lying in bed with Elvira. We work in a factory;
she has the whitest skin I have ever seen. I imagine we'll get married
one day. We are still panting, we have never mentioned it, then
suddenly she asks me, "Tell me, is it true that you . . ."

God knows who told her. I can hear the pity in her voice and go
crazy. I go into the bathroom, sit down in the tub, and start singing, to
stop myself from doing what I know I will regret after five steps.
When I come back after half an hour she asks me in surprise what

suddenly came over me, and I say, "Nothing," and give her a kiss, turn out the light, and try to fall asleep.

The whole town lies in a green belt, the surroundings are incomparable, the parks well cared for, every tree invites my memories, and I make ample use of this. But when it looks into my eyes, that tree, to see whether I have that rapturous look, I have to disappoint it, for it's not the right tree.

Jacob tells Mischa.

He hadn't come to the freight yard with the intention of telling anyone, but neither had he planned not to tell anyone. He'd come there with no intentions at all. He knew he would find it hard to keep the news to himself, almost impossible: after all, it was the best possible news, and what's good news for but to be passed on? But we know how it is: the informant is held responsible for all the consequences. In time the news becomes a promise, you can't prevent it. At the other end of town they'll be saying that the first Russians have already been sighted, three young ones and another who looked like a Tartar; the old women will swear to it and so will anxious fathers. Someone will say he heard it from so-and-so, and that person heard it from so-and-so, and someone down the line knows that it came from Jacob. From Jacob Heym? Inquiries will be made about him, everything connected with this most vital of all questions must be most carefully investigated; an honorable, reliable fellow, seems respectable enough, is said to have once owned a modest restaurant somewhere. Rejoicing seems to be in order.

Then days will pass, weeks, if God finds it necessary — two or three hundred miles are a fair bit of country — and the looks Jacob encounters will no longer be quite as friendly, not quite. On the other side of the street there will be whisperings; the old women will commit the sin of wishing him ill. The ice cream he has sold will gradually turn out to have been the worst in the whole town, even his famous raspberry ice cream, and his potato pancakes never quite kosher, this can happen.

Jacob is lugging crates with Mischa to a freight car.

Or let's look at another possibility. Heym says he has heard that the Russians are advancing, are already two hundred and fifty miles from the town. So where does he claim to have heard that? That's the point: at the military office. At the military office?! A look of horror may follow, answered by a slow nod, a nod that confirms the suspicion. Who would ever have believed that of him, Heym of all people, never! But that's how wrong you can be about a person. And the ghetto will have acquired one more suspected informer.

Well, anyway, Jacob didn't come to the freight yard with any firm intentions. It would be wonderful if they already knew about it without him, if they had met him with the news: that would be ideal. He would have rejoiced with them, wouldn't have let on that there were three people already in the know: Rosenblatt, himself, and Piwowa. He would have kept his mouth shut and, at the most, asked after a few hours who had brought the news. But as soon as Jacob arrived at the freight yard he realized that they didn't know yet; their backs were enough to tell him. The lucky break hadn't happened, indeed it would have been crazy to count on it; two lucky breaks in such a short time can only happen to Rockefeller on a Sunday.

They haul the crates to a freight car. As a carrying mate Jacob is not particularly sought after; no one is eager to have him; making pancakes is hardly conducive to muscle-building, and the crates are heavy. The yard is full of such people no one is eager to have; the big fellows are scarce. Everyone is eager to have them, but they don't negotiate, preferring to haul together. Don't talk to me about camaraderie and all that stuff; anyone who talks like that has no idea what goes on here, not the slightest. Personally I am not one of the big ones; I've cursed and hated them like the plague when I've had to haul with another fellow like myself. But if I had been one of them, I would have behaved exactly the same, exactly the same and not one bit differently.

Jacob and Mischa are hauling a crate to the freight car.

Mischa is a tall fellow of twenty-five, with light blue eyes, a great rarity among us. At one time he did some boxing at the *hakoah*, but only three fights, two of which he lost, and once his opponent was disqualified for hitting below the belt. He was a middleweight or, rather, more of a light heavyweight, really, but his trainer advised him to lose those few pounds in training, there being too much competition in the light-heavyweight class. Mischa took his advice, but it didn't help much; he didn't do all that well even as a middleweight, as was proved by his three fights. He was already toying with the idea of eating himself into a heavyweight; maybe he would have done better in that class. At about one hundred and eighty-five pounds the ghetto interfered with his plans, and ever since then his weight has gradually been going down. Even so, he is still in pretty good shape; he really deserves a better partner than Jacob. Many people believe that one day his good nature will cost him his head, but no one tells him that; maybe someday that person will suffer a similar fate.

"Stop gawking and look where you're going, or we'll both trip and fall," says Jacob. He is furious because the crate is so heavy, in spite of Mischa, and what annoys him most is the knowledge that Mischa will be the first person he tells; the trouble is, he doesn't know how to begin.

They heave the crates onto the edge of the freight car; Mischa's mind really isn't on his work. They go back to the pile to pick up another crate. Jacob tries to follow Mischa's gaze: the fellow is driving him crazy the way he keeps looking sideways. The yard looks the same as always.

"That freight car over there," says Mischa.

"Which one?"

"On the next-to-last track. The one without a roof." Mischa is whispering, although the nearest sentry is at least twenty yards away and not even looking in their direction.

"What about it?" asks Jacob.

"There are potatoes in that car."

Jacob grumbles all through the next haul. So there are potatoes in it, what's so special about that? Potatoes are only interesting when you have some, when you can cook them or eat them raw or make pancakes out of them, but not when they're lying around in some freight car or other at a yard like this one; potatoes in that freight car over there are the most boring thing in the world. Even if there were pickled herrings in there or roast goose or millions of pots of *tsholnt* . . . Jacob goes on and on, trying to get Mischa's mind off the subject and draw him into conversation.

Only Mischa isn't listening; the sentries' relief will soon show up, something they always turn into a little ceremony, standing at attention and reporting and shouldering arms, and that is the only moment at which to try. Jacob's objections aren't worth a second thought, Mischa says, of course there's a risk — all right, even a great risk, so what? Nobody's saying the potatoes are as good as eaten; every opportunity is a risk; must one explain that to a businessman? If there were no risk, there would be no opportunity either. Then it would be a sure thing, and sure things are rare in life; risk and the chance of success are two sides of the same coin.

Jacob knows that time is running out; Mischa is in a state in which no normal conversation is possible with him. And then he sees the relief column marching up: now he has to tell him.

"Do you know where Bezanika is?"

"Just a moment," says Mischa tensely.

"Do you know where Bezanika is? I said."

"No," says Mischa, his eyes following the column as it covers the last few yards.

"Bezanika is about two hundred and fifty miles from here."

"Oh yes."

"The Russians are within twelve miles of Bezanika!"

Mischa manages to tear his gaze for a moment from the marching soldiers; his unusual eyes smile at Jacob; actually this is very nice of Heym, and he says, "That's nice of you, Jacob."

Jacob almost has a fit. Here you overcome all your scruples, ignore all the rules of caution and all your misgivings, for which there are reasons enough, you carefully choose a blue-eyed young idiot to confide in, and what does that snot-nose do? He doesn't believe you! And you can't simply walk away, you can't leave him standing there in his stupidity, tell him to go to hell, and simply walk away. You have to stay with him, save up your rage for some later occasion, and you can't even relish the vision of such an occasion. You have to beg for his indulgence as if your own life depended on it. You have to prove your credibility although you shouldn't need to; he's the one who needs to. And you have to do all that terribly fast, before the sentries face each other, slap their rifles on their shoulders, and exchange the information that there is nothing special to report.

"Aren't you glad?" asks Jacob.

Mischa smiles at him kindly. "That's fine," he says in a voice that, while sounding a little sad, is intended to convey a certain appreciation of Jacob's touching efforts. And then he has something more important to watch again. The column is approaching, it has already passed the little redbrick building used by the railway men and the sentries.

Mischa is trembling with excitement, and Jacob tries to get his words out faster than the soldiers can approach. He tells his story in a shortened version — why hadn't he started it earlier? He tells about the man with the searchlight, about the corridor in the military office, about the door that opened outward and hid him. About the report he heard coming from the room, word for word as he has been repeating it to himself a thousand times during the night, nothing added and nothing withheld. He omits his brief imprisonment in the doorjamb, keeps to essentials, nothing either about the man who took him to the duty officer, a minor figure in the story, only about the duty officer himself, who must have been human and hence a weak link in the otherwise logical chain of evidence. He had looked at the clock like a human being and then, like a human being, told Jacob to go home.

And then to his horror Jacob sees that there is no stopping Mischa now. The only way is through certainty, and already the soldiers are facing each other. The enemy must be caught off guard, when his attention is at a low point. Mischa is crouching, ready to leap, certainty and the Russians are far away; the only thing left for Jacob to do is grab Mischa and hold on to his leg. They both fall to the ground, and Jacob sees the hatred in Mischa's eyes: he has ruined his chance, at least he is trying to. Mischa wrenches himself free, nothing can stop him now, and he thrusts Jacob away.

"I have a radio!" says Jacob.

It's not the sentries who have fired. So far, busy with their changeover ritual, they haven't seen a thing — Jacob has fired, a bullet straight to the heart. A lucky shot from the hip without taking proper aim, yet it found its mark. Mischa sits there motionless: the Russians are two hundred and fifty miles from here, near some place called Bezanika, and Jacob has a radio. They sit on the ground staring at each other: there never was any freight car with potatoes, no one has ever waited for the sentries to be relieved, quite suddenly tomorrow is another day. Although it is still true, of course, that opportunity and risk are two sides of the same coin, one would have to be crazy to forget that there must be some sort of healthy relationship between the two.

They go on sitting for a bit, Mischa with a blissful smile in his eyes, the result of Jacob's handiwork. Jacob gets up; they can't sit there indefinitely. He is angrier than ever. He has been forced to launch irresponsible claims, and it's that ignorant idiot who has forced him, just because he didn't believe him, because he suddenly had a craving for potatoes. He'll tell Mischa the truth all right, not this minute but sometime today, no matter whether that freight car is still there tomorrow or not. Within an hour in fact, an hour at most, maybe even sooner, he'll tell him the truth. Let the fellow enjoy a few more carefree minutes, not that he deserves them. Soon he won't be able to live without that happiness, then Jacob will tell him the truth, and Mischa will have to believe what went on at the military office. After all, that doesn't change anything about the Russians; he'll have to believe it.

"Pull yourself together and get up. And above all, keep your trap shut. You know what that means, a radio in the ghetto. Not a soul must find out about it."

Mischa couldn't care less what that means, a radio in the ghetto. Even if a thousand regulations were to prohibit it on pain of death, let them — does that matter now, when suddenly tomorrow is another day?

"Oh, Jacob . . ."

The corporal in command of the sentry detail sees a lanky fellow sitting on the ground, just sitting there, hasn't even collapsed, propping himself on his hands and staring up into the sky. The corporal straightens his tunic and comes striding toward them, little fellow that he is.

"Watch out!" Jacob cries, nodding toward the danger approaching in all its dignity.

Mischa regains his senses, comes down to earth, gets up, knows what is about to happen but can't keep the look of pleasure off his face. He busies himself with the crates, is about to tip one on its side, when the corporal hits him from the side. Mischa turns toward him; the corporal is a head shorter than he and has trouble reaching up to hit Mischa in the face. It almost verges on the comical, not suitable for a German newsreel, more like a scene from an old slapstick silent movie when Charlie the little policeman tries to arrest the giant with the bushy eyebrows, and, try as he will, the big fellow doesn't even notice him. We all know that Mischa could lift him off the ground and tear him to pieces. If he wanted to. The corporal hits him a few more times — by now his hands must be hurting — then shouts something or other that nobody's interested in and only lays off when a thin trickle of blood runs out of the corner of Mischa's mouth. Then he straightens his tunic again and belatedly notices that in the excitement his cap has fallen off; he picks it up, puts it on, goes back to his men, and marches away with the off-duty sentry detail behind him.

Mischa wipes the blood from his mouth with his sleeve, winks at Jacob, and reaches for a crate.

"All right, let's get on with it," he says.

They lift up the crate, and, as they carry it, Jacob's anger flares up again, almost tearing his teeth apart. He's not superstitious, and there's no such thing as a higher power, but in some inexplicable way — perhaps only because it verged on the comical — he feels that Mischa deserved the beating.

"Oh, Jacob . . ."

We know what will happen. We have some modest experience in the course events are apt to take; we have some imagination so we know what will happen. Mischa won't be able to keep his mouth shut. Never mind that he has been forbidden to talk. It won't be spite that will make him break his silence or make him not even try to remain silent; it won't be some malevolent desire to get Jacob into trouble — it will be joy, pure and simple. Stop taking your own lives, you'll soon be needing them again! Stop living without hope, our days of misery are numbered! Make an effort to survive, you've had plenty of practice, you're familiar with all the thousands of tricks that can cheat death — after all, you've managed so far. Just survive the last two hundred and fifty miles, then survival will be over, then life will begin.

Those are the reasons why Mischa won't be able to keep his mouth shut. He'll be asked for his source; he will reveal it, what's wrong with that? Soon even the children in the ghetto will know the big secret, in the strictest confidence of course, they will hear about it when their parents in their joy forget to whisper. People will come to Jacob, to Heym the possessor of a radio, and want to hear the latest news; they will come with eyes such as Jacob has never seen before. And what on earth is he going to tell them?

Half a day has passed, the big crates have been stowed away in the freight cars, now it's time for the smaller ones, the kind that one man can carry alone, and Jacob has lost sight of Mischa. Well, not literally lost sight of him, they see each other every few minutes but always a few feet apart, in passing, with their backs under a load or on their way to pick up another crate. The opportunity for a word of explanation hasn't come yet; he can't just take Mischa aside and say, This is how things really are. Whenever they see each other, Mischa winks at him or smiles or makes a face or waves surreptitiously; whether carrying a crate or not, it hardly makes any difference, each time some confidential gesture: we both know what it's all about. Once Jacob forgets himself and winks back, but he recovers immediately — that would be going too far, that would block the way to the opportunity. But he can't help himself; each time they pass his anger subsides. After all, the fellow has a right to be happy. Why shouldn't he be happy after all that has happened?

The day is bright blue, as if specially chosen for the joyous occasion. The sentry by the wooden shed is sitting on a few bricks, having taken off his rifle and placed it beside him; he is leaning his head against the wall with his eyes shut, basking in the sun. He is smiling; one could almost feel sorry for him.

As Jacob walks past he gets a good look at him. Walking quite slowly he studies that face with its closed eyes; he takes note of the smile, the prominent Adam's apple, the wide gold signet ring on the sentry's little finger. Jacob walks on and discovers, so he has told me, that he has changed. From one day to the next his senses are suddenly far more alert; he is beginning to observe. The apathetic despair has not survived the excitement of the previous night; nothing is left of that numbness. Now it is as if one must remember everything exactly as it was so as to be able to tell about it afterward. Afterward.

Jacob invents an innocent little game. On his way to the freight car or on his way back to the crates he always passes very close to the drowsing sentry. So close that he almost walks over his outstretched legs, each time depriving him for a brief moment of the sun. The sentry, of course, doesn't notice, doesn't even open his eyes although he is not asleep; he moves his head once slightly or twitches his mouth — in annoyance, it seems to Jacob — or does nothing at all. But each time Jacob passes him he loses a moment of sunshine. Jacob carries on his little game until he has to turn to another pile of crates. The sentry is no longer in Jacob's path; he would have to make a detour, and for that the joke is too slight and the risk too great. Jacob sees with satisfaction that a few little clouds are carrying on his prank. Then it is noon.

A man in railway uniform emerges from the redbrick building, the same man ever since we've been working here. He has a stiff leg that makes a noise with every step like a pebble falling into water, obviously a wooden leg. We call him the Whistle, not at all disparagingly, for we know nothing about his human or professional qualities. The only thing we have against him is that he happens to be a German, which, strictly speaking of course, should not be reason enough for a low opinion, but that's how unfair our plight can make us. As soon as he emerges from the building he pulls from his breast pocket a whistle fastened with a black cord to his buttonhole and proceeds to blow it at a remarkable volume, a signal that it is now noon. This is the only sound we have ever heard from him, apart from the *pit-pat* of his wooden leg. That's why we call him the Whistle. For all we know he may be mute.

We form a line, very disciplined and with no jostling. That's how they've taught us, under the threat of no food. It must look as if at the moment we had absolutely no appetite: What, already time to eat again? A fellow hardly has a chance to settle into the job before he is interrupted yet again by another of these many meals. So we form a line, without haste; we look around and make sure we're all standing in an imaginary straight line. With outstretched arm you check the distance to the man in front of you, then correct it by a few inches to create the impression that you are among well-mannered people here. The spoon is taken out of the trouser pocket and held in the left hand against the left trouser seam. Then the handcart appears around the corner of the shed, with the tin bowls piled beside the two steaming green cauldrons. The cart stops at the head of the greedy line. The first man steps forward, opens the cauldron (invariably burning his fingers as he does so), and begins doling out the contents. The Whistle stands to one side, mute and staring fixedly, to see that everything is done fairly.

On this bright blue day I do the doling. I know nothing, I'm always the last to find out, the sun gets on my nerves, I'm furious. I'm annoyed at the extra work, my burned fingers are hurting, I'm the last to get my food. I slap the ladleful of soup into their bowls, the men move off, I discover nothing unusual in their faces, in none of them, but then I'm not paying attention. I don't even see whom I happen to be giving soup to; I just look down at the bowls.

Jacob has drawn his ration, as they put it; he is looking for Mischa, who was far ahead of him in the line. Noon would be such a good opportunity for a private word with him, a little correction that does nothing to alter the actual facts. Mischa is nowhere to be seen; it is a large area, and the men have spread out with their bowls. The break is too short for a long search. Jacob sits down on a crate and swallows his hot soup. He's only human, his thoughts roam far away from the bowl, what's going to happen and how long will it take, and then what. The sun is shining on him, and no one is casting a shadow. Then Kowalski arrives.

Kowalski arrives.

"Is there a spot of room for me here too?" asks Kowalski.

He sits down beside Jacob and begins to spoon up his soup. Kowalski is marvelous. He thinks he is a real fox of a fellow who knows all the ins and outs, yet his expression can conceal nothing; it tells all. You only have to be slightly acquainted with him to know what he's going to say before he has even opened his mouth. His words are always merely the confirmation of long-held assumptions, if you're only slightly acquainted with him. At the freight yard everyone is slightly acquainted with Kowalski, and Jacob has known him since they were at school together. Here, in these grim times, they have rather lost sight of each other, which is easy enough to explain. Neither of them is one of the big fellows; a crate doesn't get any lighter when the one at the other end is an old friend, so their estrangement is simply due to circumstances. And otherwise there is virtually no opportunity. Two people get thrown together, or they don't. Jacob and Kowalski hardly ever did, and now here comes Kowalski with his bowl, saying, "Is there room for me here too?" and sits down beside Jacob and starts to eat.

Kowalski had been Jacob's most frequent customer. Not his best, his most frequent. Every day, just before seven, the shop bell would tinkle and, sure enough, there was Kowalski. He would sit down in his usual place and eat potato pancakes until the sight made you dizzy. Never fewer than four or five, usually followed by a little glass from under the counter, since Jacob didn't have a license for schnapps. Most shopkeepers would have been ecstatic over such a customer, but not Jacob, for Kowalski never paid, not a penny, not once. Being schoolmates wasn't the reason for Jacob's generosity — what kind of a reason would that be? — and generosity simply didn't enter into it. In a stupid moment one tipsy evening they had made a bargain. Kowalski's barber shop was only a few doors away; they met almost every day anyway, and the bargain had seemed advantageous to both of them. You don't pay at my place, and I don't pay at yours. Later they both regretted it, but a bargain is a bargain, and one man alone can't ruin another man. Not that they didn't try.

At first, potato pancakes were Kowalski's favorite dish, a fact that probably accounted in part for his proposing the deal, but that soon changed. After a while he grew sick and tired of them, and the only reason he went on eating four at a time was that, out of habit,

Jacob set them down in front of him without a word. Much more important to him by this time was the little drink that followed.

Jacob, on the other hand, suffered at first from the inescapable fact that, although a fellow can eat potato pancakes every day, he can't have his hair cut every day. After much thought Jacob hit on the idea of going regularly for a shave. He even sacrificed his sparse little beard, although he felt bad about that. His best times were the summers; fortunately Kowalski's stomach could not tolerate ice cream, and for a while Jacob was the only beneficiary of their bargain. However, as time passed his ambition subsided; other worries were really more important. He let his beard grow again, and the whole thing quietly petered out except for an occasional flare-up.

But that's old history. Kowalski is sitting beside him, spooning up his soup — how much longer in silence? — a single suppressed question imprinted in red spots on his gaunt cheeks. Jacob stares into his empty bowl, thinking. Perhaps it's only a coincidence; funny coincidences do happen. How are you? would sound idiotic, he thinks. He carefully licks his spoon clean and puts it in his pocket. There's no reason to get up yet; they still have a few minutes left on their break. The last men in line are just getting their soup. Putting his bowl aside he leans back, props himself on his hands, tilts his head back, and closes his eyes: to be a sentry for a few moments and enjoy the sun.

Kowalski stops eating; through his closed eyes Jacob can hear that his bowl is not yet empty; he hasn't scraped the bottom yet. So Jacob can hear that Kowalski is looking at him. It can't go on much longer; Kowalski just has to figure out how to begin.

"Any news?" he asks casually.

When Jacob looks at him he starts eating again, the ulterior motive still on his cheeks but his innocent eyes fixed on the soup. It sounds as if you've just entered his barbershop, sat down on the only chair facing the only mirror, while he shakes the black hairs of the previous customer from the cape and ties it around you — as always, much too tight. "Any news?" Mundek's son has won his first court case; it looks as if he's going to do well, but that's no longer news, Hübscher was talking about it yesterday. But what you don't know yet: Kvart's wife has left him, no one knows where she's gone, but then no normal person can get along with Kvart. It sounds so familiar that Jacob feels tempted to say: "Not as short in the back as last time, please."

"Well?" Kowalski asks, his eyes threatening to drown in the soup.

"What do you mean, news?" says Jacob. "Why ask *me?*"

Kowalski raises his face toward Jacob, that fox's face that is like an open book. He turns it toward Jacob with an expression of mild reproach, of some understanding of Jacob's caution, and the implication that in this particular case caution might well be considered misplaced.

"Jacob! . . . Aren't we old friends?"

"What's that got to do with it?" says Jacob. He's not sure whether his attempt to play dumb is convincing; after all, Kowalski has known him a long time. And he can imagine that basically it doesn't much matter whether he's convincing or not: if Kowalski knows something, no acting talent in the world is going to help. If Kowalski knows something, he won't let go; he can hound you almost to death.

Moving a little closer, Kowalski lets his spoon float in the soup and grabs Jacob's arm with his free hand to prevent him getting away.

"All right then, let's speak plainly." Lowering his voice to the level at which secrets are discussed, he whispers, "Is it true about the Russians?"

Jacob is shocked at the tone. Not at the whispering: people whisper on all sorts of occasions, that doesn't frighten him. He is shocked at the seriousness; he can see that it's not going to be a picnic, nothing to be taken lightly; he is shocked at the quaver in Kowalski's voice. It holds an expectation that will not tolerate ridicule; certainty is demanded here. A man is asking — a man who wants only this one question answered, and there's no escape — just this one question, nothing else, for all time. And yet Jacob makes one last, vain attempt.

"About what Russians?"

"About what Russians! Do you have to insult me like that, Jacob? Have I ever done you any harm? Remember, Jacob, remember who's sitting beside you! The whole world knows he has a radio, and to me, his only, his best friend, he refuses to tell anything!"

"The whole world knows?"

Kowalski backs down. "Not exactly the whole world, but one or two people do know about it. Has someone told me, or do I have second sight?"

In Jacob's head, one annoyance displaces the other. Kowalski is upstaged by Mischa: that blabbermouth is going to land him in an impossible situation. Suddenly it is no longer necessary to take Mischa aside for a correction — totally superfluous. The fire can no longer be contained — who knows how many others would now have to be taken aside! And even if he were to try his best with every single one of them, try with the patience of an angel to explain to each individual the crazy route by which the glorious news has fluttered into the ghetto, into their very ears, what else could they do but not believe him, with all due respect and much sympathy for his situation? Or does anyone seriously believe that Kowalski could afford to be fobbed off with a story so manifestly full of holes?

"Well?"

"It's true about the Russians," says Jacob. "And now stop bothering me."

"Are they twelve miles from Bezanika?"

Jacob rolls his eyes and says, "Yes!"

He gets to his feet: that's how they sour one's joy, yet Kowalski is as entitled to it as all the rest of them. He would give anything for Kowalski to have been spotted by the sentry on the Kurländischer Damm, Kowalski or anyone else. What on earth made him go there? All good citizens are in bed, but at that dark hour he has to roam the streets because the walls of his room are closing in on him, because once again Piwowa and Rosenblatt have become unbearable, because a stroll after work seems to bring a strange, faint whiff of normal times. A stroll in a town you know, have known since they used to sit you up in your baby carriage with a pillow at your back. The buildings tell you about almost forgotten trifles: over there you once fell down and sprained your left ankle, at this corner you finally told Gideon the truth to his face, in that building there was once a fire in the middle of winter. A longed-for whiff of normal times, that's what he had promised himself; he hadn't been able to enjoy it for long, and now this.

"Will you at least keep it to yourself?"

"You know me!" answers Kowalski, who wants to be left in peace, for the time being. The break is short, and he has enough just coping with his own emotions and with what is suddenly looming ahead of him.

Jacob picks up his bowl from the ground and walks away. He carries Kowalski's expression with him, the face tilted to one side, the eyes fixed on a distant point that no one else can see; no war far and wide. He hears Kowalski's lips whispering rapturously, "The Russians . . ." Then Jacob reaches the handcart. He adds his bowl to the others and glances back again at Kowalski, who is now fishing his spoon out of his soup. The whistle shrills, even Kowalski hears it, and a little tower of bowls is quickly erected. To Jacob it seems that all the men are looking at him strangely, differently from the day before, somehow with the secret in their eyes. Maybe it's an illusion; in fact it must be: they can't possibly all know about it already, but there may well be one or two who do.

 I would like, while it's still not too late, to say a few words about how I came by my knowledge, before any suspicions arise. My principal informant is Jacob; most of what I have heard from him will turn up in this story somewhere, I can vouch for that. But I say "most," not all; I say it deliberately, and in this case the reason is not my poor memory. After all, *I* am telling the story, not Jacob: Jacob is dead, and besides, I'm not telling his story but a story.

He told me the story, but I am talking to you. That's a big difference, because I was there. He tried to explain how one thing followed another and that he couldn't have acted any differently, but I want you to know that he was a hero. Not three sentences would pass his lips without his mentioning his fear, but I want you to know about his courage. About those trees, for example, about those non-existent trees I'm looking for, that I don't want to think about but have to, and my eyes grow moist when I do. He had no inkling of that; that's simply and solely my concern. I can't quite piece it all together, but there are some things that he knew nothing about, when he might have asked me how I got such ideas in my head, but somehow I feel that it is all part of it. I would like so much to tell him why I feel that, I owe him an explanation, and I think he would say I was right.

Some things I know from Mischa, but then there is a big gap for which there are simply no witnesses. I tell myself that it must have happened more or less in such and such a way, or that it would be best if it had happened in such and such a way, and then I tell it and pretend that's how it was. And that *is* how it was; it's not my fault that the witnesses who could confirm it can no longer be found.

For me, probability is not a determining factor; it is improbable that I of all people should still be alive. Much more important is my feeling that it could or should have happened this way, and that has nothing whatsoever to do with probability, I can vouch for that too.

It wasn't at all a bad idea of Mischa's to speak to Rosa during the ration card distribution, to pluck up his courage and ask her whether they couldn't walk part of the way home together, and luckily she agreed. At first it was only her face that loosened his tongue — how many girls have been addressed merely because of their bright eyes! — but one thing led to another, and today, about a year later, he loves all of her, just the way she is. The first steps were awkwardly silent; his head felt hollowed out. He received no help at all from her, not even an encouraging glance; she looked straight ahead shyly, apparently waiting for something important to happen. But nothing happened until they reached her front door; her mother was already standing anxiously at the window, wondering what was keeping her only daughter. With lowered eyes Rosa hurriedly said good-bye, but she must have had just enough time to hear where exactly he would be waiting for her the next day.

At any rate she did show up, much to Mischa's relief. He reached into his pocket and gave her his first gift. It was a little book of poems and songs; by that time he knew them all by heart, and it was the only book he happened to own. Actually he had wanted to present her with an onion, if possible one with a bluish skin; right from the start he was very serious about Rosa, but the idea was too ambitious. In such a short time he was unable to find one, try as he would. At first she was a little coy about accepting the gift at all, the way unsophisticated girls often are, but then of course she did accept the book and tell him how pleased she was. At this point he introduced himself — the day before they had been too excited to get around to that — and now for the first time he heard her name: Rosa Frankfurter.

"Frankfurter?" he asked. "Are you by any chance related to that famous actor Felix Frankfurter?"

As could later be readily established by means of theater programs, this was something of an exaggeration. Frankfurter the actor never got beyond supporting roles. But Mischa, never having seen Frankfurter onstage, had not meant it ironically. He had been to the theater only once, and he knew of Felix Frankfurter only from what he had read and heard. And Rosa didn't take it that way either. She blushingly admitted that such was indeed the case, that Frankfurter the actor was her father. They went on to chat a bit about the theater, about which he knew practically nothing, until he managed gradually with great skill to bring the conversation around to boxing, about which she in turn knew practically nothing. In this way they had a marvelous time together, and that same evening she did not resist Mischa's first kiss on her silky hair.

When Mischa arrives, Felix Frankfurter is sitting at the table playing a game of checkers with his daughter. He is a big man, tall and gaunt; Mischa described his appearance to me with loving detail. What was once a massive corpulence has left the old man's skin in folds, which is greatly emphasized by the clothes he is wearing, which date from considerably stouter times. Photos prove that some years ago man and skin formed a well-balanced entity: Frankfurter had pressed a weighty album on Mischa during his very first visit, for he couldn't possibly allow the unfavorable impression, of which he was fully aware, to remain. Around his neck a scarf, artistically yet casually arranged with one end in front and one on his back, and in his mouth a pipe, a meerschaum that has long since forgotten the taste of tobacco.

He is seated at the table with his daughter; the game looks hopeless for Rosa. Mrs. Frankfurter is sitting with them, paying no attention to the game. She is altering one of her husband's shirts, making it smaller and perhaps dreaming of some quiet happiness. When Mischa arrives, Rosa has just been grumbling that the game with her father is so boring because he takes ages to contemplate each move, and he has been trying to explain to her that it is better to win one game in two hours than lose five in the same amount of time.

"But why are you taking so long now?" she had asked. "You're ahead anyway."

"I'm not ahead 'anyway,'" he had answered. "I'm ahead because I give each move so much thought."

She had made an impatient gesture; any pleasure in the game was now gone. Only obedience keeps her from sweeping the pieces from the board, plus the fact that Mischa hasn't yet arrived, but at that moment there is a knock at the door. She hurries to open it, and Mischa comes in. Greetings are exchanged, Mr. Frankfurter offers Mischa a chair, Mischa sits down. Rosa quickly clears away the board and pieces before Mischa can take over her losing game. Many a time he has taken her place, looked for a way out, and in the end had to give up and ask for a return match. Frankfurter would agree, and then they would both sit there lost in thought, and suddenly it was so late that Mischa would have to leave before Rosa could spend any time with him.

"Have you been playing?" asks Mischa. "So who won today?"

"Who do you think?" says Rosa, making it sound like a reproach. Mr. Frankfurter draws on his meerschaum pipe, as content as circumstances permit, and winks at Mischa. "She plays faster than she thinks. But I'll bet you've noticed that yourself on other occasions, right?"

Mischa disregards the little joke. Today he is not coming empty-handed; he is merely wondering how to convey the news with the greatest possible effect, for there's nothing Frankfurter enjoys more than a story that ends with a punch line. When he talks about the theater, where, if one is to believe him, the wildest things have happened, every step, every glance he describes carries some special implication: someone falls down or makes a fool of himself or messes up the performance or doesn't understand why the others are laughing. If that weren't so, Frankfurter probably feels, there would be no point in telling the anecdote in the first place.

"What can one offer a guest these days?" Frankfurter says to his silent wife. And then to Mischa: "What can one offer a guest apart from one's daughter?"

He smiles, having brought off his little joke, then draws on his pipe again. Anyone can draw on an empty pipe, nothing to it, but not the way Frankfurter does. Included in his performance are the enjoyment, the pleasurable richness of the smoke. Someone not looking too closely might be tempted to wave the smoke away.

There is a thoughtful silence. Any moment now Mr. Frankfurter will tell a story, one of his anecdotes at the end of which he puts on such a display of mirth that he slaps his thigh: for instance, the one about the actor Strelezki, otherwise said to have been a divine Othello, whose false teeth fell out just as he was bending over Desdemona to strangle her. Rosa lays her fingers on Mischa's hands, her mother goes on making the shirt smaller, Frankfurter is rubbing his knees, perhaps he's not in the mood today, and here comes Mischa with such good news, still wondering how best to tell them, as if pondering a checkers move.

"Have you heard the latest?" Rosa asks him suddenly.

Startled, Mischa looks from one to the other; he gives up his search and is surprised that Mrs. Frankfurter doesn't even look up from the shirt. They already know, yet he hasn't noticed till now that they know. He is surprised to find that everything in the room looks just as it did on his last visit. He is amazed at the speed: it was only this morning that he heard it from Jacob, and now it's already here at the Frankfurters, by way of who knows how many intermediaries. But strangest of all is that Rosa should wait till now to bring up the subject. She can't have forgotten it and only just remembered it: impossible. Something's wrong — maybe they have a reason not to believe it.

"You already know?"

"They were talking about it at work today," says Rosa.

"And you're not glad?"

"Glad?" says Mr. Frankfurter. "We're supposed to be glad? What are we supposed to be glad about, my boy, eh? Before, they could have been glad about it, gathered all the relatives together, got drunk, but today there are a few little things that have changed. In my opinion, it's all a big calamity, my lad, almost a disaster for those people, and you're asking why I'm not glad?"

Mischa instantly realizes that they are talking about something quite different, the only explanation for their mood. Otherwise Frankfurter has taken leave of his senses and doesn't know what he's saying.

"It will be hard to bring up a child," says Mrs. Frankfurter between two stitches.

The first clue. Renewed astonishment in Mischa's eyes: they are talking about some child, so news doesn't travel all that quickly. Apparently two crazy people have brought a child into this world, without having heard the news — in normal ghetto times, certainly a subject for discussion. But as of yesterday the times are no longer normal, a different wind is blowing, we can tell you about things that will make you forget child and husband and wife and eating and drinking: as of yesterday, tomorrow will be another day.

Now Rosa is surprised: first she is surprised, then she smiles at Mischa's expression.

"So you really don't know about it yet," she says. "But that's what he's like. He can't stand it if other people know more than he does. He's such a know-it-all, while the truth is he doesn't know anything. A child has been born in Witebsker-Strasse. Actually there were twins, but one of them died almost at once. Last night. When all this is over they intend to have the boy registered under the name of Abraham."

"When all this is over," says Frankfurter. He lays his pipe on the table, gets up, and starts to pace the room, head bowed, hands behind his back. His disapproving glances are directed at Mischa — surely the boy isn't grinning? They take everything so lightly, including Rosa; perhaps they are too young to grasp it. They speak of the future as if it were a weekend that can't fail to arrive — the whole family goes off to the country with a picnic basket, rain or shine. "When all this is over the child will have died and the parents will have died. All of us will have died, that's when this will be over."

Frankfurter has finished his pacing and sits down again.

"I think David sounds nicer," says Mrs. Frankfurter gently.

"Dovidl . . . Do you remember? That's what Annette's son was called. Abraham sounds so terribly old, not at all like a child. Yet it's only for children that names are important. Later, by the time they're grown up, names don't matter so much anymore."

Rosa tends to favor Jan or Roman; she feels it's time to get away from the traditional names. When it's no longer necessary to wear the yellow star, why not choose different names? Frankfurter shakes his head over such women's talk, and suddenly Mischa wishes he had arrived at this moment instead of earlier, blurting it out the moment he arrived. For if he starts telling them now, they will feel just as he did in his error: Why did he wait till now to tell us? He can't have forgotten it! He's been sitting and sitting while they talk themselves ever deeper into their gloomy mood. Either he doesn't tell them till tomorrow and then pretends that it's the latest news, or he'll have to think up some story to explain why he's telling them only now and not as soon as the door was opened. He decides on today. It'll be a little extra punch line for Frankfurter. Mischa gets up, affects reluctance, even he doesn't know whether it's simulated or real, looks diffidently at Frankfurter, who is already wondering about the lengthy prelude, and formally requests the hand of his daughter.

Rosa discovers something on her fingernail that claims her undivided attention, something so important that her face turns fiery red: they have never exchanged so much as a syllable about it, which, of course, is really the way it should be. Mrs. Frankfurter bends lower over the shirt, which is nowhere near small enough yet, most of the work being required by the collar because of the great importance of a perfect fit. Mischa relishes his inspiration, successful or otherwise; Frankfurter is taken aback and is about to say something. It is his turn to speak, since a polite question deserves an answer, and, no matter how out of place the question may seem at first, Frankfurter's answer will build a bridge to the great news, and this will at the same time explain why Mischa waited until now to tell them. That is Mischa's plan, devised in extreme haste and not so bad at that; Felix Frankfurter will build a bridge, it's his turn, they are all waiting for his answer.

So, great astonishment on Frankfurter's part, incredulity in his expression; he has just been drawing on his pipe and has forgotten to blow out the smoke. The father who would give his only daughter to no one but Mischa, loving him as he does like his own son, the man of hard facts who is nobody's fool, is staggered. "He's gone mad," he whispers. "Suffering has confused him. It's these cursed times when perfectly normal desires sound monstrous. Why don't *you* say something?"

But Mrs. Frankfurter won't say anything. A few tears drop soundlessly onto the shirt; she doesn't know what to say, all important questions having invariably been decided by her husband.

Felix Frankfurter resumes his pacing, inner turmoil, and Mischa looks as hopeful as if the next words could only be "Take her and be happy."

"We are in the ghetto, Mischa, don't you know that? We can't do what we want because they do what they want with us. Should I ask you what security you can offer, since she is my only daughter? Should I ask you where you intend to find a place to live? Should I tell you what kind of a dowry Rosa will receive from me? Surely that must interest you? Or should I give you some advice on how to conduct a happy marriage and then go to the rabbi and ask when it would suit him best to perform the *khasene?* You'd be better off racking your brain for a place to hide when they come for you."

Mischa remains confidently silent; that still wasn't an answer, after all.

"Just listen to that! His ship has foundered, he's swimming in the middle of the ocean, not a soul in sight to help him. And he's wondering whether he'd rather spend the evening at a concert or the opera!"

His arms sink to his sides; Frankfurter has said all that was to be said, even throwing in a little allegory at the end. No one need be clearer than that.

But Mischa is not impressed. On the contrary, everything has gone just as he hoped. No help in sight, that's the kind of phrase Mischa has been waiting for — soon you'll all know the real situation. It does make sense to speak of the future, Mischa isn't an idiot after all, of course he knows where we are, of course he knows that one can't get married until — and that's the real issue — until the Russians arrive.

Mischa to me: "So I simply told them (that was his word: simply) that the Russians were twelve miles from Bezanika. You see, it wasn't just a piece of news: now it was also an argument. I had imagined they would be thrilled — you don't hear that kind of news every day. But Rosa didn't throw her arms around my neck, far from it; she looked at her father almost in alarm, and he looked at me. For a long time he didn't say a word, just looked at me, so that I began to get nervous. My first thought was, Maybe they need time to grasp it, judging by the way the old man was looking at me, but then I realized it wasn't time they needed but certainty. After all, the same thing had happened to me: I too had thought that Jacob was just trying to divert my attention from the carload of potatoes, and I went on thinking this till he told me the whole truth, how he had found out. News like that without a source simply isn't worth anything, it's no more than a rumor. So I was about to open my mouth and dispel their doubts, but then I decided to wait. Let them ask, I thought: if you have to squeeze something out of another person, you can absorb it better than if he tells it to you on his own and all in one piece. And that's exactly the way it happened."

So, an endless silence, the needle paused in the middle of a stitch, Rosa's hot breath, Frankfurter's eyes, and Mischa standing there in the spotlight, the audience hanging on his lips.

"Do you know what you're saying?" says Frankfurter. "That's not something to joke about."

"You don't need to tell me that," says Mischa. "I heard it from Heym."

"From Jacob Heym?"

"Yes."

"And he? Where did he hear it?"

Mischa smiles weakly, pretends to be embarrassed, shrugs his shoulders unhappily, which they won't accept. Somewhere there was a promise. That he is not going to keep it is another matter, but the promise was made, and he would like at least to be forced to break it, he would like to have done his utmost: in my place you wouldn't have acted any differently.

"Where did he hear it?"

"I promised him I wouldn't tell anyone," says Mischa, actually quite prepared to do so, but obviously not prepared enough, at least not obviously enough for Felix Frankfurter. This is not the time to note nuances in a voice; Frankfurter takes two or three quick steps and gives Mischa a slap, a cross between a stage slap and a genuine one, but more likely genuine, for it contains indignation: we're not talking here to pass the time.

Naturally Mischa is a bit shocked — that much force wasn't really necessary — but he can't be offended now. The force, after all, had to assume some form or other. He can't sit down with a stony face, arms crossed on his chest, waiting for an apology. He could wait a long time for that. He can, and he does, remove all doubts: the moment has arrived, his plan worked — no one is going to ask now why he took so long.

"Jacob Heym has a radio."

Another short silence, a few glances exchanged, the shirt — still too big — floats unnoticed to the floor. It's all right to believe one's own son-in-law. At last Rosa throws her arms around his neck; he's waited long enough for that. Over her shoulder he sees her father sitting down exhausted and covering his deeply furrowed face with his hands. There will be no discussion; there is nothing to say. Rosa pulls his ear to her mouth and whispers. He doesn't understand, the old man still has his hands in front of his face, and Mischa looks at her inquiringly.

"Let's go to your place," Rosa whispers again.

A brilliant idea, she has taken the words out of Mischa's mouth; today one inspiration follows on the heels of another. They tiptoe out of the room with exaggerated care, the door clicks shut, no one hears it. Outside, it is already getting dangerously dark.

Then Frankfurter is alone with his wife, without witnesses. All I know is how it ended. I only know the outcome, nothing in between, but I can only imagine it to have been something like this.

His wife finally gets up, at some point. She wipes away her tears, no longer those of the marriage proposal, or she doesn't wipe them away. She goes to her husband, quietly, as if not wanting to disturb him. She stands behind him, puts her hands on his shoulders, brings her face close to his, which is still covered with his hands, and waits. Nothing happens, not even when he lowers his arms. He stares at the opposite wall, and she gives him a little nudge. She is looking for something in his eyes and cannot find it.

"Felix," she may have said softly after a while. "Aren't you glad? Bezanika isn't so far away. If they've come that far they'll come as far as here too."

Or she might have said: "Just think, Felix, if it's true! My head's in a whirl, just think! Not much longer now, and everything will be just the way it used to be. You'll be able to perform again, on a real stage, I'm sure they'll reopen the theater. I'll be waiting for you beside the bulletin board next to the porter's lodge. Just think, Felix!"

He doesn't answer. He gets up from under her hands and goes over to the cupboard. Perhaps he looks like a man who has come to an important decision and doesn't want to waste any time in carrying it out.

Frankfurter opens the cupboard, takes out a cup or a little box, and finds a key in it.

"What are you going to do in the basement?" she asks.

He weighs the key in his hand, as if there were still something to be considered, possibly the matter of finding the right moment, but the sooner the better. Nothing is the same anymore. Perhaps he tells her now what he has in mind, taking her into his confidence while still in the room, but that's unlikely since he has never been in the habit of asking for her opinion. Besides, it makes no difference when he tells her; it won't change anything, the key is already in his pocket. So let us assume that he closes the cupboard without a word, walks to the door, turns around, and says only, "Come."

They go down into the basement.

In these houses of the poor one would formerly never have set foot: the wooden stairs are worn, they creak abominably, but he walks close to the wall and on tiptoe. She follows him uneasily, also softly, also on tiptoe — she doesn't know why, just because he's doing it. She has always followed him, without asking; often she has only been able to guess what was to be done, and it wasn't always the right thing.

"Won't you tell me now what we're doing here?"

"Sssh!"

They walk along the narrow basement passage; no need to tiptoe here. The next-to-last cubicle on the right is theirs. Frankfurter turns the key in the padlock and opens the wire door in its iron frame, which is no good as fuel and so is still there. He goes in, she follows hesitantly, he closes the wire door behind her, and there they are.

Felix Frankfurter is a cautious man. He looks for a piece of sacking or a sack with holes that he can tear or, if there is no sack, he takes off his jacket and hangs it across the door, just in case. I imagine that for a moment he puts his finger to his lips, closing his eyes and listening, but there is not a sound. Then he goes to work on the little pile filling one corner of the space, a little pile of useless stuff, a small heap of memories.

At the time they received the notice, they spent two days with their heads together considering what they should take along — apart from the prohibited things, of course. The situation was very serious, no doubt about that; they didn't expect it to be a paradise, but nobody had any definite knowledge. Mrs. Frankfurter thought in practical terms, too practical for his liking, solely of bed linen and dishes and things to wear, but he was reluctant to part with many items that she regarded as superfluous. Such as the drum on which at a highly successful performance he had announced the arrival of the heir to the Spanish throne; or Rosa's ballet slippers from the time when she was five years old, to this day almost unworn; or the album of carefully pasted-in reviews in which his name is mentioned and underlined in red. Give me one good reason why I should part with them: life is more than just eating and sleeping. The problem of transporting them? In great haste he bought a handcart, at an exorbitant price, for at that time prices for handcarts shot up overnight, and now the little pile fills a corner of their basement.

He lays aside one item after another, his wife watching him silently, seething with curiosity: What is he looking for? Maybe for a moment he studies the framed photograph of all his fellow actors at the theater, his portly figure over on the right, between Salzer and Strelezki, who in those days wasn't yet so well known. But that's not what he's looking for; if he did study the picture, he puts it aside again and goes on reducing the pile.

"That Jacob Heym is a fool."

"Why?"

"Why! Why! He heard some news, marvelous, but that's his affair. Some good news, very good news in fact: then he should just be glad and not drive everyone else crazy with it."

"I don't understand you, Felix," she says. "You're not being fair to him. Surely it's a great thing for us to know about it. Everybody should know about it."

"Women!" Frankfurter says angrily. "Today you know about it, tomorrow the neighbors know, and the next day the whole ghetto is talking about nothing else!"

She may nod, surprised at his fury. But so far he's given no reason at all to reproach Heym.

"And all of a sudden the gestapo knows!" he says. "They have more ears than you think."

"Oh, Felix," she interrupts him, "do you seriously believe that the gestapo needs us to find out where the Russians are?"

"Who's talking about that! What I mean is, all of a sudden the gestapo knows that there's a radio in the ghetto. And what will they do? They'll immediately turn every street upside down, house by house. They won't give up till they've found the radio. And where will they find one?"

The pile has been leveled. Frankfurter lifts up a cardboard box, white or brown, in any case a cardboard box containing the reason for a just and valid death sentence. He opens the lid and shows his wife the radio.

She may give a little shriek, she may be horrified, certainly shocked; she stares at the radio and at him and is at a loss.

"You brought our radio along!" she whispers and folds her hands. "You brought our radio along! They could have shot all of us for that, and I knew nothing about it. . . . I knew nothing. . . ."

"Why should you?" he said. "Why should I have told you? I've trembled enough alone, and you've trembled enough even without a radio. There were days when I forgot it, simply forgot it, sometimes even for weeks at a time. So one happens to have an old radio in the basement and stops thinking about it. But whenever I did remember I would start trembling, and I've never been reminded of it as I was today. The worst part is that I never listened, not a single time, not even in the early days. Not so that you wouldn't notice — I simply didn't dare. Sometimes I wanted to; my curiosity would almost get the better of me. I'd pick up the key, and you remember how from time to time I'd go down to the basement. You would ask me what I wanted down there, and I told you I wanted to look at photos or read the old reviews again. But that was a lie; I wanted to listen to the radio. I would go down into the basement, hang something across the door, and didn't dare. I would sit down, look at the photos or read the reviews, just as I'd told you, and I didn't dare. But that's all over now!"

"I had no idea," she whispers to herself.

"That's all over, once and for all!" he says. "You were right all the time, it was useless stuff, I don't need it anymore. There'll be nothing left, nothing to suggest a radio. Then let them come and search."

He takes the radio apart, piece by piece, probably the only radio in the hands of any of us; without much fuss he destroys it. The tubes are trodden to dust, an indestructible piece of wire is wound as a harmless cord around a box, the wooden casing is put aside piece by piece and will have to wait a few weeks before being burned. At this time of year any smoking chimney is suspect, but that's no great tragedy: wood is wood, after all.

"Did you also hear them say that the Russians have almost reached Bezanika?" Mrs. Frankfurter asks in a low voice.

He looks at her in astonishment.

"Didn't I tell you I never listened?" he may have answered.

Mischa enters his room with Rosa, and that is a whole story on its own. If it is a story when somebody must be lied to in order to make her a little bit happy, that's what happened with Rosa; if it is a story when bold ruses must be employed and fear of discovery is present, and there must on no account be any slipups, and one's expression must remain solemn and innocent throughout; if all this yields a serviceable story, then Rosa's going with Mischa to his room is also a story.

In the middle of the room is a curtain.

Fayngold is the name of the man sleeping in the other bed, it's because of Isaak Fayngold that they have to go to all this trouble, even if he couldn't care less. He's wiped out with fatigue anyway every night, he's over sixty and his hair is snow white; he really does have other worries, but go ahead and do what you like. At first only the wardrobe had divided the room; to Mischa this seemed enough and to Fayngold more than enough, but for Rosa it hadn't been sufficient. She told Mischa that, even if Fayngold is deaf and dumb, he still isn't blind, and the moon shines so brightly into the room, and in any case the wardrobe is too narrow. Mischa cheerfully removed the piece of cloth from the window and fastened it to the ceiling beside the wardrobe. Now the moon could shine in more brightly than ever, but not for Fayngold. The main thing was that Rosa was reassured.

Fayngold is no more deaf and dumb than I or Kowalski or anyone else who knows how to use his ears and tongue, but for Rosa he is as deaf and dumb as a clam. It was clear to Mischa from the start that Rosa would not set foot near his bed because there was another bed next to it with a strange man in it; the understanding landladies and the discreet little hotels with their hall porters who tactfully look the other way and ask no questions — these can be found only in some other town. He knew that under the circumstances she could only say no, she's not that kind of girl, that's out of the question. Neither is he that kind of fellow. But if renunciation is to be the ultimate option, there is still ample time for brooding. No one can fault him for that, and Mischa did plenty of it.

One blessed night he was lying awake in bed thinking of Rosa, with Fayngold about to fall asleep in the other bed, and Mischa began to tell him about Rosa. Who she was and how she was and what she looked like and how much he loved her and how much she loved him, and Fayngold merely sighed. That's when Mischa confessed his burning desire to have Rosa with him for one night.

"By all means," Fayngold answered, without going more deeply into the problem. "I don't mind. And now, do let me go to sleep."

Mischa didn't let him go to sleep. He explained to Fayngold that the point was not whether Fayngold agreed but whether Rosa agreed. Also that he hadn't mentioned Fayngold to her, he hardly dared to, and if they didn't come up with a solution, presumably nothing would come of the whole idea. Fayngold switched on the light and stared at him for a long time.

"You're not serious!" he said in a shocked whisper. "You can't expect me to hang around in the street until you're finished. Have you forgotten the regulations?"

Mischa didn't expect any such thing, and he hadn't forgotten the regulations either. He was simply looking for a solution, which was nowhere in sight. Fayngold switched off the light and soon fell asleep: it's not we who must come up with something, but Mischa, all by himself.

After an hour or two Mischa woke Fayngold, patiently put up with his abuse, and then told him his idea. As Mischa has said, Rosa will never spend the night with him if she finds out that there is another man in the room, regardless of whether he's twenty or a hundred. If Mischa doesn't tell her, maybe she will come, then she'll see Fayngold, so she'll leave again and never forgive Mischa. No matter which way you look at it, the only solution is for Fayngold to remain in the room and yet be as good as not there.

"You want me to hide?" was Fayngold's weary response. "You want me to spend night after night under my bed or in the wardrobe?"

"I'll tell her you're deaf and dumb," Mischa announced.

Fayngold protested; for days he bitterly resisted the idea, but eventually Mischa managed to convince him of the urgency. At night a person can't see much anyway, and if she is also sure that you can't hear anything, we should be able to manage. So with distinctly mixed feelings Fayngold gave his consent: If it means so much to you. And ever since then, for Rosa he has been as deaf and dumb as a clam.

For Mischa, though, there was another worry: from a few hints dropped by Fayngold he became aware that Fayngold had once been listening. True, Rosa hadn't noticed anything and Fayngold had kept his mouth shut, but he must have heard a thing or two not intended for his ears. After all, when two people lie in each other's arms, quite a few words are spoken that are not meant for other ears, and it was very embarrassing for Mischa. Since then he has been studying Fayngold's sleep, often deliberately lying awake to listen to the pitch of his breathing and snoring. No one has ever heard himself sleep; no one can imitate his own sleep. A person can imitate sleeping as such but cannot know anything about his own sleep. And Mischa knows what Fayngold's sleep sounds like: he could swear, he says, that he knows it in every detail. And during the rare nights when Rosa is with him, Mischa always first listens intently as he lies beside her, and only when he is quite sure that Fayngold is asleep behind the screen does he begin to caress her and kiss her, and Rosa forgets her disappointment and stops wondering why he has kept her waiting so long.

On one occasion something terrible happened: while deeply asleep, in the midst of a confused dream, Fayngold suddenly began to speak, clearly audible individual words, ignoring the fact that deaf mutes must be deaf and dumb in their sleep too. This woke Mischa, whose heart almost stopped beating; he looked anxiously at Rosa, who lay asleep in the moonlight and merely turned her head from one side to the other. He couldn't call out, Fayngold, shut up! He could only lie there motionless and hope, and luckily Fayngold stopped his fantasizing before there was a disaster. Dreams last for only a few seconds, people say, and it never happened again.

So much for the miniature comedy. All in all, we see that some bold paths have led Rosa to this room, right beneath these covers, not merely straight down one street, then a turn to the left and a turn to the right. Mischa has found a way, Fayngold has cooperated, Rosa is happy to be here.

She is lying on her back, I know, her hands under her head, tonight as always, even though that's a bit selfish since with a big fellow like Mischa the bed has more than enough to cope with: he has to make do with the edge. There she lies, a faraway look in her eyes; the evening, the most wonderful yet, is over. They have already whispered their sweet nothings into each other's ears. Although Fayngold is deaf and dumb, they always whisper, as people do who lie as Rosa and Mischa do now. They would whisper even on a lonely island, if, that is, it were absolutely necessary to speak. The night is far advanced; the mute Fayngold has long since been asleep behind the screen of wardrobe and curtain. The hot weather and the news must have worn him out: tonight he was only a brief impediment. After only a few minutes Mischa was satisfied with the sounds coming from the other side and could lavish his entire attention on Rosa.

Rosa gently nudges Mischa, her foot against his foot, persisting until he is sufficiently awake to ask her what's up.

"My parents will be living with us, won't they?" she says.

Her parents. They had never come as far as this room. There had always been only the night when Mischa and Rosa were lying together and making love — that particular night and no other. All the following ones were yet to come, and there was no use wasting time thinking about them. But now that the parents are here, let's look briefly at what may one day happen, let's peek through the hole in the curtain. Her parents are here, along with an idea of what the future may hold; they can't be thrown out, Rosa is adamant.

"They won't be living with us," says Mischa in the darkness.

"And why not? Do you have something against them?" Rosa raises her voice — these are not matters that demand to be whispered — raises it so rebelliously, perhaps, that Fayngold might wake up, but of course she never suspects this danger.

"Good heavens, is that so important that you have to wake me up in the middle of the night?"

"Yes," says Rosa.

All right. He props himself on his elbows. She can pride herself on having finally chased away his sleep; he sighs, as if life wasn't already difficult enough.

"All right. I have nothing against them, nothing whatsoever. I really like them very much indeed, they won't be living with us, and now I want to sleep!"

He heaves himself onto his other side, a minor demonstration in the moonlight: their first tiff. Not yet a real quarrel, merely a foretaste of everyday worries. A few silent minutes pass during which Mischa notices that Fayngold has woken up.

"Mamma could look after the children," says Rosa.

"Grandmas always spoil children," says Mischa.

"And I don't know how to cook, either."

"There are books."

Now she sighs, Let's quarrel later, we'll have all the time in the world. Rosa has to lift her head slightly because he is pushing his reconciling arm under it: now a kiss to make up, then finally back to sleep. But she can't simply close her eyes and run away. What she sees she sees: we've been waiting a long time for this glimpse into the future. When they knock, when they are standing in the doorway, those Russians, good morning, here we are, now we can start, by that time it's too late, we can't wait till then to decide, we must know by then what has to be done first and what next. But Mischa wants to sleep, and Rosa can't. So many things are mixed up; at least some of them should be straightened out. Important matters will somehow take care of themselves; people of consequence who'll take care of those are sure to show up. Let's start with our own little affairs, no one's going to look after those for us.

From pondering, Rosa progresses to whispering. First of all there's the question of the house, one we'd feel comfortable in, but we might also discuss something other than the house, if you can think of anything, anyway let's begin with the house. Not too small, not too big, let's say five rooms, that's not asking too much. Now don't start yelling, that much one can ask for, we've been modest long enough. There'd be one room for you, one for me, and two for my parents. And a children's room, of course, where they can do what they like, stand on their heads or scribble all over the walls. We would sleep in my room, we don't need a special bedroom, that would be giving away space that would be wasted during the day. We have to think in practical terms too. When we have guests we could sit in your room: a sofa in the middle of the room, that's quite modern, a long, low table in front of it and three or four armchairs. Though I don't want too many guests, just so you know right now. Not because of the upheaval, that's no great problem, but I'd rather be alone with you. Maybe when we're a bit older. And no one's going to tell me how my kitchen should be. It has to be tiled, that's always clean and attractive. Blue and white is what I like best. The Klosenbergs used to have a kitchen like that, just like that, I can't imagine a nicer one. The floor covered with pale gray tiles, on the wall shelves for plates and jugs and ladles, and there must also be a little shelf for all those spices. Nobody knows how many spices there are — saffron, for instance. Do you have any idea what saffron is used for? That it makes cakes and noodles yellow?

The rest of it I don't know since just about here my informant Mischa finally fell asleep, in the midst of all the spices. Perhaps Fayngold could have told me more about this particular night, perhaps he lay awake all the way from basement to attic, but I never asked him.

Then at last it is daytime again, daytime at last. We hurry this way and that in the freight yard with our crates; only a few years earlier it would have been described as cheerful, bustling activity. The sentries behave quite normally, shouting or dozing or shoving as usual; they show no alarm or don't feel it yet. Maybe I am mistaken, but I seem to remember that day very well, although nothing unusual happened, at least not to me. As if it were today, I am standing, so I recall, on a freight car; my job is to take the crates and stack them so that as many as possible will fit into the car. There is another man with me, Herschel Schtamm, and that, come to think of it, *is* something unusual. For Herschel Schtamm has a brother, in fact he has a twin brother, Roman, and the two of them work together and normally are always seen together. But not today. Herschel had a little accident right after starting work. He stumbled while carrying a crate, Roman couldn't hold the crate alone, crate and Herschel crashed to the ground. Herschel had to suffer the usual beating, but that wasn't the worst part: in stumbling, he sprained one foot and could hardly walk, so he couldn't go on carrying with Roman, which is why he is now standing with me on the freight car.

He is sweating buckets, I have never seen anyone sweat like that, and he won't stop sweating until the Russians have captured this damn ghetto, not a day earlier. For Herschel Schtamm is devout. In his lifetime he was a sexton in a synagogue, we call that a shammes, as devout as the rabbi himself. And then there are the earlocks, the pride of all Orthodox Jews: go and ask Herschel whether he is prepared to part with them. Not for all the money in the world, he'll tell you, looking at you as if you were mad. How can you ask such a thing? But the earlocks may only be displayed within one's own four walls, nowhere else. In the street and here at the freight yard one runs into Germans who take a dim view of them: where do we people think we're living for some of us to be running around in a get-up like that? Cases have been known where a grab was made for the nearest pair of scissors, and to the accompaniment of secret prayers and tears of laughter, the matter was taken care of on the spot, but there have been worse cases too.

Herschel has taken the only possible way out: he hides his earlocks. He is smuggling them through these times. Summer and winter he wears a hat. Presumably one is still allowed to wear a hat: a black fur hat with earflaps that can be fastened under the chin. In the sun the hat is terribly hot, but it was the only one he could get hold of, and for his purposes it is eminently suitable. We nondevout ones, even his brother Roman, smiled and made our little jokes only during the first warm week. After that we lost interest: Herschel must know what he's doing.

We hoist a crate onto the very top; he wipes the sweat from his face and asks me, while we are picking up the next one, what I think of that business. I know at once what he is talking about and tell him I'm already wild with joy and can think of nothing else. Everything I once owned will belong to me again, everything except Hannah, who was executed. There will be trees again; in my parents' garden I can see myself sitting in the walnut tree, on such slender branches that my mother is almost ready to faint; right there in the tree I stuff myself with walnuts. My fingers turn so brown from the shells that it takes weeks for the stains to disappear, but Herschel doesn't seem so enthusiastic.

Jacob lifts a crate onto the edge of the freight car. Why all the hurry? Jacob rushes back to the pile with Mischa at his heels. As of yesterday, Jacob is fortune's darling, one of the elect. Everyone is after him, the big fellows as well as the little ones; everyone wants to work with him, with the man who has a direct line to God. Mischa was the first in line, the first to lend a hand when Jacob's eye fell on a crate, and now he's running after him. The fairest way would be to raffle him off, with so-and-so many blanks and one grand prize; then everyone would have the same chance at the supreme stroke of luck, at what has suddenly become so important: being close to Jacob. Only Jacob looks disgruntled: thanks a lot for that kind of luck, five or ten times today he's already been asked — confidentially and hopefully, even by complete strangers — what the radio has been saying. Five or ten times he hasn't known how to answer, has merely repeated what he said yesterday, "Bezanika," or put his fingers to his lips with a conspiratorial "Sssh!" or said nothing and walked on in annoyance. And all this annoyance has been foisted on him by that stupid beanpole who is now scurrying after him, all innocence, in unwarranted joyous anticipation. Something no one could possibly have foreseen. They are behaving like kids, like people eagerly clustering around a bulletin board. Barring a miracle, it will be at best a few hours before the sentries start noticing. Jacob would have welcomed such a crowd in normal times; his shop was open every day except *shabbes*, all year round, and there was a radio in clear view behind the counter: people could listen to whatever they liked. But there you people mostly stayed away, each of you had to be treated like a king, otherwise you'd leave and not come back; and now you're treating *me* like a king and won't leave and keep coming back. A fellow needs a bodyguard for protection against you.

Mischa has no idea what furious thoughts are being ignited so close to him, that it is rage that makes Jacob walk so briskly. They haul a few crates, and Mischa imagines that it will go on like this until noon; he fails to notice the hostile looks directed at him from time to time, more and more often. Until the pot boils over, until Jacob stops in his tracks, in the hope that Mischa will walk on, as far away as possible. But Mischa stops too, looking puzzled: he really is totally unaware, so he might as well be told.

"Please, Mischa," Jacob says in an agonized voice, "there are so many nice fellows here. Do you *have* to haul with me?"

"What's up all of a sudden?"

" 'All of a sudden,' he says! I can't stand the sight of your face anymore!"

"My face?" Mischa smiles stupidly; so far his face hasn't bothered anyone, Jacob least of all. At most there's been the occasional remark about his blue eyes, when people couldn't think of anything better to talk about, and now suddenly this little eruption, almost an insult.

"Yes, your face! With that blabbermouth!" Jacob adds, since Mischa seems so completely in the dark. And now Mischa knows which way the wind is blowing: he is the weak link in the chain of silence — Jacob is right. Although that's no reason to make such a scene, God knows there have been worse things to endure. Mischa shrugs his shoulders: it just happened, too late to change it now. Without a word, before Jacob can get even more worked up, Mischa walks away, which is none of the sentries' business; later or tomorrow there's sure to be time for a conciliatory word.

So Mischa goes alone to the crates and quickly finds a new partner; after all, he hasn't been completely downgraded yet. His powerful arms haven't been forgotten, they are still appreciated; if you can't haul with Jacob, at least you can with Mischa. And Jacob also comes alone to the pyramid, doesn't even see who reaches with him for the crate: his eyes are still glued to Mischa, who eventually disappears without turning around, maybe offended, maybe not. But after a few steps Jacob notices that his new partner doesn't hold the crate as firmly as Mischa does, not nearly, and he looks at him and sees that the new man is Kowalski, and he makes a face and knows that he has fallen from the frying pan into the fire: Kowalski won't leave him in peace for long.

Kowalski doesn't say a word, or rather, he is not just silent, he is restraining himself: how long can he keep this up? He hauls and hauls, which is fine with Jacob. But somehow it irritates him, Kowalski being silent; the red spots on his cheeks haven't come from exertion. Three whole crates are moved in silence. If Kowalski thinks he can starve him out, he's mistaken: Jacob will never bring up the subject on his own since he has nothing to tell, but it gets on his nerves all the same. I'll outwit you, Jacob thinks suddenly. I'll set a trap for you, a harmless conversation that could make you forget the question you're still keeping to yourself. What should we talk about? The noon whistle will blow any minute, and then try and find me.

"Do you know of anything to keep from going bald?" Jacob asks.

"What do you mean?"

"Every morning my comb is full of hair. Isn't there something one can do about it?"

"Nothing," says Kowalski, clearly implying that the subject doesn't interest him.

"Surely there's something? I remember that at your shop you used to treat a customer with some such stuff. . . . I seem to remember it was green?"

"Just a racket," says Kowalski. "I treated lots of people with that, but I might just as well have rubbed water into their scalps. Some customers insist on having something rubbed in. And it wasn't green, it was yellow."

"There's nothing that'll help?"

"You heard me."

So far so good. They keep on hauling in silence. In Jacob the hope is growing that he is mistaken, that Kowalski has no intention of asking him, that he reached for the crate simply because he was the closest, and the red spots might actually be due to exertion or bedbug bites. Why do we often fail to think of the obvious? There's no reason to lose faith in all integrity on account of a few bad experiences: Kowalski also has his good side, as countless memories go to show. After all, they were almost close friends. Already Jacob looks at the sweating Kowalski more kindly, a secret apology in his glance, secret because, fortunately, the reproaches have also remained secret. Each new crate that is carried wordlessly to the freight car is leading him away from the suspicion that he has apparently been directing at an innocent person.

Then suddenly, just before noon, Kowalski puts his sneaky question. Without preamble and in a humiliatingly innocent voice he says, "Well?"

That's all. Jacob flinches; we know what is meant. Instantly all his rage returns. Jacob feels deceived; the red spots are the same old ones after all. And it wasn't by chance that Kowalski was closest to the crate; he was lying in wait, working all day toward that infamous "Well?" He didn't keep quiet for so long out of consideration — he doesn't even know what that is — he kept quiet because he saw Jacob having an argument with Mischa, and he has merely been waiting for a favorable moment, cold and calculating as he is: Jacob was to be lulled into a sense of security.

Jacob flinches; the worst thing in this ghetto is that you can't just turn your back and walk away. It isn't advisable to repeat this ploy too often.

"Anything new?" Kowalski asks more pointedly. He is not in the mood for a prolonged exchange of stares. If you don't understand my "Well?" then so be it.

"No," says Jacob.

"You're not seriously trying to tell me that in wartime a whole day passes and nothing happens? A whole day and a whole night?"

They lift the crate onto the edge of the freight car and go back to the pile. Jacob takes a deep breath, and Kowalski gives him an encouraging nod; Jacob loses his self-control and raises his voice to an undesirable pitch.

"For God's sake, stop pestering me, can't you? Didn't I tell you yesterday that they're within twelve miles of Bezanika? Isn't that enough?"

Of course it is not enough for Kowalski if the Russians are within twelve miles of some place called Bezanika and he is here: how could that be enough for him? But he has no time for logical rejoinders, not at the moment. He looks around nervously, Jacob having been less than cautious. In fact a sentry is standing quite close by. They have to walk past him, and he is already looking their way. The uniform doesn't look right on him; he is much too young for it. They have already noticed him several times. He has a loud mouth but so far hasn't done much in the way of beating.

"What have you scumbags got to argue about?" he asks as they are about to walk by him. Obviously he hasn't heard any details, only raised voices, which can be quickly explained.

"We're not arguing, sir," says Kowalski loudly. "It's just that I'm a bit hard of hearing."

The sentry looks them up and down and rocks on his toes, then turns around and walks away. Kowalski and Jacob pick up another crate without wasting a word over the incident.

"A whole day has gone by, Jacob. Twenty-four long hours. Surely they must have advanced at least a few measly miles!"

"Yes, two miles according to the latest reports."

"And you act as if you don't care? Every foot counts, I tell you, every single foot!"

"So what's two miles?" says Jacob.

"I like that! Maybe for you it isn't much, you hear the news every day. But two miles is two miles!"

The ordeal is over, Kowalski won't bother him again today; he is as mute as Fayngold now that he's found out what he wanted to know.

Jacob has to admit that it wasn't so bad; actually the words came out quite easily, as he explained to me at length. It was an important moment for him, he told me. The first lie, which may not even have been one, such a little lie, and Kowalski is satisfied. It's worth it: hope must not be allowed to fade away, otherwise they won't survive. He knows for sure that the Russians are advancing, he has heard it with his own ears, and if there is a God in heaven, they must come at least this far; and if there is no God, they must come at least this far and they must find as many survivors as possible, so it's worth it. And if we should all be dead, it was an attempt, so it's worth it. The trouble is, he has to dream up enough bits of news, for they will go on asking questions, they will want to know details, not just how many miles; he must invent the answers. He hopes his brain will be equal to it. Not everyone is good at inventing things; so far he has invented only one other thing in his life, that was years ago, a new recipe for potato pancakes with cottage cheese and onions and caraway seeds, you can hardly compare the two.

"And besides, it's important that they're advancing at all," says Kowalski reflectively. "I mean, better to advance slowly than to retreat quickly. . . ."

We're late enough coming to Lina, inexcusably late, for she is of some importance to all this. It is she who rounds it out, if one can say such a thing. Jacob goes to her every day, but we have only come now. Lina is eight years old, long black hair and brown eyes, just the way they should be, a strikingly beautiful child, most people say. She can look at you so that you feel like sharing your last mouthful with her, but only Jacob does that; sometimes he even gives her everything. That's because he has never had children of his own.

For two years Lina has had no parents: they went away, they got on a freight train and went away, leaving behind their only child, alone. Barely two years ago Lina's father was walking along the

street; no one had pointed out to him that he was wearing the wrong
jacket, the jacket without the yellow stars. It was early autumn, and
he was walking along with nothing bad in mind; they would certainly
have noticed on the job, but he never got there. Halfway to work he
met a patrol; one sharp look was enough, but Nuriel didn't know how
to interpret it.

"Are you married?" one of the two men asked him.

"Yes," Nuriel said, never suspecting what they wanted of him
with their strange question.

"Where does your wife work?"

In such and such a place, Nuriel replied. So off they went with
him to the factory and hauled her out of the building. The moment
she saw him with the two men she noticed the bare places on the
front and back of Nuriel's jacket. She looked at him in horror, and
Nuriel said to her, "I don't know what's going on either."

"Your stars," she whispered.

Nuriel looked down at his chest. Only then did he realize that
this was the end, the end or shortly before it; a much lesser reason
would have sufficed for the end, according to the rules of the ghetto.
The men accompanied Nuriel and his wife to their home, telling
them on the way what they would be allowed to take with them. Lina
wasn't playing in front of the building, neither was she in the hallway;
her mother had given her strict instructions to leave their room as
seldom as possible. But we can't know, can we, what children get up
to all day while their parents are at work: a fervent prayer that this
one time she may have been disobedient. She wasn't in the room
either, so she couldn't be surprised and ask what was the matter, why
were Papa and Mama coming home so early, and the men would have
known that Nuriel had more than a wife. They packed their few
things, the two men standing beside them to make sure everything
was being done correctly. Nuriel moved like a sleepwalker until his
wife nudged him and told him to hurry up. Now he hurried too. He
had caught her meaning: at any moment Lina might come into the
room.

Going down the stairs he had seen through a landing window that Lina was playing in the yard (all this without witnesses, but perhaps that's exactly how it was and not otherwise). She was balancing on the low wall between the two yards: God knows how many times he had forbidden her to do this, but that's the way children are. A neighbor who happened to be on night shift that week met them on the stairs, and she heard Nuriel's wife telling him that he shouldn't keep looking out of the window but should watch his step or he'd fall. So he did that, he didn't fall. Without incident they emerged into the street, and since then Lina has had no parents. Shortly afterward, a new family was allocated to the Nuriels' room: at that time there was still a stream of new arrivals.

What to do with Lina became a problem: no one could take her in permanently, and not only because of insufficient space or lack of kindness. All it needed was a spot check: What is this child doing here? For weeks everyone waited for a search to be made for Lina: someone in some office somewhere, in going through some papers, could have noticed that instead of three Nuriels only two went on that transport, but nothing of the kind occurred. Eventually a few women in the building cleaned up the little attic, her bed was moved upstairs together with a chest of drawers containing her belongings — which of course were still there — and Lina lived on the top floor. Only a stove was lacking, but none could be found. During the coldest nights, when even two blankets were not enough, Jacob, who never had any children of his own, risked taking her secretly into his bed. The natural result of this was that she belongs to him more than to anyone else; she has had two years to twist him around her little finger, more than enough time.

Tonight is not a cold night, let alone the coldest; Herschel Schtamm has been sweating profusely all day. Lina will have to sleep alone. Jacob goes up to her room; he does this every evening. Lina is lying there with her eyes closed. Jacob knows quite well that she isn't asleep, and she knows quite well that he knows, which results every evening in some new joke. He takes a paper bag from his pocket, in the bag is a carrot, which he puts down on the chest of drawers beside the bed, then he performs today's joke. He blows up the paper bag and bursts it by clapping his hands, but Lina is already laughing while her eyes are still closed: something is about to happen. So what happens is the bang. Lina sits up, gives him the kiss he has earned, and insists that she is already feeling much better. She intends to get up tomorrow, this silly old whooping cough can't last forever, but Jacob can't make that decision himself. He puts his hand on her forehead.

"Do I still have a temperature?" Lina asks.

"Maybe just a little, if my thermometer is working properly."

She picks up the carrot, asks him what that actually means, a temperature, and starts to eat.

"I'll explain that some other time," says Jacob. "Has the professor been to see you today?" No, not yet, but he said yesterday that there was some improvement, and Jacob shouldn't always put her off with "some other time": he still has to explain to her about gas masks, epidemics, balloons, martial law, she's forgotten what else, and now he also owes her about temperatures.

Jacob lets her talk; she seems quite cheerful. Perhaps he thinks a bit wistfully of the three cigarettes the carrot cost him; he must get the next one more cheaply. In the end everything turns into pure conversation, of which Lina is a master; she must have been born with that gift.

"How's work going?" she asks.

"Couldn't be better," replies Jacob. "Nice of you to ask."

"Was it also so hot where you were today? Here it was frightfully hot."

"Not too bad."

"So what did you do today? Did you ride the locomotive again?"

"What gave you that idea?"

"The other day you rode it as far as Rudpol and back again — don't you remember?"

"Oh yes, of course. But not today, the locomotive has been out of commission for the last few days."

"What's wrong with it?"

"It's lost a wheel, and there aren't any new ones."

"What a shame. How's Mischa, by the way? He hasn't been to see me for ages."

"He's very busy. But I'm glad you reminded me; he sends you his love."

"Thank you," says Lina. "Give him mine too."

"I will."

It could go on like this for hours, via twenty carrots. It doesn't matter what they chat about; they keep talking until the door opens, until Kirschbaum comes in.

If I hadn't made up my mind from the start to deal with something else, I would tell Kirschbaum's story. Maybe I will someday, the temptation is great, although we only met briefly two or three times, and he never even knew my name. I really only know him from Jacob's sparse comments; he mentioned Kirschbaum almost marginally, but he made me curious. Kirschbaum plays no major role in this particular context: the main thing is that he cured Lina. Years ago Kirschbaum was a celebrity, nothing like Rosa's father, but a genuine, bona fide celebrity heaped with honors, head of a Kraków hospital, in great demand as a heart specialist; lectures at universities all over the world, fluent in French, Spanish, and German, said to have been in intermittent correspondence with Albert Schweitzer. Anyone wanting to be cured by him had to go to a good deal of trouble; to this day he continues to exude the dignity of an eminent personage, with no effort on his part. His suits do, too: made of the best English cloth, a little worn at elbows and knees, but they're still beautifully cut; all of them dark in color as an effective contrast to his snow-white hair.

Kirschbaum has never given a thought to being a Jew; his father before him was a surgeon. What does it mean, of Jewish origin? They force you to be a Jew while you yourself have no idea what it really is.

Now he is surrounded only by Jews, for the first time in his life nothing but Jews. He has racked his brains about them, wanting to find out what it is that they all have in common, in vain. They have nothing recognizably in common, and he most certainly nothing with them.

For most of them he is something of a wizard. Kirschbaum doesn't feel comfortable with that; he'd prefer warmth to respect. He tries to adjust but goes about it awkwardly, while everyone expects something special from him, and he is so totally lacking in the humor that might help.

He comes into the attic bringing a pot of soup for Lina, his step as springy as a thirty-year-old's; the tennis club has kept him young.

"Good evening, everyone," he says.

"Good evening, Professor."

Jacob gets up from the bed, making room for Kirschbaum, who wants to listen to Lina's chest. She is already taking off her night-gown. The soup is still too hot; she is always examined first. Jacob goes to the window, which is open, a little attic window, yet from it one can see half the town. Perhaps a sunset, the buildings gray and gold, and much peace. The Russians will march along all the streets, not omitting a single one, those damned stars will be removed from the doors and leave behind light patches, like ugly pictures that have hung too long on the wall and go to their well-deserved end on the rubbish heap. At last he has, like the others, a little time for rosy thoughts, as if it were Kowalski who had reported the miracle. Some-where down there the future lies hidden: no more great adventures; let the younger generation plunge into those. No doubt the shop will need a new coat of paint, perhaps a few new tables as well. He might even get a license to serve schnapps, something that would have been virtually impossible for him before. A place for Lina could be fixed up in the storage room; he just hopes no distant relatives will come barging in wanting to take her away. Only her parents can have her, but who knows whether they are still alive? Next year she'll start school: ridiculous, a young lady of nine in the lowest grade. The lowest grade will be full of overgrown children; perhaps someone will come up with an idea so they won't have to waste too much time. It wouldn't be a bad idea to teach her a few things in advance, at least reading and a bit of arithmetic — why hadn't he ever thought of that before? But first she must get well.

"Well, now I can tell you," says Kirschbaum. "Things looked rather bad for this young lady. But when young ladies do as they are told it is usually possible to achieve something. We have pretty well repaired the damage. Take a deep breath and hold it!"

In the cupboard, right at the bottom, is an old book, a travel description of Africa or America that would do quite nicely for learning to read; it even has a few illustrations. Somehow the idea must be made appealing to her, for if she doesn't feel like it, you can talk until you're blue in the face. As soon as it's possible I'll adopt her, after searching for her parents first of course, without her knowing about it. They say adoption is not so simple; there are a whole lot of formalities and authorities if someone at an advanced age comes by a child. The Germans have their share of responsibility, and the Russians have theirs; who has the greater? I'll tell her that we're finished now with forever telling fairy tales, that there's more to life than princes and witches and magicians and robbers; reality looks quite different, you're old enough now, this is an *A*. She is bound to ask what that means, an *A*, she will want to know what it's for, she has a very practical mind, at her age questions are half of life. He can see difficult times ahead. As a child she is already eight years old, and as a father I am barely two.

Kirschbaum is holding the stethoscope to her chest and listening intently. Suddenly he registers mock surprise, looks at Lina with wide eyes, and asks: "Dear me, what have we here? Do I hear some whistling in there?"

Lina throws an amused glance at Jacob, who doesn't stop; he didn't realize he'd started, but now he carries on, not wanting to spoil Kirschbaum's meager joke, and Lina laughs at the silly professor who hasn't understood that the whistling comes not from her chest but from Uncle Jacob.

Why, one wonders, did anyone say that coming events cast their shadows before them? Far and wide no shadows, a few uneventful days pass, uneventful for the historian. No new decrees, nothing visibly happening, nothing you can put your finger on, nothing that would seem to indicate change. Some say they have noticed that the Germans have become more restrained; some say that, because nothing at all is happening, it is the calm before the storm. But I say the calm before the storm is a lie, that nothing at all is a lie, the storm, or part of it, is already there: the whispering in the rooms, the fears and speculations, the hopes and prayers. The great day of the prophets has arrived. When people argue, they argue about plans: mine is better than yours. They have all packed their belongings, all are aware of the inconceivable. Anyone who is not must be a hermit. Not everyone knows the source of the report, the ghetto is too big for that, but the Russians are on everybody's mind. Old debts raise their heads again, diffidently the debtors are reminded, daughters turn into brides, weddings are planned for the week before New Year's, people have gone stark staring mad, suicide figures have dropped to zero.

Anyone executed now, so shortly before the end, will have suddenly lost a future. For heaven's sake, give no cause now for Majdanek or Auschwitz (if causes can be said to have any meaning); use caution, Jews, the utmost caution, and make no thoughtless move.

Two parties soon form and divide every building — not every one is Jacob's friend — two parties without statutes but with weighty arguments and a platform and the art of persuasion. One group is feverish for news: what happened last night, how high are the losses on each side? No report is so trivial that one conclusion or another can't be drawn from it. And the others, Frankfurter's party, have heard enough; for them this radio is a source of constant danger, and it would be so easy for Jacob to put their fears to rest. I hear their misgivings at the freight yard and on the way home and in the

building. In your naïveté you'll be the death of us all, they warn; the
Germans are not deaf or blind. And the ghetto regulations are not
merely suggestions for good behavior; it says right there in black and
white what it means to listen to a radio, as well as what happens to
those who know that someone is listening and who don't report it. So
calm down and wait quietly in your corner. When the Russians show
up they'll show up; no amount of talking will get them here. And
above all stop talking about that wretched radio, about that potential
cause of a thousand deaths; the sooner it's destroyed the better.

That's the situation, so not everyone is Jacob's friend, but he is
not aware of this, nor has he any way of finding out.

Those who crowd around him, those greedy for news, the hundred Kowalskis, they'll be sure not to tell him because Jacob might
have second thoughts, change his mind, and suddenly decide to say
nothing; they'd rather say nothing themselves. And the admonishers
would be the last to tell him. They're not going to send any warning
delegation to him, that would be far too risky. They give Jacob a wide
berth: no one must be able to testify that they'd been seen in his
company.

The earlocked Herschel Schtamm, for example, is one of the
others, those who don't want to hear and see anymore and don't wish
to be accessories. At the freight yard, when, our hands held to our
mouths, we evaluate the latest Russian successes, fresh from Jacob's
lips, he moves a few steps away, but not too far, still within earshot I'd
say. As long as it's not a conversation in which he is seen to be
involved: that's obviously what he is worried about. Herschel's gaze
wanders aimlessly over the tracks, or lands on one of us with disapproving severity, yet it is quite possible that under the sweat-
inducing fur hat he pricks up his ears like a rabbit.

The power failure that turns Jacob's radio for days into a life-
threatening dust gatherer is, Herschel feels, his personal achieve-
ment. Not that he makes any such claim in public: Herschel is not
given to boasting, but we heard about this from his twin brother
Roman, who spends every evening and every morning in the same

room with him and every night in the same bed. He must know, after
all. When we ask Herschel how he brought off such a feat — cutting
off the power in several streets for several days isn't exactly child's
play — a benign expression spreads over his face, almost a smile as
after surviving a great ordeal, but he refuses to say a word.

And then we ask, "How was it, Roman? How did he manage it?"
The last few minutes before going to bed, Roman tells us, are filled
with prayer, quietly in a corner, an old habit established well before
the radio. Roman waits patiently in bed until their shared blanket can
be drawn over their heads. He has long ceased urging Herschel to
hurry up and come to bed, having been enlightened as to the incom-
patibility of prayer and haste. He disregards the monotonous murmuring, the chanting; to listen would be a waste of time since Roman
doesn't understand a word of Hebrew. But recently some familiar
sounds have been penetrating his ear. Ever since Herschel has had
concrete petitions to send up to God, no longer the usual pious stuff
about protecting and making everything turn out for the best, he
resorts more and more often to the vernacular. In a fragmentary way,
Roman can now listen to what is preoccupying and tormenting his
brother: nothing extraordinary — if he were to pray himself, he
wouldn't have anything very different to say. Night after night God is
informed about hunger, about the fear of deportation or being beaten
by sentries, all of which cannot possibly be happening with His
approval; would He please see what could be done about this, soon, if
possible, it is urgent, and could He also give a sign that one has been
heard? The sign is slow to appear, a test of constancy passed with
flying colors by Herschel: each succeeding day has been scanned in
vain for some modifying intervention. Until at last it did appear, that
longed-for sign, unheralded like all divine action and so potent that
any word of doubt could not but die away on the lips of even the most
hardened unbeliever.

That night Herschel's topic was the radio, at present the most
overriding of all worries. He explains to God in minute detail the
incalculable consequences that will result if thoughtlessness and

carelessness allow the gossips to overlook a German ear and, before you know it, it's happened: the gossips are called to account, in line with the present law, together with their silent accessories. And it will be claimed that we are all accessories, that the news has not circumvented a single person, and actually they will be right. Besides, it need not even be a German ear that happens to be nearby; there are also camouflaged German ears, and only You know how many informers are at large among us. Or someone wants to save his own skin and betrays on his own initiative the existence of the radio. There are scoundrels everywhere, You know that too; without Your consent they would not be in this world. Don't permit the great disaster to overwhelm us, so close to the end, seeing that all these years You have held Your sheltering hand over us and saved us from the worst. For Your own sake, don't permit it. Don't let the Germans find out anything about the radio; You know what they are capable of. Or better still, if I may make a suggestion, destroy that cursed radio; that would be the most satisfactory solution.

At this point the lightbulb below the ceiling suddenly begins to flicker. At first Herschel ignores it, but then he looks up with wide eyes: in a flash the significance of this is revealed to him. God has granted his request, his prayers have not been in vain; at the appropriate moment He sends His sign, the acknowledgment of receipt, truly a sign that could not be more practical: this proves He is God! Without power the radio will be doomed to shut up; the more ardently Herschel prays, the more the light flickers. "Don't stop now!" Roman spurs him on, but there's no need for him to say it, Herschel knows what is at stake: advice from scoffers is not asked for when bliss beckons as a reward. Fervently he exploits his contact until the crowning success: the light finally goes out, the ultimate word has been spoken. Herschel rushes to the window and scans the other side of the street: not a single curtain shows a glimmer of light, not even in Jacob Heym's building. We have silenced you, my friend, heavenly silence will reign, take your terrible box and give it to the devil; it's of no further use to you. And don't imagine that the power, the loss of which you innocently assume to be a breakdown, will be restored tomorrow: short circuits instigated by the Supreme Being take their time.

Proud and moderately happy, as far as circumstances permit, Herschel, his day's labors over, goes to bed and serenely accepts Roman's congratulations.

Worried faces wherever Jacob looks: What's going to happen? Here they sit, high and dry, with no idea what is going on in the outside world. These intolerable conditions are already in their third day; this is no longer a power failure, this is a natural disaster. Must we really be the victims of this catastrophe too? They had been rash enough to take the joyful reports for granted; they had become addicted to the advance of a few miles every morning, and all day long there was something to hope for and to discuss. And now this dismal silence. Our first step each morning has led us to the light switch; some of us even got up in the middle of the night. We have pressed the switch and obtained the dreaded response that for yet another day Jacob will be no wiser than we are. Only the electricity will make him all-knowing again, only the electricity that the powers of darkness have turned off, only when the lights go on again in all the rooms, only then will his light shine with a special brilliance. But when will that be?

The one person who is not affected by the new reason for anxiety is Jacob. For once, Jacob is not affected by this calamity. His connection with the outside world has not broken off; what does not exist cannot break off. The connection is as tenuous as it had ever been, only that at last he can admit this. No rhyme or reason the way Fortune chooses which pot will boil, even though it be a very modest Fortune disguised as a power failure. May it last until the first Russian faces take the sentries at the outskirts of the town by surprise. At least Jacob can breathe more freely now, can revert to being just one among many; nobody forces him to know more than all the others, but he must keep up the pretense, a constant pretense, he must feign regret where there is none, regret over the power failure — no easy task considering his relief: You have seen, my friends, that I was doing my best; as long as it was possible I supplied you with the latest and the best. There hasn't been a day when you have been deprived of comforting reports. How I would love to go on reporting until that longed-for hour arrives, but my hands are tied, you can see for yourselves.

Next morning Kowalski has won the race again: he is hauling with Jacob, except that this time it was no longer really a race. Overnight Jacob has become just another worker, an elderly person with two undeniably weak hands that are no longer in great demand. Kowalski has paired off with Jacob more from habit, or out of friendship; in any case they are hauling together. It is a long time since things have been so quiet between them. To Jacob the crates seem a shade lighter since Kowalski and the others have stopped plying him with questions; to Kowalski no doubt heavier now that answers are no longer forthcoming. Weight, as can be seen, is not an absolute quantity. The last question was whether in Jacob's building the light — God forbid — had also failed, to which Jacob answered simply and truthfully yes. After such a long time he was quite happy to be able to speak the unadulterated truth, and since then it has been as quiet around him as around anybody else. That's how it will remain until the electricity is restored, and no one should be surprised at Jacob's composure.

When the whistle blows for soup, they sit down side by side in the sunshine. Kowalski sighs and spoons and sighs; this is not due to the soup, which tastes neither better nor worse than on any other day. Recently Jacob has learned to dread Kowalski's presence. Kowalski was the most avid among the curious, letting Jacob neither eat nor sleep and using him simply as a vehicle for his curiosity, relentlessly. But today his presence cannot alarm Jacob; questions would be a waste of words. The sun is shining, they are sitting side by side, peacefully and silently eating, and somewhere in the distance Stalin's soldiers are approaching at an unknown speed.

"How long do you think this power failure can go on?" Kowalski asks.

"For twenty years, I hope," says Jacob.

Kowalski looks up from his bowl with an injured expression: that's no kind of answer between friends. Of course the last few days haven't been easy for Jacob, the sole connection with the outside world that everybody wanted to take advantage of, we've been assaulting and peppering you, and there's been some risk too, but can one in our situation object to that little extra effort? Who in your position would have acted otherwise? Look for him among us and you will not find him, and then in reply to our modest question we have to listen to such harsh words.

"Why are you so mean?" Kowalski asks.

"You'll never find out," says Jacob.

Kowalski shrugs and goes on eating; there's no talking to Jacob today. Maybe he's in a bad mood — as a matter of fact, there have always been days when he was strangely quarrelsome. When one came into his cheerless shop, in the old days, after entering in the best of moods and sitting down at one of the many empty tables and asking Jacob a perfectly normal question, such as "How's business?" the way anyone would, it sometimes happened that, instead of giving a normal answer, like "Business is thus and so," as might be expected from an adult person, he would snap back with "What a stupid question — can't you see for yourself?"

Not entirely by chance, Kowalski and Jacob are joined by two others. Mischa sits down beside them: he's brought along Schwoch, junior partner of Lifschitz and Schwoch, wholesale and retail stamp pads. At first Jacob assumes that they've sat down simply because there is still room here, a little unobserved spot in the sunshine, until he notices that they keep exchanging looks, Mischa's being encouraging and Schwoch's undecided. Now he realizes that it's no coincidence, some unknown factor is involved; he has learned to pay attention to the minutest nuances. Mischa's looks mean Go ahead and say it, and Schwoch's mean No, I'd rather you said it, and when all these looks threaten to go on forever, Jacob says between two spoonfuls, "I'm listening."

"We have sort of an idea," says Schwoch.

So far so good, there's always room for a decent idea, good ideas are like air for breathing. Let's hear what you've come up with, then we'll see.

But Schwoch seems tongue-tied after his tentative opening. He looks at Mischa again, and his eyes convey, I'd rather you said it.

"The thing is this," says Mischa. "We've been thinking: if the power won't come to the radio, then the radio must go to the power."

"Is this some kind of a riddle?" Jacob asks uneasily, though there's no mystery about Mischa's words. They mean no more and no less than that somewhere in some street in this ghetto the lights are still on, he'll soon hear in which street; any normal intelligence can put two and two together.

"In Kowalski's street the power is on," says Schwoch.

These propitious words, uttered for Jacob's benefit, reach Kowalski's ears just as he is scraping out his bowl. His hands stop in midair, for a brief moment he closes his eyes, his lips whisper bitterly, may Schwoch be struck by lightning, and he moves aside. Not far, just a few symbolic inches. He hasn't heard a thing, let these madmen go on saying what they like, all this has nothing to do with him.

This minor revelation is not lost on Jacob; a pity he can't smile. There are important things to do before their break is over and Mischa and Schwoch's plan begins to circulate and is judged worthy of at least some consideration. That with Kowalski they'll find themselves up against a brick wall is as clear as day to Jacob; there's no danger from that quarter. Anyone who has lived within earshot of Kowalski all these years knows what a hero does not look like. Trimming your beard in the latest fashion and arranging your hair artistically so that people in the street turn around to look at you, these may be within his scope; but listening to broadcasts on pain of death and passing on their contents — he's not that stupid. The problem certainly doesn't lie with Kowalski; the real worry is that someone else will be found — Kowalski's street is a long one. Someone else may come and say, Hand over the set, we'll let it play and sing and proclaim heaven on earth.

They must be totally persuaded to drop their plan if nothing is to come of it, and nothing will come of it: it must be the plan's fault, not Kowalski's. He must emerge from the affair as a perfectly honorable man; words must be found that disparage the very idea itself and prove its complete uselessness. So, let's have such proof, but where to find it in a hurry? Maybe Kowalski will come up with the right thing. For once he is Jacob's ally; they are sitting in the same uncomfortable boat. Kowalski, too, will gnaw away with all his strength at Mischa and Schwoch's idea; he'll say anything except that he is too scared. He has to be shoved into the water up to his neck, then he'll talk; all one can hope is that in this short time he will be able to grow the appropriate angel's tongue.

"Did you hear what they want you to do?" Jacob asks.

Kowalski turns his head toward Jacob, pretending that his thoughts were far away, and asks with perfect innocence, "Who, me?" And then he asks Schwoch: "What is it?"

"We're talking about the electricity," Schwoch explains patiently. "The radio might be taken to your place, mightn't it?"

Kowalski acts as if he has heard a bad joke. "To my place?"

"Yes."

"The radio?"

"Yes."

"Wonderful!"

These idiots want to kill me, he must be thinking; they want to ruin me, as if I don't have enough to worry about, and they talk about my doom as if it were the most natural thing in the world.

"How about you, Jacob? What do you say?"

"Why not?" says Jacob. "It's up to you. It's fine with me."

It only looks as if he's playing with fire; he knows exactly what to expect from Kowalski, and besides, if Kowalski were suddenly to turn into a hero, he could always change his mind later. But it's safe to assume that won't be necessary. Kowalski is an arithmetic problem for six-year-olds.

"Don't you realize the risk you're running?" Kowalski asks, utterly astonished at such recklessness. "And what does that mean, anyway: the radio might be taken to my place? Who by? Me? You? He? Who by? Do you intend to carry the radio through the ghetto in broad daylight? Or better still, at night, after eight o'clock maybe?"

He leans back, indignant; it verges on the comical, what they're suggesting, and they claim to be intelligent people.

"They're planning on a procession! The patrols and sentries will go to bed during that time, and when it's over we'll go and wake them up and say, 'You can carry on now, the radio is safely at Kowalski's!' "

Schwoch and Mischa exchange worried looks; taken apart, their plan no longer seems quite so brilliant, and Jacob also contributes a few significant looks, serious and full of doubt. Kowalski's outburst seems to have given even him food for thought.

"Besides, there's another important point," Kowalski goes on. "By this time many people know there is a radio in the ghetto, but who has any idea that it's at Jacob's? We four here at the freight yard and maybe his neighbors. If so far nothing has gone wrong, that's to say, if so far the Germans haven't the slightest suspicion, we can assume that there are reliable people living in Jacob's building. But what makes you think it's like that in my building? I share with three men: who can guarantee that there isn't a traitor or a coward above me or beside me or below me? And that he will have nothing more urgent to do than run to the gestapo and tell them what he knows?"

A long pause, Kowalski's words are assessed and weighed, and in a low voice Schwoch says, "Shit, he's right."

Mischa shrugs, undecided, and Jacob stands up, saying, "If that's how you feel . . ."

"Why be in such a hurry and run a risk, fellows?" Kowalski says. "The power is bound to come back on again, if not tomorrow then the day after. Then it still won't be too late for Jacob to tell us how far they've got."

By the time the Whistle summons them back to work, Mischa and Schwoch's plan is dead and buried. It has been discussed in detail, as is only proper among people endowed with intelligence; its weak points have been brought to light, and it could not withstand the light. It would have been wonderful, what a shame, but clear thinking has opened our eyes. Schwoch and Mischa put their empty bowls back on the handcart. They are almost the last; the sentry is already casting impatient and threatening looks their way.

Once again Jacob and Kowalski form a solitary pair, each relieved of an anxiety, each having survived an ordeal.

"The ideas they come up with!" says Kowalski with a grin, more to himself than to Jacob, thus closing this chapter.

Lina is standing idly in the doorway, watching Rafael and Siegfried sitting on the curb and whispering together, whispering with exaggerated caution, it seems to her. As soon as someone walks by they stop and squint innocently into the sun. Lina pricks up her ears in vain, her restraint quickly melts away, and she crosses the street to find out what the two show-offs are whispering about. She hears Siegfried maintain that there's not much time left, and Rafael says that at home they claim it can't last more than a few days.

Then she is discovered. The two boys look at her nonchalantly and wait with deadpan expressions for the interruption to end. But they can wait forever, Lina doesn't walk on; she stays where she is and smiles brightly. Until Rafael finally gets up.

"Come on. What we have to discuss is none of her business," he says.

That's just what Siegfried thinks too. Drawing himself up to his full height in front of Lina, he gives her to understand that they would beat the daylights out of her if she weren't just a runt of a girl. Lina accepts the threat impassively, since anyway the two boys turn and disappear into their own building. Lina waits for a few moments; Jacob, who has strictly forbidden her to go into strange buildings, is far away, and Lina follows them in. Carefully sticking her head through the door to the inner courtyard, she catches sight of Siegfried and Rafael going into the shed where, in happier days, Panno the carpenter used to have his workshop; to this day it still reeks of glue. There is no glass in the window of the shed, Lina knows that without checking; she was there herself when Rafael managed to hit the last remaining pane with his first throw. So the nefarious thoughts of the two boys won't remain hidden for long, not from her. She tiptoes to the dark window and quietly crouches down on the ground. She is ready; they can fire away now.

"What we could do is blow up the military office," she hears Siegfried say.

"What if they catch us?" asks Rafael.

"Don't wet your pants. The Russians will soon be here, you heard it, too. Besides, they can't catch us if we blow them up because then they'll all be dead. Only we mustn't let them spot us first."

Siegfried has always been full of hot air; Lina could bet then and there that nothing will come of it.

"D'you think the top Russian will give us something if we bring it off?" asks greedy Rafael.

"What a stupid question. A decoration, or a real pistol, or something to eat!"

"Or all three?"

"For sure! Wouldn't that be something? And we wouldn't tell anybody at home."

For a second or two there was silence. No doubt the two idiots were imagining all the things the Russians would fish out of their overflowing pockets to reward them for their heroic deeds.

Suddenly Rafael says disconsolately, "Siegfried . . . it won't work."

"Why?"

"Where are we going to get hold of some dynamite? Even if I empty my two cartridges, that'll never be enough."

"You're right. You got any more at home?"

"No."

"Nor have we."

Lina laughs and puts her hands over her mouth, which almost lets out a shriek; it's incredible how stupid two ten-year-old boys can be.

Rafael has another idea: "You know what? We'll lock 'em up!"

"Who?"

"The gestapos, who else? We'll just lock up the military office. At night they're all asleep, and then we'll lock 'em up. The doors are at least that thick, and they put bars on all the windows themselves. . . . They'll never get out! And then when the Russkies get here we'll have them all!" Rafael is panting with excitement.

"But we don't have a key!"

"We'll find one," says Rafael confidently. "In my dad's drawer there's a ring with at least twenty keys on it. One of them is sure to fit, you'll see."

"Not bad at all," Siegfried grumbles, audibly annoyed at not having thought of this brilliant idea himself. He'd be only too glad to find fault with Rafi's plan, but there's nothing wrong with it.

Just then the door to the courtyard opens and little Mrs. Bujok appears, looking for her wayward son, but she can't see him. She sees only Lina sitting on her heels and smiling. "Have you seen Siegfried?"

Lina is startled out of her absorption; she looks up at Mrs. Bujok and regains her smile. That "runt of a girl" still echoes in her ear. She might as well make hay while the sun shines: Lina gestures with her thumb to the shed behind her. Mrs. Bujok looks menacingly at the shed, pauses for a moment to take a deep breath, then marches in. Lina hears a none-too-gentle slap, then "Ow!" and "How often do I have to tell you to stay close to my window!" and finally one more slap and "You go home too, you rascal!"

As silence settles over the yard, Lina gets up and brushes off her skirt; the performance is over. Mrs. Bujok emerges from the shed; anger has made her red in the face. Siegfried is hanging on to her with one hand while holding the other against his cheek. At least he's not howling. They quickly leave the yard; Siegfried doesn't notice Lina.

Lina also goes toward the courtyard door. She is in no hurry. She could stay, actually, but since Rafael is alone, her listening post has lost its value. He might even deign to make do with her now, but she couldn't care less about that; she no longer feels like it. Let him sit there by himself and stew over which of the twenty keys will fit; nothing's going to come of it anyway.

So she leaves, turning back once more in the doorway. Rafael is taking his time.

"You're both pretty stupid!" she shouts across the yard toward the shed, which doesn't make her exactly popular.

And the resistance, I will be asked: Where is the resistance? Could it be that the heroes are gathering in the shoe factory or in the freight yard, at least a few? Is it possible that at the ghetto's southern limits, which are the least clearly defined and hence the hardest to keep under surveillance, dark passages have been discovered through which weapons can be smuggled into the ghetto? Or are there in this wretched town only hands that do exactly what Hardtloff and his sentries demand of them?

Condemn them, go ahead and condemn us; those were the only hands there were. Not a single righteous shot was fired, law and order were strictly maintained, there was never a trace of resistance. I suppose I should say that I believe there was no resistance. I am not omniscient, but I base this assertion on what is called probability bordering on certainty. Had there been anything of the kind, I would have been bound to notice it.

I would have participated, I can swear to that; they need only have asked me, if only for Hannah's sake. Unfortunately I am not one of those rare individuals who raises the battle cry; I cannot inspire others, but I would have participated. And not only myself: why didn't the man emerge who could cry, "Follow me!"? The last few hundred miles would not necessarily have been so long and so hard. The worst that could have happened to us would have been a meaningful death.

I can tell you that I have since read with awe about Warsaw and Buchenwald — another world, but comparable. I have read much about heroism, probably too much, I have been gripped by senseless envy, but I don't ask anyone to believe me. Be that as it may, we remained passive until the last second, and there's nothing I can do about it now. I am not unaware that an oppressed people can only be truly liberated if it contributes toward its liberation, if it goes at least a little bit of the way to meet the Messiah. We did not do this, I did not take a single step, I learned the rules by heart and adhered strictly to them, and only asked poor Jacob from time to time what new reports had come in. I will probably never come to terms with this; I haven't deserved any better. My whole thing about the trees no doubt has something to do with it; as well as my fatal sentimentality and the generosity of my tear ducts. Where I was, there was no resistance.

They say that what is good for your enemies is bad for you. I don't intend to argue about this; anyway, it only makes sense with concrete examples, such as the one I now have, but I don't want to argue about it. My example is the electric current. Jacob doesn't mind in the least doing without it; in fact he manages splendidly without it. Doing without? No one would ever have thought how good no electricity can be. Apart from the Russians and good health for Lina, there is nothing Jacob wishes for as much as no electricity. But Jacob is only one, and we are many. We want electricity. We are at the mercy of our imaginations: if not our saviors, then let it at least be electric current.

The Germans, to return to the example, also want electricity, and not only because at the military office they are ruining their eyes with candlelight. The fine-tuned plans have been thrown into disarray; not a chair, not a sideboard leaves the furniture factory, there are no pliers or hammers or screws coming out of the tool factory, no shoes, no trousers: the Jews are sitting around twiddling their thumbs. Two groups of hurriedly assembled electricians swarm out in search of the damage, double rations of bread and cigarettes, day and night they test fuses and whatever else can be tested, dig up streets, expose cables, accompanied by our good wishes. After five fruitless days Hardtloff has them shot; there is talk of sabotage, which is sheer madness. The electricians were all in one way or another Jacob's customers and had a personal interest in eliminating the problem. They are executed in the square in front of the military office. Anyone is free to watch: Let this be a warning and do what is demanded of you.

Then a German special detachment arrives on a truck, like men from Mars. Equipped like deep-sea divers, they are seen to laugh and relish their importance: We'll take care of it all right, let's see what's stumped these Jewish bunglers. Two days, and the trouble spot is exposed: a swarm of rats has been gnawing at a cable and succumbed to their greed. A new cable is lowered into the ground, and once again there are chairs, shoes, pliers, screws, Jacob's radio.

We want to know whether it is true that they intended to sell us for ransom. If so, where's the money? We want to know whether it is a fact that a Jewish state is to be founded. If so, when? If not, who is obstructing it? Above all we want to know what's taking the Russians so long. For three weeks you've been making our mouths water the way you never managed to do with your pancakes. Tell us how they are breaking through the front, what tactics they are employing, whether they are treating prisoners as prisoners or as convicts, whether the Japanese are being a big nuisance to them in the east, whether the Americans can't at least relieve them of that burden if they aren't landing in Europe. And we also want to know what kind of a career Jan Kiepura is having, how he's getting along in America. By this time a whole lot of news must have accumulated. Fair enough, so they won't broadcast a special news summary for us, they've no idea how we've been suffering from the power failure, but there are a few things one could find out about other than the latest news. Please don't leave out anything, do you hear, nothing, please.

Jacob deserves our sympathy. He should have a well-equipped office, a headquarters with three secretaries, better still with five, a few contacts in all the important capitals who punctually and reliably relay every little detail they have managed to ferret out to headquarters, where secretaries are slaving away at sorting the details, scanning all the leading newspapers, listening to all the radio stations, and extracting from all this a summary that they submit to Jacob as the person ultimately responsible. Only then could he truthfully answer roughly a third of the questions — to the extent that newspapers and radio stations and contacts are to be trusted.

A newspaper is tucked into the Whistle's pocket. The Whistle emerges from the redbrick building and, dragging his wooden leg, walks past the freight cars and right through all the Jews, who are not even aware of what is limping past them. Why care about newspapers? We have Jacob. Only Jacob sees and cares, the magnifying glass in his eye is glued to the precious object in the railway man's pocket, some pieces of paper containing truthful or fabricated reports of actual events — at any rate, infinitely more valuable than a nonexistent radio. Respite for his exhausted powers of invention, if he could bring off a bold exchange of ownership.

Beyond the last track the Whistle reaches his goal, a wooden outhouse for Germans only: it says so on the door, right under the little heart-shaped opening they carved into it, as is the custom in their own country, I imagine.

Jacob refuses to be distracted by his job with Kowalski and keeps one eye firmly on the outhouse. If the newspaper is intact so far, as appears to be the case, and the railway man is not too wasteful, there should be some left over. If the railway man isn't stingy, he should leave some of it behind. He mustn't be wasteful, he mustn't be stingy, there's no way of knowing one way or the other; when Jacob gets a chance, he will go and take what's left. Yet whatever the chance, it would inevitably mean risking his life. What business has a Jew using a German outhouse? For you, my brothers, I'll risk life and limb. I don't intend to steal potatoes like Mischa, who is a more practical type and thinks realistically; if all goes well I'll carry off a few ounces of news and turn them into a ton of hope for you. If my mother had endowed me with a smarter brain, gifted with as much imagination as Sholem Aleichem — what am I saying, half that much would be enough — I wouldn't need to resort to such petty theft. I could dream up ten times as much as they can write in their newspapers, and better too. But I can't, I can't, I am so empty it almost frightens me. I'll do it for you, my brothers, for you and for myself; I'll do it for myself too, for one thing is certain: I can't survive as an individual, only together with you. That's what a liar looks like from behind. I'll go into their outhouse and take what's left, hoping there is something left.

At last the Whistle emerges into God's sunshine, takes a few deep breaths, and lights a cigarette, for which in that wind he needs four matches. He takes enough time for Jacob to want to throttle him, but the pocket, the all-important pocket, is empty. What were newspapers like in the old days? Ours usually had eight pages, four sheets; let's assume his also had four, that's a reasonable assumption. You tear one sheet in half, then once again, then a third time, that means per page — let's see — eight small pieces per page. You can also tear it four times, but then the pieces turn out rather small, so let's stay with three times; after all, he has plenty of paper. Four sheets times eight, that makes thirty-two pieces, no healthy person needs that many; you tear up only one page and put the others aside for reading. But even if he has torn them all up, there's bound to be something left over, unless in his ignorance he has tossed the remainder down the hole.

"What do you keep mumbling about?" Kowalski asks.

"Me, mumbling?" says Jacob.

"All the time. Four and sixteen should make so-and-so much — what are you figuring out?"

The Whistle at last disappears into the brick building. Jacob looks at the sentries: one is standing by the gate, looking bored; another is sitting on the footboard of a freight car, reassuringly far away; the third is nowhere in sight, presumably he's inside the building or hiding somewhere in order to take a nap since nothing ever happens. And there are no more than three.

"Go on working and don't turn around to look at me," Jacob says.

"Why?" asks Kowalski. "What's going on?"

"I'm going to use their outhouse."

Kowalski, astonishment in his face, stops working: Next thing you know, this lunatic will be going into the redbrick building for schnapps and tobacco, trying to borrow money from a sentry, and they'll put him up against the wall for that just as they will for what he's about to do now.

"Are you crazy? Can't you wait till soup time and then go behind the fence?"

"No, I can't."

Jacob ducks and runs off like a professional; the stacked crates shield him almost all the way from eyes in the brick building, except for the last few feet, but they're part of it and he manages them too. Jacob closes the outhouse door behind him. Not a word about the smell or the graffiti on the walls: beside the hole lies the rich booty. But first a glance out through the little heart: no one has noticed anything; in the freight yard framed by a heart everything looks normal. The booty consists of the expected remainder, the German has not been wasteful, there are a good number of neatly torn squares of paper, as if cut with a knife, and under the squares a double sheet, intact. Jacob stuffs the squares under his shirt, as flat as he can so they won't rustle while he is working, better on his back than on his stomach. The double page is worth nothing, or rather, it *is* worth something: four pages, filled from top to bottom with death notices bordered in black, gratifying in one way but short on information. Killed in action . . . killed in action . . . We'll leave those behind, we don't want to carry around any ballast; they're not hard to memorize, four pages of the dead, let the next visitor enjoy them too. But we'd better not linger, as if we were in our own outhouse, we won't risk spending too much time in here, we want to return to work, we're impatient to get it over with. Then we'll go to our unobserved room, free our back of its burden, and play our new radio. And tomorrow you can come again and ask as long as the supply lasts.

Jacob looks outside once more to see whether the coast is clear. It's not clear at all, far from it, the way back is strewn with mines: a soldier is walking toward the outhouse, purposefully one might say. His fingers are already fumbling with his belt buckle; in his mind's eye he is already sitting down and feeling better. It's too late for anyone to leave the outhouse without his noticing. What do you do now? Jacob's knees remind him emphatically that he is no longer young, no matter how speedily he covered the ground to get here; one always finds this out too late. The door can't be fastened, some idiot has ripped off the loop for the hook; if you try to keep it closed, one shove of the shoulder and the man will be inside and gape and do God knows what to you. Theoretically we should keep a cool head, remain calm, the advantage of surprise is on our side, and he still has eight whole steps to go. The planks of the back wall will take at least five minutes and make far too much noise, five steps to go, and all that's left for you is the little oval hole, down into their crap. To which you can't bring yourself, though you're skinny enough.

The soldier opens the door, which offers no resistance; to his dismay he sees before him an opened double sheet of newspaper, trembling moderately, although at such an embarrassing moment this doesn't particularly strike him.

"Oh, excuse me!" he says, quickly closing the door, without having seen the disintegrating Jewish shoes beneath the newspaper or the want of a display of lowered trousers that would have rounded out the picture, a maneuver, however, for which the head had been not cool enough and the time too short. Perhaps just as well, too much camouflage can be damaging too, the main things being that the soldier has shut the door devoid of any suspicion: he prepares for a brief wait, his belt is already looped over his arm, and he walks up and down, that being less uncomfortable than standing.

For how long a wait should Jacob prepare? Over the edge of the newspaper and through the little heart he sees the gray uniform walking up and down. The only thing that can help now is a miracle, any old miracle will do, no need to cudgel the brain; true miracles are not calculable. There are at most two more minutes for the unexpected to materialize, and if it fails to do so, and there's no reason to expect otherwise, then the proverbial last hour will look this ridiculous.

"Hurry up, comrade. I've got the trots," he hears the soldier pleading.

The squares of paper on his back are beginning to stick; they will have to be dried before use, if by some miracle everything turns out well. And Jacob tells me that suddenly he is tired, suddenly fear and hope slip away, everything becomes strangely heavy and light at the same time, his legs, his eyelids, his hands, from which the four pages of heroes fallen for the Fatherland slide to the ground.

"Did you hear that Marotzke's got another furlough? Smells fishy to me! He must know some people right at the top, eh? He's always going off, while guys like us have to wait and wait and hang around with these garlic eaters."

My God, garlic, if a fellow could have just one clove, spread very thin on warm bread. You idiot, you think some Schulz or Müller is in the outhouse, someone who's no friend of Marotzke's, which is true enough, in a way, whoever Marotzke is. Jacob leans back against the back wall and closes his eyes; if they expect some heroic resistance from him, they can wait a long time, he is beyond that. It's up to the comrade outside; he has to keep the action going. He's welcome to leave or stay. Tormented by stomach cramps he can fling open the door, gasp, and shoot; the man he hits will not be taken by surprise. What follows is his business.

Who could possibly suspect that the miracle is already in the works, the rough outline already designed? There is still Kowalski, Kowalski with two horrified eyes in his head, he knows what's going on, he's aware of the situation. He sees the soldier in dire need and the door still presenting a barrier; he knows who's inside and can't be set free without his help, assuming he hasn't already died of fear. Salvation lies in distracting the German, not merely by throwing a pebble against the wall to make him turn around to see who threw it: something has to happen that requires his immediate intervention. The first thing that comes to mind is the stack of crates, some six feet high and rather wobbly. If two crates are pulled out from below, the stack will cease to stand there all proud and ready for transport, its balance will be destroyed, and that could provide a fine distraction. But what will happen to the numskull who is responsible for such clumsiness, what will happen to Jacob if there is no clumsy oaf far and wide, what are forty years of friendship worth? Calculations facing Kowalski.

Jacob hears a low rumbling in the distance, the ears can't be closed as the eyes can, then he hears military boots hurrying away. Reason enough to open the eyes wide again: that's exactly what a miracle sounds like. Arms and legs reassuringly regain their former weight; things are on the move again. The glance through the heart tells him that the coast looks clear; the Jews visible through the opening in the door have paused in their work and are all staring in one direction, toward the spot where the miracle is presumably happening.

Kowalski has successfully penetrated the stack of crates. His strength was only just sufficient, and one crate fell on his head. The soldier rushes blindly from the outhouse into the trap and flings himself upon the bait, Kowalski. It may be said that rarely has sleight of hand been more successfully performed. Although the blows find their mark — the crate falling on his head was nothing in comparison — Kowalski merely whimpers as he tries to protect his face with his hands and apologizes profusely for his unforgivable blunder.

The rest of us stand as if rooted to the spot and grind our teeth; one man beside me claims he saw Kowalski toppling the stack deliberately. The soldier goes on punching and beating, Marotzke has been granted a furlough again and he hasn't; maybe he is genuinely outraged over such clumsiness, but suddenly he stops in the midst of his task. Something is moving inside him, not pity and not exhaustion: it is his diarrhea demanding its rights, as is plain for all to see. He grimaces and runs in long strides to the outhouse that has meanwhile been vacated for his benefit, or rather, first he calls out: "I want to see it all stacked up again when I come out, got it?" Only then does he perform his long leaps, which, in spite of everything, look very comical. The matter permits no delay: now he would insist that any newspaper reader vacate the position, immediately, instantly, otherwise there'll be a minor disaster. But he can save himself the trouble: he flings open the door onto an empty latrine. The minor disaster was prevented in the very nick of time.

Not one of us looking on dares help Kowalski or comfort him. The place is for work, not for comforting. He wipes the blood from his face and tests his teeth, which are still there except for one; all things considered, it could have turned out considerably worse. The pain will pass, Jacob has been preserved for us, after the war we'll present him with his own private outhouse where he can sit for hours to his heart's content and think about his good friend Kowalski. The man so miraculously rescued comes around what remains of the stack of crates, behind Kowalski, who is still feeling himself all over. Jacob plucks up the courage to face him, for Kowalski must not find out the true reason for the daring expedition. He of all people; he has deserved not to be bothered with this reason; for him it must remain an inexplicable whim of Jacob's, a whim that came within a hair of costing him his life.

"Thank you," Jacob says in an emotional voice. *Emotional* is the right word, emotional for the first time in forty years; you don't have your life saved every day, and then by someone you have known for such a long time and of whom, to be quite honest, you wouldn't have expected it.

Kowalski doesn't deign to glance at him; getting up with a groan he sets to work on the crates, which had better be stacked up before the soldier returns from his urgent business and checks to see how much his word is worth here. They could all still be standing in neat rows, like the few teeth in Kowalski's mouth, if Jacob were a normal person, if he hadn't yielded so irresponsibly to some wondrous yearning for which others must pay bitterly.

Jacob makes his hands fly: one crate by Kowalski is matched by three of his, which in Kowalski's case is due partly to the question of guilt, partly to fury, and no doubt also to pain. "Did you at least have a good shit?" Kowalski inquires, making an effort not to shout. "Have a look at my face, have a good look. I bet it's quite a sight! It wasn't him, it was you! But why am I getting excited? The main thing is you had a high-class shit, that's all that matters. There's just one thing I'll swear, Heym: just try that again! Go ahead, try it, then you'll find out who helps you!"

Jacob takes shelter behind his work; Kowalski is right, of course, from his point of view. The words that would calm him down Jacob mustn't say, and any others would lead to a new outburst. Later, Kowalski, when all this is behind us, when we two are sitting quietly over a glass of schnapps, when the pancakes are sizzling in the pan, then I'll tell you everything. At our leisure, Kowalski, you'll hear the whole truth; we'll laugh and shake our heads to think how crazy the times once were. You'll ask why I didn't tell you right away, tell you, at least, my best friend, and I'll answer that I couldn't because you would have told all the others, and they would have taken me for one of those thousands of liars and rumormongers and would have been without hope again. And then you'll put your hand on my arm, because maybe you'll have understood, and you'll say, "Come, Jacob my friend, let's have another vodka."

When, after quite some time, the outhouse door opens again, the stack of crates rears up proudly, as if no one had ever brought about its collapse. The soldier strolls over, his hands clasped behind his back, uniform all adjusted; he has been expected. Not exactly with longing, merely to have the matter finally over and done with. But the way he approaches and then stops and holds his head, his whole manner, is enough to make one uneasy, for he looks more benign than critical. Somehow he is looking at the world with different eyes; how a few good minutes can change a person. The crates, he's completely forgotten about the crates, he has eyes only for Kowalski's swollen face, which for the time being is red but on which one can already divine blue and green and purple, and the soldier looks concerned. If Jacob can trust his eyes, he looks concerned. What's one to make of that? Without a word he turns around and walks away. Jacob is thinking, Lucky he didn't discover his soft heart until now and wasn't a good person from the beginning or he would never have dashed away from the outhouse door; he would have stayed there and very soon his goodness of heart would have undergone much too severe a test.

In passing, the comrade drops two cigarettes, Junos, without tips. He drops them either by mistake or on purpose, a question that will never be resolved, any more than his motives, assuming it was deliberate. Anyway the cigarettes belong to Kowalski; he has paid for them, after all.

A few minutes later the Whistle emerges from the brick building and trills for the midday break: the railway man whom up to this hour none of us has heard say a word, but who nevertheless is the most informative among our Germans because he left behind a halfway useful radio. It all started with the Whistle today, and he suspects nothing, whistles as usual for soup time, and has no way of knowing how shamelessly his forgetfulness, or whatever it had been, was exploited. Only Jacob knows, reminded by the little squares of paper under his shirt, and the double page that meanwhile has suffered an uncertain fate and shouldn't really have been left behind unused.

"By the way, did I tell you that the Germans are suffering huge losses?" Jacob asks.

They are already lining up; Kowalski turns around to him, and in the midst of his bruises, a hint of a grateful smile — grateful in spite of everything — blooms fleetingly.

The radio turns out to be not particularly fruitful. Jacob arranges the squares side by side on his table, nine of them altogether, and Piwowa and Rosenblatt refrain from disturbing him. Today they are what they are, long since dead, due to cat meat and a guard; today they don't interfere in Jacob's business, for he has to concentrate on his game of patience.

The name of the newspaper appears nowhere, nor does the date; blind chance has seen to that. The nine squares of newspaper yield not a single coherent page, the Whistle having picked up squares at random, which means extra work for Jacob. He tries this way and that but can find scarcely two scraps that fit together. At the end of all his effort he is faced with two extremely patchy pages, the gaps revealing the color of the tablecloth: two pages that look as if a circumspect censor had cut out everything worth knowing and taken care that only items of no consequence find their way into the hands of unauthorized persons. The sports section, for instance, has been perfectly preserved: how happy the Jews will be that the Luftwaffe boxing team has defeated a Navy team ten to six. Or that once again the Berlin soccer team, as so often in the past, didn't have a chance against the Hamburg eleven. Then the uncommunicative page divulges the earth-shattering news that a *Gauleiter* whose name has been torn off has made some favorable comments about an art exhibition somewhere, that His Excellency the Spanish ambassador would like to see a further expansion of mutual friendly relations, and that, in a people's court trial of two agents in the pay of Jewish world capitalism, justice has prevailed.

You sit there looking disappointed; you hadn't ever expected much — a little favorable wind for your poor brain, the occasional hidden allusion from which with a bit of skill a feast could be prepared — but you hadn't counted on quite so little. Not a word about Bezanika, through which the Russians must long since have advanced; not so much as a hint that the Germans are encountering difficulties. Instead, those nitwits are playing soccer and putting on exhibitions and meting out justice.

Let us at least try to be fair and admit the possibility the newspaper is old or that the best part of it was used by the Whistle, but still, one way or another, it was idiotic to have had such high hopes. Anyone who gave it a mere five seconds' thought would have known what to expect. We all know what kind of newspapers those people can produce; years ago there was a German paper in our area, the *Völkischer Kurier,* and don't ask me what that was worth. No one ever bought it. Throwing away money is a sin, but sometimes you did run across it, whether you wanted to or not. At the market they wrapped fish in it, at the dentist's there was a copy in the waiting room, and at the insurance office as well, of course, and occasionally at Kowalski's barbershop, because he wanted to make a cosmopolitan impression. He was told; Kowalski, we told him, if you leave that filthy rag lying around any longer, you'll ruin your business. Or do you really think some German customer will happen to stray into your place so that your Yiddish fingers can fiddle around with his Kaiser Wilhelm mustache? That's none of your business, Kowalski replied in an offended tone. Do I tell you how much sawdust to mix into your potato pancakes? That's how Kowalski was, and may my hands fall off right here and now if this slander is true. Anyway, a glance at the *Kurier* was enough to show what kind of rag it was. The Germans were constantly feeling threatened and humiliated and discriminated against by God and the world; according to them, it wasn't they who humiliated us, but we them. The question of how long Germany was to go on suffering from the shameful consequences of the last war obsessed them in every issue, three times a week. And on the last page, alongside the picture puzzle, there were poems so unintelligible that you almost thought you had forgotten their language.

Only the classified advertisements weren't so bad; they had a certain flair for that section. Every other Wednesday or Tuesday the two middle pages were closely printed with classified ads, and if you needed something that was hard or impossible to find on the market, say a few nice-looking chairs with woven rattan seats, perhaps, or a modern standard lamp or a sizable lot of plates because dishes never lasted long in the shop, then a glance at the *Kurier* wouldn't do any harm. Of course, it was essential to pay attention to the name of the person offering the goods. If it was Hagedorn or Leineweber, you didn't even bother to go; if it was Skrzypczak or Bartosiewicz, you went with great reluctance; and if it was Silberstreif, you simply went. For when it came to advertising, the *Kurier* people weren't choosy. They took from anyone; what counted was the ability to pay. But, as I said, that was only the classified section, every other Wednesday or Tuesday; the rest was sheer unadulterated rubbish.

All this might have been remembered in time to avoid sticking one's head in the noose, to no avail, and only getting it out again through a miracle wrought by a friend. That's how they used to produce newspapers, and that's how they produce newspapers to this day; so far nobody has shown them a better way. Only the talent for successful classified sections has apparently stayed with them, and the four abandoned pages filled with death notices would seem to indicate that there are still people on the job who know their business.

Jacob turns over each square, one by one, all is not yet lost; there is still an unread reverse side that has as many gaps as the front but may tell us a little more. There is an item about a hero such as only our nation can produce, a pilot with a French name who shoots down enemy planes like sparrows out of the African sky. The Führer has replied to a message from the Duce, and in Munich a truck collided with a streetcar, causing a traffic jam for several hours. A cartoon. A man holding a lighted match over a sandwich. Question: What does this mean? Answer: Sandwich under fire. And a fat headline claiming, Victories on All Fronts! One can believe it or not, we'd rather not, the lower half is missing. As a claim it hangs in the air, so to speak, and we know they have been trying to tell us that they were already not far from Moscow. It was the Germans who claimed that, not us, but we heard with our own ears that there is fighting near Bezanika. There's quite some distance between the two; if that's what a victory looks like, you're welcome to hundreds more of the same.

That's all very well; Jacob can figure out for himself that they tell a few fibs, but how is he to answer the questions that will rain down upon him first thing tomorrow morning? His notion of what it would be like, he told me with a sigh, had been far too naive: one reads their slanted reports, he had thought, sees through them with no effort, or very little effort, simply turns everything around, and right away one's mouth is bursting with news ready to be released at the appropriate time. But now try just turning things around. The Luftwaffe boxers didn't win against the Navy, they lost; the *Gauleiter* with the torn-off name declared the art exhibition to have been atrocious; the German hero didn't shoot down a single plane in Africa; the streetcar in Munich skillfully avoided the truck; and the Führer didn't reply to the Duce's message because he never received one. I tell you, nothing but rubbish. Perhaps I can make something out of the cartoon, I think; Sandwich under fire means they're firing at Sandwich, and Sandwich, if I'm not mistaken, is a town in England, and if they're firing at England, then England will be firing back, which seems reasonable. Wonderful, they'll tell me tomorrow morning, so England is defending itself, but England is far away, and what about us? Perhaps I could turn the victories on all fronts into defeats, but what do I know about fronts, where they are or how many there are? Defeats must be substantiated with details, and I don't know any. What would you have done in my place?

Jacob comes to a crucial decision. The power failure was a divine respite, the only drawback being that we had no influence on its duration. We'll gain another respite for ourselves, but without the drawback, because the interruption we have in mind has no end. When they ask us, What's the latest, Jacob, our shoulders will droop and we'll put on our saddest expression and whisper in a despairing voice: Just imagine, Jews, last night I sit down with expectant ears at my set and turn the knob, like I always do, but not a sound! Not one! Yesterday it was still singing like a little bird, and today not a murmur. It's no use wringing our hands, Jews. You know how temperamental a radio can be, and now it's dead.

The radio is dead. Jacob scrunches up the squares of newspaper, all nine of them, into a little heap; he is able to contain his annoyance at not having had this brilliant idea earlier. It is far surpassed by the joy of discovery: if the toilet paper had been of no other use than to enlighten him, then, in spite of everything, it was worthwhile, then the price paid by Kowalski was not too high. No longer will he be lying night after night with wide-open eyes, racking his brain over what lies to tell them next morning. Now he can spend night after night with wide-open ears, listening, like everybody else, for whether the longed-for distant rumble of cannon has finally broken its silence. The radio is dead, the scraps of newspaper are tossed into the stove, Jacob will set a match to them when it becomes necessary to heat the room, the lid is firmly closed.

Just in time, for in his haste Jacob has forgotten to lock his door: it opens, and a smiling Lina enters without knocking.

"Did you forget about me today?" she asks.

"Of course not," says Jacob, giving her a kiss, and at least now he locks the door. "I was just about to come up to see you, but I had something to do first."

"What was that?"

"Nothing you need to know about. Have you had your supper?"

"Yes, what you put out for me."

Lina looks around the room, not in search of anything special but just to make sure everything is tidy and not dusty. She draws her finger across the cupboard, inspects it; the result is not that fantastic.

"I'll tidy up your room tomorrow," she says. "I don't feel like it today."

"No, you won't," Jacob says sternly. "The professor said you weren't supposed to move around too much yet."

Lina doesn't reply. With a smile she sits down at the table; Jacob knows as well as she does that she is going to tidy his room. For some time it has been quite clear who sets the tone here; it's no longer a subject of discussion. Jacob's job is to provide the food and clothing and in winter the heating; she is responsible for everything else, even though occasionally he still makes a bit of a fuss. She hasn't come into the room to argue about matters long since settled, or out of fear he might have forgotten her; she knew he wouldn't. The reason for her coming goes back a few days, when she heard much and understood little; there was something that was rather unclear to her.

"Have you heard what they're all talking about?" Lina asks.

"About what?"

"That the Russians will be here soon?"

"You don't say!"

Jacob goes to the cupboard, takes out his weekly bread ration, breaks off enough for his supper, and starts eating.

"Who's talking about that?"

"Oh, Siegfried and Rafael and Mrs. Sonschein and Mrs. London — everybody. Haven't you heard anything?"

"No."

Jacob sits down opposite her, sees the disappointment in her face; she had hoped for enlightenment, and he knows nothing. He divides his bread and holds out one half of it to Lina as compensation. She accepts it, even starts eating, but the bread is not nearly as good as his lack of knowledge is bad.

"Or rather, I did hear something," says Jacob. "But nothing definite. What's so important about it?"

Her eyes gradually grow resentful; how stupid does he think she is, as if she were a baby, she who takes care of all the housework. Everybody is talking about something tremendous, and what's so important about it?

"What's it going to be like when the Russkies are here?"

"How should I know?" says Jacob.

"Better or worse?"

Jacob is ready to groan. You've managed to escape the hyenas at the freight yard for today, even forever if the idea of the broken-down radio stands the test. But already you have to look for some other means of escape, for within your own four walls a new tormentor is taking shape — albeit a much-loved one, but she can ask more questions than you have hairs on your head. Or you don't look for an escape, you submit to your fate: a child of less than nine, surely you can cope with her. You'll tell her, as best you can, something about the world of tomorrow, after all that interests you too, and to have a rough idea of what is in store for her certainly won't do her any harm.

"Will it be better or worse?"

"Better, of course," says Jacob.

"But how better? What will be different?"

"We won't have to wear stars anymore. Lina can wear whatever she likes, and no one will stop her in the street and ask where she has left her yellow star."

"Is that all?"

"Of course not. You'll get enough to eat. . . ."

"As much as I like?"

"As much as you like. Just imagine: there's all kinds of food on the table, you take whatever you happen to fancy, and when you can't

eat any more the table is cleared, and at the next meal it's all there
again."

"You're pulling my leg," she says, because it would be quite nice
if he confirmed it to her all over again.

"That's the solemn truth. And you'll have pretty dresses, we'll
go shopping together, and —"

"Wait a minute. What kind of food will there be on the table?"

"Whatever you like best. Pâté with butter and challah and hard-
boiled eggs and fish. You can choose."

"Will you be making potato pancakes again?"

"I certainly will."

"In your shop?"

"In my shop."

"You haven't forgotten your promise, have you? That I'll be
allowed to help you in the shop?"

"Of course not."

"You'll stand behind the counter making the pancakes, and it'll
be my job to take them to the customers, in my white apron. And in
the summer I'll serve them ice cream."

"That's how it'll be."

"I can hardly wait!"

Lina can hardly wait, and whenever she is in that mood she
hunches her shoulders up to her ears. At last Jacob can get on with his
supper, starting with the dry bread, until after some thought she
frowns because she has suddenly foreseen a snag.

"But what's going to happen about school? You've also told me
that later on I'll have to go to school. And if that's true, I won't have
any time for the shop, will I?"

"School is more important," Jacob decides. "While you're there
I'll be able to handle the customers by myself. After school you can
come and help me, if you still feel like it."

"But I'd rather help right away!"

"What have you got against school, anyway? Has some idiot
been telling you bad things about it?"

She shakes her head.

"There you are then. School is a wonderful, wonderful place, where all kinds of stupid kids go in and all kinds of clever kids come out. But if you think I like you better stupid . . ."

"Will Siegfried and Rafael have to go to school too?"

"Of course."

After this reassurance there is a knock at the door. Lina jumps up to run to the door and unlock it, but Jacob holds her back and places his finger on his lips. A knock is always suspicious; not every suspicion is confirmed. It might be Kirschbaum, for instance, come to discuss Lina's recovery, or his neighbor Horowitz to borrow a spoonful of malt coffee till the next distribution, word of honor. It may be quite an ordinary knock, we'll soon find out, but even so there's no need for Lina to be seen; she's nobody else's business. Jacob puts his arm around her shoulders, draws her to the window, points behind the bed.

"Hide behind there," he whispers. "Don't move till I tell you. Right?"

Right. Lina crouches down and doesn't move, and Jacob opens the door. Who should be outside but Kowalski, standing there with his swollen face, trying to smile.

"Can't get rid of me, can you!"

Jacob would gladly dispatch him right there at the door; tell me quickly what's up and then good-bye. But Kowalski clearly gives the impression of having all the time in the world. Walking past Jacob, who is still holding the door handle, he sits down at the table and says: "Aren't you going to close the door?"

Jacob closes the door rather loudly; Lina, as ordered, makes no sound. He has no choice but to sit down on the other chair, and he tries hard to look pressed for time.

"I see you're just having supper," Kowalski observes. "I hope I'm not disturbing you?"

"Aren't you ever going to tell me why you're here?"

"Is that the way to treat a guest?" Kowalski asks amiably.

"No, it isn't. I'll rush down and bring up some wine from the cellar!"

"Why so impatient? That always was your problem, Jacob. You weren't pleasant enough with your customers, they often used to tell me as much while I was cutting their hair. That's why you were getting fewer and fewer customers."

"Thanks for the advice. But did you come here to tell me that?"

From behind the bed comes a soundless giggle, audible only to someone who knows there is another person in the room.

"Believe it or not, I've nothing special in mind. At home the walls are closing in on me; a man can't spend evening after evening in the same room. I'll go and have a chat with Jacob, I thought, he'll be in the same boat, I thought, he'll be glad. In the old days people used to meet after work, didn't they? Everybody found that quite normal. Shouldn't we gradually start getting used to something normal again?"

Before Jacob can reply that the old days were the old days and today is today, and that he wants to be left in peace and to go to bed because the work at the freight yard is getting to be too much for him, Kowalski digs into his pocket, brings out the two cigarettes, and puts them on the table, one in front of himself and one in front of Jacob, and thus momentarily silences him.

"That's very kind of you," says Jacob. Kowalski may believe that Jacob is referring to the visit, but Jacob is looking at the cigarettes; perhaps he actually means both.

"Besides, you've told me very little today," Kowalski says after a suitable pause. "The news about the losses was pretty encouraging, but you can imagine that other things interest me just as much. And there hasn't been a word about those today."

"For crying out loud, Kowalski, why do you keep badgering me? Aren't things difficult enough? Do you have to keep harping on that? I can't take it anymore! When I know something I'll tell you, but surely in my own room at least you can leave me in peace!"

Kowalski nods a few times thoughtfully, rolling his cigarette between his fingers, and pushes out his lower lip, the swollen one. He has come with a suspicion that seems to contain some truth. "You know, Jacob," he says, "I've noticed that you always get impatient with me. You even lose your temper when I ask you for news. You never volunteer anything, so I have to ask, and the moment I do, you get furious. I simply don't understand it. I can't see any logic in it. Imagine if it was the other way around, Jacob, if I had the radio and you didn't. Wouldn't you also be asking me then?"

"Are you mad? In front of the child!"

Jacob jumps from his chair and turns toward the window. Lina has been crouching and listening long enough, and, as agreed, she emerges from her uncomfortable hiding place; after all, in a way he did call her. She is grinning from ear to ear.

"Good God!" stammers Kowalski in a shocked voice as he claps his hands together. But no one pays any attention to him; this is a matter between Jacob and Lina. They exchange glances, Lina winks: Now you're in trouble, I bet you weren't counting on that! Jacob abandons his faint hope that she might not have heard anything, children are often God knows where with their thoughts, or that at least she hadn't understood; she is a wide-awake young rascal, she winks, and everything is crystal clear. It'll take him a good while to think his way out of this one, every day a fresh disaster, once again he can forget about listening for the rumble of cannon in the night. But night has yet to come, and Lina is still standing there, enjoying the little triumph which that fool of a Kowalski has so unthinkingly handed her. Jacob can't take root and sweat blood and water forever; he has to give some kind of sign of life.

"Run upstairs now, Lina. I'll be up to see you later," says Jacob wearily.

First, though, she goes over to him and pulls down his head. Jacob thinks this is for the kiss that is part of even the briefest separation. But he can think what he likes, Lina's mind is not on kissing, not now; she pulls down his head because his ears are attached to it, and into one of them she whispers, "So they've all heard it from you! You were pulling my leg!"

Then she is out of the room, Jacob and Kowalski are again seated at the table, Kowalski expecting a flood of reproaches while feeling completely innocent. For nothing would have happened if Jacob hadn't hidden his child from him, from his best friend. And if he did have to hide her because he couldn't be sure who was knocking at the door, he should have let her out when he saw who it was. But no, he leaves her there in her corner, probably he's forgotten her. I ask you, how can anybody forget a child? No one's clairvoyant, after all, and now he's angry and about to let loose his accusations.

"A fine job you've made of it! It's not enough that the whole ghetto is yacking about it, now she knows about it too!" Jacob does in fact say.

"I'm sorry, but there was no way I could have seen her. With this eye . . ."

Kowalski points to his eyes: Jacob can take his pick, both are orientally narrow, impressively framed in dark blue. Yes, Kowalski is pointing to his eyes, a discreet reminder of this morning's lifesaving operation, no need to press the point; if reproaches are in order here, the question is by whom to whom. Or we can both be a bit generous and forget about what happened; it's all water under the bridge anyway. And the ploy is successful; the eyes are superbly effective. Instantly the mood at the table changes, becomes a few degrees warmer, instantly Jacob responds to the demand made on his pity; he shifts a little closer and looks with new eyes at the damage he has caused.

"Doesn't look too good."

Kowalski makes a dismissive gesture: it'll soon heal up; if Jacob wants to be conciliatory, Kowalski won't be petty either, he's in a generous mood. There lie the cigarettes, still cold, but Kowalski has thought of everything, even matches. As a final surprise he takes some out of his pocket and lights one on the worn striking surface: now the time has come for a smoke, brother. Come on, lean back and close your eyes, let's not spoil the pleasure by talking, let's take a few puffs and dream of old times, which will soon be back again. Come on, let's think of Chaim Balabusne with his thick steel-rimmed glasses and the tiny shop where we always bought our cigarettes, or rather the tobacco to roll our own. His shop was closer to yours than mine was, and closer to mine than yours was, it was between our two shops, yet we never became real friends with him, but that was his fault. Because he wasn't interested in pancakes and ice cream, or in a haircut or a shave. Many people said he let his red hair grow so long out of religious piety, but I know better; it was out of stinginess, nothing else. Ah well, never mind, better not speak ill of the dead. Balabusne always had a good selection — cigars, pipes, cigarette cases with little flowers, gold-tipped cigarettes for the rich — always tried to persuade us to take a more expensive brand, but we stuck with Excelsior. And the stand with the little gas flame and the cigar cutter on the counter, the brass stand he was always polishing when you went into his shop, it's that brass stand you always remember when you think of the old days, though we only bought tobacco from him once a week at most and never used the stand.

"Are you thinking about Chaim Balabusne too?"

"Why bring up Chaim Balabusne all of a sudden?"

"No special reason. Maybe the smoking."

"I'm not thinking of anything."

The last pull, one more would burn the lips. The smoke has tickled the lungs gloriously and made them a little woozy, like after a few little glasses too many; the world is circling leisurely, but they are firmly seated, hands on the table. A bit of sighing, a bit of groaning, the smoke is still floating around the room. "And now let's get to the point, Jacob," says Kowalski. "How do things look out there? What's the news about the Russians?"

Jacob remains calm. It was only a matter of time anyway before Kowalski brought up the real reason for his visit; the cigarette couldn't deceive anyone. Now there's no Lina hiding in the background, now it's possible to speak freely, I've already concocted an answer for you and your kind, brace yourself. So, bring on the despairing expression, bring on the sad, drooping shoulders, now comes the last act in our question-and-answer game, Kowalski, and you won't like it. But I can't worry about that anymore, I've been doing it long enough, I'm just another tormented human being.

"I didn't want to tell you. . . ."

"They're being pushed back!" cries Kowalski.

"No, no, it's not that bad!"

"What then? For God's sake tell me!"

"Can you imagine," says Jacob in a low voice, offering a perfect picture of distress, "a while ago I sit down at my set and turn the knob like I always do, but not a single sound comes out. I mean, yesterday it was still working perfectly, and today it's completely silent! It's hopeless, my friend, a radio is a miraculous object, and now it's broken."

"Good God!" exclaims Kowalski in horror; for the second time tonight Kowalski exclaims, "Good God!" and even claps his hands together, probably because for him one is not possible without the other.

"If only we could have a smoke!" Jacob says longingly, for it is the next day, and the cigarette, the Juno without a tip, lives on only in his memory. He is standing in a boxcar, doing a *yontev* job, a holiday job, as it may well be called, which consists of taking from us Jews the bags that we are privileged to carry today. We carry the hundred-pound bags to him across a distance of fifty yards or more; all he has to do is move them along in the freight car and stack them up neatly against the walls, hence holiday job, also because there are two of them to do it, Jacob and Leonard Schmidt. The day, incidentally, had started out surprisingly enough when we were shown what we were to do; we had looked at each other in amazement and thought, they don't know what they want. Well over two weeks ago a whole trainload of bags of cement arrived as if they were planning to put up some buildings; we unloaded every last one and covered them with tarpaulins, and today we are suddenly told to load the bags back onto the cars. Well, it's their business. We obediently reload the bags, just the way they want them, we lug them over to the cars, in one of which Jacob is doing his *yontev* job and saying, "If only we could have a smoke!" and Schmidt answers him, half amused: "If that's all you've got to worry about, Mr. Heym . . ."

Leonard Schmidt. The fluke that had brought him to this ghetto transcended anything he could ever have imagined, since Schmidt could look back on a life that deserved to have continued on the other side of the fence. His presence in our midst was, for him, one of the few mysteries on this earth.

Born in 1895, in the town of Brandenburg, the son of a wealthy father and a monarchist mother, attended an excellent high school in Berlin where his father had moved two years after Leonard's birth for business reasons (acquisition of a textile factory); joined the army immediately on completing school, Flanders offensive, Verdun, occupation of the Crimea and later Champagne when the army was short of men: such was Schmidt's war. Then he received an honorable discharge from the defeated army as a proud lieutenant decorated for bravery in the face of the enemy and whatever else, and he turned his attention to his future career. University was the next step, as was expected of privileged sons: studying law first in Heidelberg and then in Berlin. The results couldn't have been better, passed all his exams with flying colors, most of them even with honors. Three obligatory years of clerking, then the professional card LEONARD SCHMIDT, ESQ., and finally the longed-for moment, the opening of his own law practice in the best part of town. Good clients were quick to show up; his father's connections more or less propelled them there. Soon he had to engage two juniors for the less important cases, and he made a name for himself ten times as fast as many another lawyer. A love match, two beautiful fair-haired daughters, the world respectfully doffed its hat to him every day, until an envious fellow member of the bar association conceived the fateful idea of looking into his family tree, then chopping away at it and allowing everything to reach its disastrous conclusion. His wife, his two daughters, and his bank account made it safely to Switzerland because good friends had warned him, but he himself was too late. He was still busy settling his most urgent affairs when there came a peremptory knock at his door.

In Schmidt's mind the whole thing persists like some idiotic joke; perhaps he'll wake up one morning to find clients once more sitting in his waiting room. He had been well on the way to becoming a German nationalist. But they didn't let him, they knocked on his door and told him not to make a fuss while the maid stood looking horrified between the white-shrouded, plush-covered armchairs. They brought him here because his great-grandfather attended the synagogue and his parents had been stupid enough to have him circumcised, although by now they had forgotten why. Joke or no joke, he suffers doubly and triply. In the first few days, when he was still a newcomer, he told me his life story, and added miserably, "Can you understand that?"

And a short time later — it was possible, insofar as one thought about him at all, to imagine that he was gradually getting used to life in the ghetto — he turns up at the freight yard, and what we see makes our hearts stand still. On his shirt is a pin from which hangs a small object, black and white, that on closer inspection proves to be an Iron Cross. "Have some sense!" someone tells him. "Take that cross off and hide it or they'll shoot you down like a mad dog!" But Schmidt turns away and starts working as if nothing were wrong. We all give him a wide berth, no one wants to be involved, he's beyond help, and from a safe distance we don't take our eyes off him. It is a good hour before a sentry notices the enormity, swallows a few times, stands mutely before Schmidt, and Schmidt stands pale faced before him. After an eternity the sentry turns on his heel; it really looks as if he had been rendered speechless. He goes into the redbrick building, returns immediately with his superior, and points at Schmidt, the only person to have resumed work. The superior beckons Schmidt over; no one will give two cents for his life now. The superior bends down to the pin and carefully inspects the object like a watchmaker examining a tiny damaged part.

"Where did you get that?" he asks.

"Verdun," says Schmidt in a shaky voice.

"We can't have that here. It's against regulations," says the superior. He removes the decoration from Schmidt's chest, puts it in his pocket, doesn't make a note of any name, doesn't shoot any malefactor. Treats the incident like a nice diversion that will cause general mirth in the bar that night. He returns cheerfully to the brick building, the sentry has his eyes elsewhere again, nothing more is said about it, Schmidt has had his fun and we have had our spectacle. Thus, not long after arriving, he achieved an odd notoriety; so much for the life story of Leonard Schmidt.

"Never in my life have I had anything to do with a court case," says Jacob.

"I see," says Schmidt.

They make an easy day of it, picking up each bag together after we have lifted it onto the edge of the car, then hoisting it with a "One, two!" onto the right spot. Even the rain doesn't bother them since their boxcar has a roof. In the brief intervals that occur they lean against the wall, wipe from their brows the sweat that has inexplicably appeared there, and chat just like in peacetime. When Kowalski or the Schtamms or Mischa pantingly unload their bags, look at them enviously, and snidely remark that if they don't watch out they'll work themselves to death, they smile. "Don't worry about us!"

"Actually, I once was a witness," says Jacob.

"I see."

"But not in court. Only in the office of the district attorney who was handling the case."

"What case?"

"It had to do with whether Kowalski owed money to Porfir the usurer or not. Porfir had miraculously mislaid the promissory note, and I merely had to testify that Kowalski had paid him back the money."

"Were you actually there at the time?" asks Schmidt.

"Oh no! But Kowalski had already explained the whole thing to me in detail."

"But if you were not there and thus knew the facts merely from hearsay, you should not have appeared as a witness at all. How could you be certain that Kowalski had actually returned the money? I don't wish to insinuate anything, but after all, it is conceivable, isn't it, that Kowalski might have lied to you so that you would testify in his favor?"

"I don't think so," Jacob says without hesitation. "He has many faults, nobody knows them as well as I do, but he's not a liar. He told me right away that he hadn't paid Porfir back. Where would he have got the money?"

"And although you knew that, you testified before the district attorney that he had paid it back in your presence?"

"Naturally!"

"Well, it's hardly that natural, is it, Mr. Heym?" Schmidt says with a smile; he is undoubtedly wondering about the remarkable notions of justice harbored by these quaint people to whom he is supposed to belong.

"Anyway, it helped quite a bit," Jacob went on, bringing his story to a close. "That cutthroat Porfir had no luck with his accusation. His money was gone, but what am I saying, *his* money! Over the years he had gradually managed to fleece every one of us small businessmen. Thirty percent interest, can you believe it? The whole street broke into cheers as Porfir and Kowalski came out of the courthouse after the verdict, Porfir seething with rage and Kowalski beaming with joy!"

Kowalski of the many-hued eyes tips his bag onto the floor of the car; with half an ear he has caught something about Kowalski beaming with joy, and he asks, "What kind of stories are you telling about me?"

"That old business of Porfir's mislaid promissory note."

"Don't believe a word he says," Kowalski tells Schmidt. "He gives me a bad name whenever he gets a chance."

Kowalski pads back for the next bag, drenched to the skin, after giving Jacob a come-off-it look. Schmidt and Jacob, both comfortably dry, also make some effort — without chatting, for a change — to see how many bags will fit into one car. Until the next little interruption, until Schmidt remembers something important, until he asks: "I hope you don't mind my curiosity, Mr. Heym, but what has Mr. Churchill to say about the present situation?"

"Who?"

"Winston Churchill, the British prime minister."

"I have no idea what he has to say. Haven't you heard? My radio's on the blink."

"You must be joking!"

"What do you take me for?" Jacob says seriously.

Schmidt seems stunned and looks narrowly at Jacob, just like the others he'd had to tell that very morning, with drooping shoulders and despairing voice, the only real news of the day. Schmidt, who is a bit stuck up and whom some wit has dubbed Leonard Assimilinski, this same Schmidt seems to feel a stab to the heart like all the others; suddenly he is no different from the rest.

"How did it happen?" he asks in a low voice.

The answer to this question had been reworded that morning; there hadn't been time to present it to each one as it had been handed to Kowalski, wrapped in tissue paper. Jacob had to settle for some major deletions. How did it happen? "How do you think? The way a radio like that goes on the blink, that's how. Yesterday it was still working, and today it isn't."

Reactions had been mixed; some cursed an unjust God, others prayed to Him, and some consoled themselves with the thought that radio and Russians were two entirely different things. One man had wept like a child, his tears blending with the raindrops running down his cheeks. One of them said: "Let's hope that isn't a bad omen."

Jacob couldn't say yes and couldn't say no; he had to leave them to their minor anguish rather than expose them to the whole truth. Neither has he any words of comfort now to whisper to the disconsolate Schmidt. His store of comfort is exhausted. At this point we should remind ourselves briefly that Jacob is just as much in need of consolation as all the other poor souls around him, just as cut off from all further supply of news, that he is tormented by the same hopes. Only a freak coincidence has turned an equal person into a special person and prevented him thus far from laying all his cards on the table. But only thus far: today I have let you glance up my sleeve, you have seen how empty it is, there is no trump card inside. Now we are all equally informed, there is no difference between us anymore, except for your belief that I was once a special person.

"There's nothing to be done, Mr. Schmidt. We have to carry on. Right now in fact!"

Across the freight yard, through the rain that has abated somewhat, booms an unfamiliar voice, "Keep your hands off that!"

Jacob and Schmidt hurry to the door to see what is happening outside. Herschel Schtamm, one of the twins, is standing on the siding beside an ordinary-looking boxcar that is still closed. Thinking no doubt that this was the next one to be loaded, he hears the unfamiliar voice that can mean only him, and he snatches his hand away from the bolt, which he was just about to raise. The only remarkable thing about the incident so far is the voice, but it is indeed very remarkable: it is the Whistle's, hence unfamiliar. The Whistle in his railway man's uniform advances, as quickly as his wooden leg allows, on Herschel Schtamm, who backs away in fear. The Whistle stops beside the boxcar and checks the bolt, which is still firmly closed.

"Didn't you hear before? This car is not to be touched, goddammit!"

"Yessir!" says Herschel Schtamm.

Then the Whistle turns toward all the Jews, who have paused in their work to enjoy the thrill of a totally new sound. Raising his voice, he turns toward them and shouts, "Have you all got it into your heads now, you scumbags? This car is not to be touched! Next time there will be a bullet!"

 So that's what his voice sounds like, not a very impressive premiere I'd say, a weak baritone I'd say, the tone leaves a lot to be desired. The Whistle stalks back to the brick building, Herschel Schtamm resumes work as fast as he can so as to get out of the limelight, and we do the same. The incident, which wasn't a genuine one, has come to its temporary conclusion.

"What kind of a boxcar do you suppose that is?" asks Schmidt.

"How should I know?" Jacob replies.

"Mr. Schtamm can count himself lucky to have got away with it. Actually the sentry did order us this morning to leave that boxcar alone. You must have heard that too."

"Yes, of course."

"So why did he go over there?"

"How in the world am I supposed to know!"

Schmidt has no instinct for when a conversation has come to an end. He expresses his views on the advisability of strictly obeying orders, on the increased chances of survival resulting from such adherence, then delivers a brief lecture on the factual legal situation deriving from the present power configuration. Jacob listens with only half an ear. Frankly, he doesn't find Schmidt particularly likable; without ever actually saying so, Schmidt considers himself superior and more intelligent and more cultured — he probably wouldn't have had the slightest objection to the Germans' establishing the ghetto at all if they hadn't picked on him to be put in it. When he makes an effort to gloss over social differences, which he usually does, the impression is inescapable that he is pretending: Look how nice of me, I'm just behaving as if we were all of the same kind. The differences are there, he can't fight them: if only in the way he looks at a person or speaks or eats or talks about the Germans or the past, but above all in the way he thinks. One can't choose one's fellow sufferers, and a fellow sufferer he undoubtedly is; he trembles no differently from anyone else for his portion of life — well, yes, a bit differently perhaps, in his special way, a way that our kind don't happen to find all that pleasant.

Soon Herschel Schtamm appears lugging a sack, wearing the soaked fur cap under which he hides his piety, and Jacob asks him, "What was all that about, Herschel?"

"You won't believe it, but I heard voices in that car," Herschel says.

"Voices?"

"Voices," says Herschel. "As true as I'm standing here, human voices."

He may be feeling a cold shiver down his spine, especially since he is always much too hot under his fur cap. He puffs out his cheeks and nods anxiously a few times: you can imagine what that must mean. Jacob can; he reacts to Herschel's announcement by sighing despairingly, closing his eyes, and raising his eyebrows. They are carrying on an inaudible little dialogue, and Schmidt stands beside them without understanding a single syllable.

Mischa comes up to them, sets down his bag of cement, and says quietly, "You'd better go on working, the sentry's already looking this way."

Suddenly Jacob is all thumbs, the bag slips from his hands, and Schmidt says in annoyance: "Watch what you're doing!"

Jacob does have to watch himself. He feels, as he remembers later, like you do just after dreaming of happiness and quiet little places, and then someone comes and pulls away your warm blanket, and you lie there naked and trembling from the impact of cold reality.

"You're very silent," says Schmidt after a while.

Jacob persists in his silence; deeply distressed, he picks up the bags as they are handed to him, merely casting an occasional furtive glance at the innocuous-looking boxcar on its siding, behind whose walls human voices have been heard. Ventilation holes right up under the roof, no one is tall enough to look out, and no one is screaming, from neither inside nor outside, why isn't anyone screaming, the bags need to be carefully stacked. Standing there reddish-brown on its siding as if forgotten, but they won't forget it, in some ways they can be relied upon. Yesterday it wasn't here, tomorrow it'll be gone, just a brief stop on its way to somewhere. A car like that — loaded and unloaded and loaded by us a hundred times, crates, coal, potatoes under strict surveillance, machinery, stones, boxcars exactly like that, but this one isn't to be touched, or they'll shoot.

"Do you think it's true?" asks Schmidt.

"Think what's true?"

"About those voices."

"Don't ask such stupid questions. Do you think Herschel Schtamm is trying to impress us?"

"But who can possibly be inside that car?"

"Who do you think?"

Schmidt's mouth opens; suddenly he is seized by a dreadful suspicion. "You mean . . . ," he whispers.

"Yes, I do!"

"You mean, they're still sending people to the camps?"

Unfortunately that's how it is. Schmidt is not at home in the game of hints where certain things aren't mentioned and yet are said. He'll never be at home; in his heart he is and always will be an outsider. He needs to be told everything in blunt, unequivocal terms.

"No, they're not sending anyone anymore! The war is long since over, we could all go home if we wanted to, but we don't want to because we're having such a good time here!" says Jacob, rolling his eyes. "Are they still sending people! Do you imagine there are none left? I'm left, you're left, all of us here are left. Just don't get the idea it's as good as over!"

Schmidt interrupts the well-deserved lecture with a quick gesture, pointing outside in alarm and exclaiming: "Look! Schtamm!"

Herschel had never attracted much attention, except for his praying, which at the time he was convinced had led to the power failure. Now he's making up for it: he is standing on the siding beside the boxcar. The sentries haven't noticed him yet. Herschel is pressing his ear to the wall of the car and speaking: I can clearly see his lips moving, see him listening and then speaking again, our pious Herschel. His brother Roman happens to be standing next to me, his eyes like cartwheels: he makes a move to dash over to Herschel and bring him back before it's too late. Two men have to restrain him by force, and one of them has to whisper: "Calm down, you idiot, you'll only draw their attention to him!"

I can't hear what Herschel is saying or what the people inside are telling him, it's much too far away, but I can imagine it, and this is not a case of vague conjectures. The longer I think about it, the surer I am of his words, even though he never confirmed them to me.

"Hello! Can you hear me?" Herschel begins.

"We can hear you," a voice from inside must surely answer. "Who are you?"

"I'm from the ghetto," Herschel says. "You must hang on; only for a short time, you must hang on. The Russians have already advanced past Bezanika!"

"How do you know?" they ask from inside, all quite logical and predictable.

"You can believe me. We have a secret radio. I have to get back now!"

The people locked up inside thank him, utterly bewildered; a little white dove has strayed into their darkness. What they say is of no consequence; maybe they wish him happiness and riches and a hundred and twenty years of life before they hear his footsteps moving away.

Everyone is watching spellbound as Herschel starts on his way back. Crazy fools that we are, we stand there gaping instead of getting on with our work and behaving as if everything were normal. First we keep Roman from committing a stupid blunder, then we commit one ourselves. Perhaps Herschel wouldn't have escaped them anyway, who can tell in retrospect? In any event we do nothing to distract their attention from him. Only now does he seem to have discovered fear; so far everything has gone as if of its own volition, according to the unfathomable laws obeyed by sleepwalkers. Cover is pitifully inadequate, almost nonexistent. Herschel has good reason to be afraid. A stack of crates, another empty boxcar, otherwise nothing along his path where he would need the protection of a convoy. I see him sticking his head around the corner of the boxcar, inch by inch; with his eyes he has already reached us; I can already hear him telling us about his great journey.

So far the opposition is quiet. The sentry by the gate is standing with his back to the railway tracks; there is no sound to rouse his attention. The other two sentries have disappeared, are inside the building presumably, driven in by the rain. I see Herschel making his final preparations for the great sprint; I see him pray. Although he is still standing beside the boxcar and moving his lips, it is obvious that he is not talking to the people inside but conversing with his God. And then I turn my head toward the brick building: it has a little window in the gable. The window is open, and on the sill lies a rifle being aimed, very calmly and deliberately. I can't make out the man behind it, it is too dark in the room; I see only two hands adjusting the aim of the barrel until they are satisfied: then they are still, as in a painting. What should I have done, I who have never been a hero, what would I have done if I were a hero — given a shout, that's all, but what good would that have been? I don't shout, I close my eyes, an eternity passes, Roman says to me: "Why are you closing your eyes? Look, he's going to make it, that crazy fool!"

I don't know why, but at this moment I think of Hannah, executed in front of a tree whose name I don't know. I'm still thinking of her after the shot is fired, until the men around me are all talking at the same time. A single dry shot; the two hands had, as I said, plenty of time to prepare everything all the while Herschel was praying. It is a strange sound — I have never heard a single shot before, always several at a time — like a naughty child stamping its foot in a tantrum, or a toy balloon being blown up too hard and bursting, or even, since I am already indulging in images, as if God had coughed, a cough of dismissal for Herschel.

Those locked behind the reddish-brown walls of the boxcar may be asking: "Hey, you there, what's happened?"

Herschel is lying on his stomach, across the track and between two ties. His clenched right hand has fallen into a black puddle; his face, of which at first I can see only one half, has a surprised look with its open eye. We stand silently around him; they allow us this little respite. Roman bends down to him, pulls him off the track, and turns him over on his back. Then he removes the fur cap, his fingers fumbling awkwardly with the flaps under the chin. He thrusts the cap into his pocket and walks away. For the first time in this freight yard, Herschel's earlocks are allowed to wave freely in the wind; many of us have never seen them before, have merely been told about them. So this is what Herschel Schtamm really looks like, without disguise. For the last time his face, darkly framed by wet earth and black hair, someone has closed his eyes. I won't lie, why should I, he was no beauty, he was very pious, wanted to pass on hope, and in so doing he died.

Unnoticed, the sentry from the gate has come up behind us; it is time to divert our thoughts, and he says: "You've been gawking long enough, or haven't you ever seen a dead man before? Come on, back to work on the double!"

At the end of the day we will take him with us and bury him; that's permitted, without its being printed in black and white in one of the many regulations; it has simply become accepted. I look once more up to the window, which is now closed again: no rifle, no hands. And no one emerges from the building, they pay no further attention to us, for them the incident is closed.

Life goes on; Schmidt and Jacob start moving the bags again. By this time Schmidt has understood enough to hold his tongue and not let on why Herschel insisted on dashing over to the boxcar although the railway man emphatically and specifically warned him earlier.

In Jacob's head, self-reproaches follow one upon the other; the part he has played in this drama is frighteningly clear. You construct some scanty consolation for yourself; you visualize a huge scale with two trays, on one you place Herschel while on the other you pile up all the hope you have been spreading among the people. Which side will go down? The problem is, you don't know how much hope weighs, and no one is going to tell you. You must find the formula by yourself and complete the calculation alone. But you calculate in vain, the problems mount. Here's another: who can divulge to you how much harm was prevented by your inventions? Ten disasters or twenty or only a single one? What has been prevented will remain hidden from you forever. Only the one you caused is visible: there it lies beside the tracks in the rain.

Even later, during the lunch break, Jacob hasn't come one bit closer to the solution of the problem with all its unknown factors. He sits apart as he swallows his soup; today everyone leaves everyone else in peace. He has avoided Roman Schtamm. Roman hasn't sought him out; only beside the cart where the empty tin bowls are always deposited do they find themselves suddenly face-to-face. They look each other in the eye, especially Roman. Jacob tells me, "He looked at me as if I had shot his brother."

The evenings belong to Lina.

A long time ago, Jacob stopped with her in the corridor outside his door and said: "Listen carefully, Lina, so that, if anything should happen, you'll be able to find the key to my room" is what he said. "Here behind the doorframe is a little hole in the wall, see? I'll put the key in here now, then wedge this stone in front of it. It's quite easy to remove — if you stand on tiptoe you'll be tall enough. Try." Lina tried; she stretched up her arm, removed the stone, barely managed to grasp the key, and held it out proudly to Jacob. "Wonderful," Jacob said. "Remember the place carefully. I don't really know

why, but maybe someday it'll be important. And one more thing —
never tell anyone about this place."

By now Lina no longer has to stand on tiptoe; for two years she
has been tirelessly growing up toward the little hole behind the
doorframe. If anything should happen, Jacob had said; today something had happened. Lina retrieves the key, unlocks the door, and
stands with bated breath in the empty room. She is a bit nervous, but
that will pass; if Jacob comes in unexpectedly she'll simply tell him
she's tidying up. The motives driving her are adventurous, he would
hardly approve of them, and what he doesn't know won't hurt him.

In her path lie two obstacles, she is under no illusions: the first is
the hiding place, still unknown; the second is that she doesn't know
what a radio looks like. Hiding places are not unlimited in this room;
in a few minutes it could be turned upside down. The second
obstacle seems much more difficult to her. There are all kinds of
things that Jacob has explained to her. She would have no difficulty,
for instance, in describing a bus, although she has never been face-to-
face with one; she could talk about bananas, airplanes, teddy bears
that start to growl when you lay them on their backs. During the
recent power failure, Jacob even traced with her the highly mysterious path traveled by the light from the coal mine to the little bulb
under the ceiling, but not a single word has he ever uttered about a
radio. There are a few scanty clues: everyone is talking about it, it is
forbidden to own one, it reveals things not known before, it is small
enough to be easily hidden.

"Will you show me your radio tomorrow?" she'd asked him the
previous evening, when he came up to the attic to see her after
Kowalski's futile visit.

"No," he said.

"And the day after tomorrow?"

"No!"

"And the day after the day after tomorrow?"

"No, I said! And that's enough!"

Even her normally infallible look of wide-eyed entreaty had no effect; Jacob didn't even notice it. Hence her new attempt after a resentful pause: "Are you ever going to show it to me?"

"No."

"Why not?"

"Because."

"Will you at least tell me what it looks like?" she asked then, her plan already half-formed in her mind. But he refused to answer this either, so her half-formed plan became a whole one.

In a nutshell: Lina must look for an object of which all she knows is that Jacob keeps it hidden away, an object without color, shape, or weight, the only good thing being that Jacob can't have that many unfamiliar objects in his room. The first one she finds and has never seen before can confidently be assumed to be called a radio.

Lina starts with the obvious hiding places: under the bed, on top of the cupboard, in the table drawer. Quite possibly a radio is too big to fit into a table drawer — perhaps anyone watching would laugh out loud to see Lina looking in there for a radio. But it's not her fault that Jacob remains so obstinately silent, and besides, no one is watching. It's not in the drawer; there's nothing in it. All she finds under the bed and on top of the cupboard is dust. All that's left is the inside of the cupboard; there's no other hiding place. The cupboard has two doors, one at the top and one at the bottom. She can forget about the top one; behind it are the two soup plates and two flat plates, the two cups of which one lost its handle when Lina dropped it on the floor while doing the dishes, also a knife and two spoons, the ever-empty sugar jar, and behind all that the food, when there is any. Behind this door Lina is at home; she often sets the table, serves the meal, and clears it away. She can forget about that one, but her project must not fail for want of thoroughness. She looks: the four plates, two cups, sugar jar, knife and spoons, plus some bread and a small bag of dried beans, no surprises.

Now for the bottom door. Lina hesitates: her fingers are already around the key and can't make up their mind. If what she is looking for isn't in there, then it's nowhere. So far she'd never had any reason to look inside. "That's where I keep my stuff," Jacob had said. Nothing could sound more harmless. His stuff: only now is it clear what is concealed behind two such innocent words.

There is a limit to her hesitation, and Lina finally opens up; outside in the corridor footsteps hurry by. Locking the door won't do: if Jacob comes he won't ask what she's doing here, he'll ask why she has locked herself in, and there's no answer for that. Lina takes everything out: a pair of trousers and a shirt, a needle and thread, a saucepan — why isn't that in the top section? — a box of nails and screws, an empty picture frame, the book about Africa. She allows herself a brief pause; the book has more to offer than the words and letters to which Jacob has recently been attaching such strange importance. The pictures do deserve a few moments' attention, regardless. The woman with those amazingly long breasts, so flat and dried-up looking, and the ring stuck through her nose — Jacob has promised to explain the meaning of that later. The naked men who have painted their faces all over, carry long spears, and on their heads wear enormous structures of feathers, hair, and ribbons. Or the skinny children, with round, protruding stomachs, animals with horns and stripes and endless noses and even longer necks: all this can certainly cause delay, but not enough to make one forget one's real purpose.

Lina crawls waist deep into the cupboard; a final obstacle is removed, a modest pile of underwear with a green towel on top, and then. . . . The path has been cleared to that as yet unseen object, a proud smile of triumph, there it stands, inconspicuously in the corner, mysterious and forbidden. She brings it out to the light, some delicate latticework, a little knob, glass, and round; she places it reverently on the table and sits down facing it. Now something will happen. His stuff, Jacob had said; while she is staring at it the minutes tick away: what will be revealed now that she didn't know before? Does this thing speak like an ordinary person, or does it deliver up its secrets in some other way, in some miraculous way? After a prolonged, expectant silence, Lina realizes that, left to itself, it will reveal nothing, it must be made to speak; maybe she just has to ask it something. If so, then not, she hopes, by means of some prearranged formula like with Ali Baba outside the cave of Sesame.

"What is my name?" Lina starts off with the simplest words she can think of, but already this seems to be too much for the thing. Lina allows it plenty of time, in vain. Her disappointment makes way for the thought that she has to ask for something unknown, for something she doesn't already know — after all, she does know her own name. "How much is thirty times two million?" she asks. When this evokes no reply either, she takes a new approach; she remembers the light that can be switched on and off according to one's fancy. Perhaps this thing can be switched on in the same way, let's try the little knob. It's rusted, can hardly be moved; after much effort, just a tiny squeak, and already her fingers are sore. At that moment Jacob appears in the doorway and asks, as predicted: "What are you doing here?"

"I," says Lina, "I wanted . . ." she says, having to recover from the shock, "I wanted to tidy up your room. Don't you remember?"

Jacob remembers; he looks at the Sodom and Gomorrah in front of the cupboard, then back at Lina, who had wanted to tidy up; before he can open his mouth she knows it won't be all that bad. "But I hope you haven't finished yet?" asks Jacob.

Of course she hasn't finished yet, she's only just begun. She jumps up and stuffs saucepan and book and underwear back into the cupboard, so quickly that his eyes can scarcely follow her. Next, the picture frame, in her haste the nails fall out of the box, in no time they're gathered up, then come the needle and thread, where are the needle and thread, she'll find them next time, the cupboard door is slammed shut, and already the mess is forgotten. Only that thing remains on the table. He has seen it anyway; there stands his only secret, and he is still not giving vent to his anger.

"You're not cross with me, are you?"

"No, no!"

Jacob takes off his jacket, then washes the dirt from the freight yard off his hands. Lina grows uneasy: the thing is standing there being ignored.

"And what did you really mean to do here?"

"Nothing. I was tidying up," she says, knowing that it's hopeless.

"What were you looking for?"

Now he does begin to raise his voice, but she finds the question too silly for words: he's sitting in front of the thing, asking in pretended innocence what she has been looking for, and to that we refuse to give the obvious reply.

"What's the lamp doing here?"

"What lamp?"

"This one. Do you see any other?"

When Lina remains silent and wide eyed, staring at the alleged lamp, and the wide eyes gradually fill with tears, Jacob draws her close and asks in a much gentler voice: "What's the matter?"

"Nothing."

He pulls her onto his knee; she doesn't often cry. Who is to know what's going on in a little mind like that, a mind that has all day to brood alone? "Come on, tell me what's the matter. Does it have anything to do with the lamp?"

"No."

"Have you ever seen it before?"

"No."

"Would you like me to explain how it works?"

Lina stops her tears: after all, Jacob can't be blamed for her mistake, and besides, tomorrow is another day, somehow she'll find the hiding place that she overlooked today. She attends to eyes and nose with her sleeve, which is not quite adequate; Jacob's handkerchief hurries to her aid.

"Would you like me to explain?"

"Yes."

"Well, then. This thing is a kerosene lamp. In the old days all the lamps were like this, before there was any electric light. This is where you pour in the kerosene, into this little bowl. This is the wick, it sucks up the kerosene, and only its tip sticks out. It can be made longer or shorter, with this knob here. You hold a match to the wick, and then the room is lighted up."

"Could you do it for me?"

"I'm sorry, I don't have any kerosene."

Lina slips off Jacob's knee; she picks up the lamp in both hands and looks at it from all sides: so that's why it was no use waiting for an answer. At home, in the Nuriel family, there had been no kerosene lamp and no radio; mistakes arise from lack of experience. After one last look she puts the thing back in the cupboard. Order is completely restored, also with Lina. She even discovers a funny side to her unsuccessful voyage of discovery.

"Do you know what I thought it was?"

"Well?"

"But you won't laugh at me?"

"I wouldn't dream of it."

"I thought it was your radio."

Jacob smiles; he remembers how, as a very little boy, he had believed an old woman who lived next door, a hunchback, to be a witch, a similar mistaken conclusion; but soon his smile gradually fades. Lina was looking for the radio, she admits that. It wouldn't have been a bad idea to leave her to her belief: what difference does it make to a lamp to be taken for a radio? He would have sworn her to secrecy: Now at last you've found it, now you know what it looks like, now not another word about it, above all not to strangers. And for weeks there would have been peace for him, at least at home. But he had let the opportunity slip by; Lina hadn't betrayed herself until it was too late, and he hadn't had enough presence of mind to size up the situation in the room and the lamp on the table and the significance of her tears. Any minute now she will ask, All right, so that was a lamp, now where's the radio? Any minute now, or in an hour, or tomorrow at the latest, she's already itching with impatience. Telling her it's broken won't satisfy her, Then show me the broken one, and unfortunately he's not one of those who can answer awkward questions with the occasional slap. There is still, of course, one way out, a very simple one: Jacob could claim to have burned it, a damaged radio, if found, being no less dangerous than an intact one.

He could say that, then he'd be happily rid of the radio, for Lina and all the world, but it so happens that the day just past at the freight yard also plays a certain role. The dead Herschel Schtamm, his brother Roman with the tormenting gaze, the unknown people locked up on the siding: they all have a right to speak before the radio is finally destroyed. And the individual Jews who arrived hopefully in the early morning with their questions and left again in dismay, without the news to which they are entitled. By this time they will already be home, relatives and friends will be knocking on their doors, what's the latest news at the freight yard? Nothing, they'll be told, the radio says nothing anymore, it's broken, yesterday it was still working, and today not a sound. The relatives and friends leave, spread the latest news throughout all the buildings and streets, which soon will once again seem as wretched as they did before that night when the searchlight picked up Jacob about seven-thirty on the Kurländischer Damm. There's a lot to be considered before making frivolous decisions, before buying the peace that is no peace.

"Will you show me the radio now?"

"I already said no yesterday. Has anything changed since then?"

"I'll find it anyway," says Lina.

"Then go on looking."

"Want to bet that I'll find it?"

She is switching to open attack, let her search rather than ask questions, Jacob is not going to talk her out of the next radio she finds. And the radio that she'll never find will for the time being be saved from the fire, for many reasons, the first being Herschel of the earlocks: that very morning, as he lay in the rain between the railway ties, he had as good as repaired it.

Jacob goes to work with a light heart. Anyone observing his posture and his brisk walk and drawing comparisons with yesterday or the last few days is struck by the change: there goes a man of poise. With a light heart, for the hours in bed had been rich in important decisions; contact with the outer world has been restored. The radio had been on half the night, right after Lina had been shaken off it went on and stayed on until sleep came unbidden, and by that time his ear had picked up a number of reports, and not to be sneezed at either. With a light heart, for the little flame of expectation must not go out. Thus Jacob's resolve; he had spent half the night looking for wood and kindling to keep it going. He has succeeded in achieving a substantial advance, he and the Russians; he has quietly let them win a great battle on the banks of a little river, the Rudna, which, although it doesn't babble along right outside the front door, is gratifyingly closer than the town of Bezanika.

In reviewing the news items supplied thus far, Jacob noticed that, when looked at more closely, these had consisted only of extended trifles; except for the very first item about Bezanika, nothing substantial. He had turned every little idea into a tremendous story, often transparent and lacking in credibility. Doubts had so far not arisen merely because hope had made the people blind and stupid. But during the night before the battle of the Rudna an insight was gained: Jacob has at last discovered the source of his difficulties. In other words, hardly had he turned out the light when it came to him in a flash why his inventions had become so laborious and eventually failed him almost entirely. He was too modest, he suspected; he had always tried to keep his news items within a sphere that at some later date, after life resumed its normal course, cannot be verified. With each news item some inhibition had stood in his way, some pang of conscience; the lies had come stumbling reluctantly from his lips, as if looking for a hiding place they could crawl away to in a hurry before anyone took a closer look at them.

But this procedure was fundamentally wrong, as he came to

realize last night; a liar with pangs of conscience will always remain a bungler. In this type of activity, restraint and false modesty are inappropriate; you must go the whole hog, you must exude conviction, you must act the part of a person who is already aware of what they are going to hear from you the very next moment. You must throw out figures and names and dates right and left; the battle of the Rudna is merely a modest beginning. It will never go down in history, but in our history it will be given a place of honor. And when all these tribulations are over, when anyone who is interested can look up the true events of the war in books, he will be free to come and ask: "Hey you, what kind of nonsense did you tell us back in those days? When was there ever a battle of the Rudna?" "Wasn't there?" will be your surprised answer. "Let's have a look at that book. . . . You're right, there never was. It's not in here. So I suppose I must have misheard at the time, I'm sorry." They will probably forgive you, at worst they'll shrug and walk off, and perhaps there will even be some among them who will thank you for the error.

As regards the progress of the fighting, Jacob has done some preliminary work, and for this his local knowledge has come in very handy. The battle of the Rudna and its aftermath are to suffice for the next three days; we mustn't go overboard, for the crossing of the river isn't altogether without its problems. We're not going to make it that easy for the Russians: the Germans have blown up the only bridge, Jacob has thought it all out. Before the advance can be continued, a temporary pontoon bridge has to be built, and this will take three or four days. When that's been taken care of, the Russians will march on the little town of Tobolin, which the Germans have turned into a kind of fortress. Tobolin, in turn, resists for three days; it is surrounded, softened up by the artillery, and stormed by the infantry. In a hopeless situation Major Karthäuser, a splendid name with a credible rank, signs the document of surrender: Tobolin is liberated. Incidentally that will please Mischa — he has an aunt living there who, it is hoped, will live to see this victory. The aunt, Lea Malamut, owned a haberdashery and, when Mischa was a boy, always used to send him a little box of colored buttons and threads for his birthday. But let's not linger in Tobolin, it's a long way from there to the district town of Pry, the next town in our direction. Some forty miles; they have already been planned in rough outline but aren't yet ready in every detail. That will be Jacob's night work for a while. As far as Tobolin everything is clear, and today at the freight yard the result of the glorious battle of the Rudna will be announced.

With a light heart Jacob goes off to work, and a little added touch occurs to him that he could apply to the events at the Rudna. Might not secret German plans have fallen into Russian hands, thus revealing all the enemy's actions on this front for weeks to come and rendering them ineffectual? That would be a few raisins in Jacob's cake, but immediately doubts arise in terms of probability, for would secret plans be kept in such an insecure place? After all, the Germans are no fools. Neither are the Russians: even if they did capture plans of that kind, they're not going to broadcast the fact to the world over the radio. They'll keep it carefully to themselves and discreetly make their preparations. So we'll dispense with the added touch. What we already have is enough to give the Jews a bit of the poise with which Jacob continues on his way to work, with a light heart.

At the corner of Tismenizer-Strasse he sees Kowalski waiting for him, nothing special about that, Kowalski often waits for him here, he lives here. As he approaches, though, it turns out that Kowalski is not alone; with him is a young man, which *is* somewhat unusual, especially since Jacob has never seen the young man before.

From some way off, Kowalski points at Jacob; the young stranger follows the finger with his eyes, as if Kowalski were explaining, That's the man, the one in the dark gray jacket.

Jacob comes up to them, they shake hands, and all three walk on; there have been no introductions yet. "You're late today," Kowalski says. "We've been waiting quite a while for you."

"Had we arranged to meet?" Jacob asks. He looks out of the corner of his eye at the young man, who doesn't say a word and seems a bit awkward and embarrassed, staring straight ahead. A blind man would be aware that there is some special significance to his presence. Kowalski has said, "We've been waiting," so the young man is not here by chance. Kowalski has a hand in this; he must have told him to come.

"Won't you introduce us?" says Jacob.

"You've never met?" asks Kowalski with a show of surprise. "This is Josef Neidorf."

"I'm Jacob Heym."

"I know," says the shy young man. So his name is Neidorf. His first words convey nothing.

"You don't work at the freight yard?" asks Jacob.

"No."

"Where, then?"

"At the tool factory."

"But then you're heading the wrong way. You should be going in exactly the opposite direction."

"We start later than you do," Neidorf says, and it is obvious that he is not comfortable with his explanation.

"I see. And since you have some time to spare, you choose to accompany us all the way to the freight yard. Stands to reason."

Neidorf suddenly stops, the way one does before running away; he looks haunted and says in a low voice to Kowalski, "Can't you really manage without me? You see, I don't want to have anything to do with this whole business. I'm scared, you see."

"Oh, don't start that again! Didn't I already explain it all to you till I was blue in the face?" Kowalski says impatiently, taking him by the arm before he can get away. "Can't you get it into your head? He won't say a word, *I* won't say a word, and *you* won't say a word. Apart from us three, not a soul will ever find out about it. So what can happen?"

Neidorf still looks most unhappy, but he stays when Kowalski cautiously lets go of him.

"What won't I say a word about?" asks Jacob, who by now has become curious.

Kowalski gestures to him to be patient. The gesture means many things: that you can see what a state the boy's in, that we must allow him a moment or two to come to terms with himself and his fear, for Kowalski's gestures can be highly expressive. He gives Neidorf an encouraging wink, which with his swollen eyes isn't easy, and says, "Now you can tell him what you are."

Neidorf still hesitates. Jacob is quite intrigued, a surprise early in the morning that makes a young man afraid and about which they must — although so far for unknown reasons — keep silent: Kowalski can't bring off one like that every day.

"Actually I'm a radio repairman," Neidorf finally says in an agonized voice.

A radio repairman.

There is no chair waiting for Jacob: looks fly back and forth, pleased ones and withering ones. An insane rage toward Kowalski almost chokes Jacob. Trying to play God, this cretin of a friend arranges for repairs without the vaguest idea of their extent and, what's more, undoubtedly expects you to feel grateful to him for his enterprising efforts. It couldn't have been easy, after all, in a single short evening that is already over by eight o'clock, to dig up someone who knows something about radios, but not too difficult for a friend like Kowalski. There he stands, beaming expectantly: Haven't I done a good job? Magnificent of course. Any more help like that and you might as well go and hang yourself right away. And it is for him that you have just helped to win the battle of the Rudna; you're tempted to burn the radio after all. Right after they parted yesterday evening, he must have dashed off and driven the whole ghetto frantic. He hadn't known this Neidorf before, you would have known if he had, for unfortunately Kowalski's friends are also your own. He must have sidled up to one person after another, asking confidently in his penetrating voice, "Do you happen to know anybody who can repair a radio?" "A radio? Why on earth do you need someone to repair a radio?" "Why do you think?"

Someone or other must have then put him on to this poor fellow Neidorf, who has more intelligence in his little finger than Kowalski has in his whole head; the boy's fear is the best proof. Kowalski has told him God knows what to reassure him, then dragged him here and contrived this highly embarrassing situation, and now you're confronted with a radio repairman in the flesh.

"What a splendid profession!" says Jacob.

"Yes, isn't it?"

Kowalski is as pleased as Punch. There is simply no end to his deeds of friendship — the other day the miraculous rescue from the outhouse, today the second noble deed. He dares anyone to match it, in a place where there is so little room for kind actions. But he's not looking for any special gratitude; among true friends such things are taken for granted: they don't waste much time on talk, they act. And because time is getting on, and because so far no visible signs of joy or comprehension are noticeable in Jacob, Kowalski explains to him: "He's going to fix your radio, you see. And don't worry, the lad's trustworthy."

"I'm glad to know that," says Jacob.

"Of course, I can't guarantee anything," Neidorf says with modest eagerness. "If, say, a tube's gone, there's nothing I can do about it. I have no spare parts — I told Mr. Kowalski that right away."

"Just go there and have a look at it," says Kowalski.

Jacob has only minutes to find a way out; one would imagine that it gets easier from one time to the next, seeing that practice makes perfect, but actually it always remains just as difficult. Ruefully he remembers all the decisions he reached last night, more easily made than carried out when obstacles of this kind show up, but Jacob pulls himself together. Happy news requires a happy face, but Jacob can't manage one: the sight of Kowalski the demon helper precludes all possibility of a smile. With a great effort, Jacob stretches his lips from side to side and forces a look of grim affability into his eyes as he tries to convey that something of immense importance has just occurred to him.

"Of course, you couldn't know!" he says. "You've gone to all that trouble for nothing. The radio is working again!"

"You don't say!"

"But I appreciate your efforts all the same."

"How did it happen? Did you fix it yourself?" Kowalski asks, and it's impossible to tell whether he is genuinely glad or whether he is disappointed at his helpfulness having gone for nothing.

"It's working again. Isn't that enough?"

"But how?" asks Kowalski. "A radio can't repair itself, can it?"

If Neidorf weren't with them, Jacob could tell Kowalski anything — a tube had come loose, or he had banged it a few times with his fist and it came on again — Kowalski knows as little about radios as he does. But unfortunately this Neidorf with his expert knowledge is still there; not only does he look relieved because his help isn't needed after all, but there is also a gleam of professional interest in his eye. And now it's up to you to improvise a suitable explanation that will satisfy nitwit and expert alike. You must know, after all, how you repaired your radio: tell them quickly and look cheerful about it.

"It was one of the wires in the electrical cord. I just shortened it a bit."

So everything has worked out splendidly, Jacob is quite proud of himself, all three parties are satisfied. As he leaves, Neidorf shakes hands with Jacob, many thanks again for your trouble, he walks off in the direction of the tool factory and doesn't have to be scared anymore.

Kowalski and Jacob continue on their way to the freight yard: Jacob is thinking up a revenge for the ruined morning that had started out so well, namely, the battle of the Rudna will be withheld from Kowalski; let others bring him the joyful news. Friends who never miss a chance to torture a person nearly to death don't deserve battles won during sleepless nights of torment. Even if no harm was intended. What Kowalski has inflicted on you today, the difficulties he lands you in with no harm intended, are getting alarmingly out of hand; you can't stand idly by watching this trend. Two days ago Kowalski forced him to cope with Lina, today with Neidorf, and among all the questioners Kowalski is the most tireless, so the countermeasure of a single suppressed battle is surely appropriate.

"Was there any news last night?" asks Kowalski.

"Nothing."

A few men they know say good morning as they pass, the street is the only one leading to the freight yard, and it gradually becomes crowded. Jacob notices people looking at him narrowly, at Kowalski too apparently. Kowalski is basking in Jacob's glory and whispers to someone: "The radio is working again!" As if he had been instrumental, and the other fellow quickens his step and whispers it to others. Soon many are turning to look at Jacob and seem to perk up. Jacob nods imperceptibly — that's right; you heard correctly — and the repaired radio will probably arrive at the freight yard before its owner.

"I meant to ask you," Kowalski says, "I've been wondering whether the time hasn't come to think of some other things."

"Such as?"

"Such as business."

"Business? What kind of business?"

"I'm a businessman," Kowalski says. "Isn't this the best time to prepare at least mentally for the future?"

"What do you mean, business? And what do you want to prepare? Isn't your barbershop standing there waiting for you?"

"That's what I'm wondering about. I've been thinking for a long time that maybe I should try something different in the future."

"Something different, at your age?"

"Why not? Just between ourselves, I've got some money tucked away. Not exactly a fortune, mind you, but maybe there's some better way to invest it than in my old shop, which I never really liked, anyway. Any more than you did, if you're honest. And if I go ahead with something like that, I want to be sure I'm not throwing my money away."

"And where do I come in?"

"From time to time there must surely be some business news on the radio."

"There is."

"Hasn't there been anything that could be taken as a guideline? Some hint or other?"

"I'm not interested in such things."

"Not interested in such things — look who's talking!" says Kowalski. "I'm sure you must have heard something!"

"What is it you want to know, then? So far I haven't understood a single word."

"I simply want to know which line of business has the best prospects."

"Sometimes you're positively childish, Kowalski. Do you seriously think that they announce over the radio: 'We advise you to invest your money after the war in such and such businesses'?"

This makes sense to Kowalski, and he says: "Well, all right, then I'll simply ask you as a friend. If you had some money, where would you be most likely to invest it?"

So Jacob considers it too; an investment like that deserves a lot of consideration: where would he be most likely to invest it? "Alcohol, or tobacco, perhaps? If you remember, after the last war no one could get enough of them. And David Gedalye, you must have known him too, built himself a magnificent house in those days from schnapps."

"He did, he did," says Kowalski, "but where to find the raw materials? Do you really think that, right after the war, there'll be enough potatoes to make schnapps?"

"That's not the way to look at it. There'll be no raw materials for anything. What you need for postwar commerce is not logic but a good nose for business."

Kowalski is still doubtful, his nose doesn't favor schnapps, his money's too good for that.

"Actually, textiles shouldn't do too badly. There's always a need for clothing," he says.

"You may be right. For years they only made clothing for soldiers: soldiers' trousers, soldiers' socks, soldiers' tunics, soldiers' overcoats. Ordinary people went on wearing their old clothes. And what does that mean?"

"Well?"

"There'll be a demand."

"That's only half the truth, Jacob. Don't forget that during the same period a lot of clothing has been lying unused in cupboards — I mean, all the soldiers' civilian clothes. And today they're as good as new."

"Hm," Jacob says pensively.

And so on, while they consider two or three other possibilities, and Kowalski even toys with the idea of joining forces with Jacob and establishing a large restaurant with all the frills. But Jacob thinks this is too big a risk; besides, he is sure Kowalski isn't really serious. Jacob reverts to his first suggestion, which is that Kowalski is to remain in his old shop, and if he doesn't know what else to do with that bit of money tucked away, he can have the place modernized, and for heaven's sake get some new chairs — demand or no demand, hair and beards will go on growing. By the time they reach the freight yard, Kowalski is almost back to being a barber again.

Lina wins her bet, for in the long run Jacob is no match in the unequal battle: he shows her the radio.

After some days of fruitless searching — there was nothing left she didn't already know — she resorts to pleading. No one can plead like Lina, and she particularly knows how to plead with Jacob, with flattery, tears, hurt looks of a special kind, more tears, and all this with incredible perseverance. Jacob has held out for a few days, then his strength is exhausted: one predictable evening Lina wins her bet. For me, probably the only one who is still alive and able to reflect on the matter, that evening is the most incomprehensible of the whole story. Even when Jacob explained it to me, as best he could, I didn't fully understand it; I asked him: "Didn't you go a bit too far? Couldn't she have betrayed you and everything would have been over?" "Of course not," Jacob replied with a smile, "Lina would never betray me." I said, "I mean without the slightest intention. Children so easily let fall a thoughtless remark, and someone or other picks it up and builds a whole house out of it." "Lina is always very careful about what she says," Jacob replied, and I had to believe him.

But there was also something else that I found almost impossible to understand. "There's something else, Jacob. How could you be sure that she didn't see through the whole thing? She could so easily have noticed what was actually going on — she's a clever girl, you've said so yourself. Wasn't it an outrageous stroke of luck that she didn't see through it?" "She did see through it," Jacob said, his eyes lighting up with pride. "You know, I really didn't care whether she noticed or not. I simply wanted to give her pleasure, regardless of the consequences: that's why I went down into the basement with her." And after a pause, which was much too short to allow me to understand that evening, he added, "Or rather, I did care. I believe that at the time I wanted her to know about everything. I had reached a point where I simply had to show my radio to someone, and I would rather it was Lina than anyone else: with her it was like a game. Anyone else would have been horrified by the truth, but she was happy afterward. So that evening I said to her, 'Come down now into the basement; we'll listen to the radio together.' "

And at this point I suddenly smiled and said: "If I'd known at the time all the things you're capable of, I would have come to you and asked you to show me a tree." Which in turn Jacob couldn't understand. Let's listen to that evening.

Considerable suspense, Lina hangs on to Jacob's jacket, the basement corridor is long and dim. The metal doors that are passed on tiptoe are all locked, as if to hide riches of incalculable worth. The air is damp and cold, although it's August outside. With anxious foresight, Jacob has insisted on a winter dress, stockings, and a scarf for Lina; from ceiling and walls hang droplets that glisten like tiny, feeble lamps.

"Are you scared?"

"No," she whispers firmly, and it's not that much of a lie; her curiosity will make her forget everything else. After all, at the end of the passage waits the thing she has been searching for in vain for days and that she has almost given up as a lost cause, and who is she to say now, I'm scared, let's go back?

At last Jacob stops, at almost the last locker in the long row. Taking the key from his pocket, he unlocks the door and turns on the light, which is only slightly brighter than no light at all.

The locker has to be described: twelve feet square with no window. Its most noticeable feature is a partition built right across it, making almost two out of it and leaving only a narrow passage: the builders must have had a coal bin in mind. The inventory is quickly listed: an iron bedstead with rusty springs, the remains of an old stove with some leftover tiles, green and brown, and a few stovepipes, including an elbow. And in the corner by the door, the only treasure worth locking up: a small, carefully stacked pile of firewood in which Piwowa, the demanding poacher, had been sleeping some months ago while it still represented a piece of furniture. Then a glance behind the partition: more stove debris, bricks, a spade, a bucket with holes in it, and an ax. That's all: I'm being so accurate not because these items are of any significance but because later I was there, during my search for witnesses and traces and nonexistent trees. Just as I have measured the distance between the military office and the next corner with my tape measure, just as I went into Jacob's room where by that time an old woman was living by herself who knew nothing about the fate of any former tenants — the housing authorities had allocated the room to her on a temporary basis — I have also been in this locker; it still belongs to that room. Mrs. Domnik handed me the key without question, saying merely that she had never been down there, she didn't own anything that needed to be kept in the basement, so I mustn't be surprised at the dust or at any mess I might find there, she wasn't responsible for that. And indeed it was dusty, with cobwebs everywhere, that is the truth, but I didn't notice any mess, I found everything just as Jacob had described it to me. The bedstead, stove debris, ax and bucket; even the chopped-up wood was still by the door.

Jacob locks the door from the inside; he says, "So nobody will disturb us." Then he goes on: "And now sit down here," pointing to the iron bedstead.

Lina has already looked around a bit, so far without any result, yet she sits down without protest; under these circumstances he could demand a much greater display of obedience from her.

"Where do you keep the radio?"

"It won't hurt you to wait."

He squats down in front of her, takes her chin in one hand, turns her face toward him, forcing her to look at him, and starts off with the necessary preparation: "Now listen carefully to what I have to say. First of all you must promise me you'll be good and do everything that I'm now going to ask of you. Sacred word of honor?"

The sacred word of honor, intended only for occasions of the utmost importance, is given impatiently; her eyes demand that he cut short the preliminaries.

"You'll sit here keeping perfectly still. The radio is behind that partition. I'll go behind there now and turn it on, then we'll both hear it play. But if I notice you getting up, I'll shut it off again immediately."

"Can't I see it?"

"Absolutely not!" says Jacob firmly. "Actually little girls like you aren't even allowed to hear it either, it's strictly forbidden. But I'm making an exception with you. Agreed?"

What can she do, she's being blackmailed and must submit. Hearing is better than nothing, although she had been looking forward to actually seeing it. Besides, she still might, she might, you never know.

"What is your radio going to play?"

"I don't know in advance, I have to switch it on first."

The preparations are completed, nothing more can be done to protect himself. Jacob stands up. He goes to the partition, pauses in the little passage, and looks once more at Lina, with an expression intended, if it were possible, to chain her to the bedstead; then he finally disappears. Jacob's eyes must first get used to the unfamiliar light, which hardly reaches beyond the partition, and he knocks the bucket with his foot.

"Was that the radio?"

"No, not yet. It'll be another moment or two."

Something is needed to sit on, for the stunt may take a while once it gets started. Jacob turns the bucket bottom side up and settles down on it. At this late stage he is faced with the question of what kind of program the radio has to offer, Lina having already touched briefly on this, and the time is ripe for an answer. He should have thought about this earlier, should have done all sorts of things, perhaps even practiced a bit, but as things are the radio will have to play whatever comes to mind, whether it be music or talk. Jacob remembers how, eons ago, his father could imitate an entire brass band, with tuba, trumpets, trombones, and a big drum, enough to send the family into fits of laughter. After supper, if the day had passed without any major annoyance, he could sometimes be persuaded. But Jacob wonders whether he can manage to produce an orchestra like that the very first time; his father spent hours polishing his act. Lina is waiting silently in her winter dress, and Jacob is already sweating, although the performance hasn't even begun yet.

"Here we go," says Jacob, ready for whatever suggests itself.

A fingernail flicks against the bucket, that's how radios are switched on, then the air is filled with buzzing and whistling. He skips the warming-up period, a detail for connoisseurs, Jacob's radio has the correct temperature right away, and the station is also quickly selected.

An announcer with a high voice — the first thing to suggest itself, as has been said — comes on the air: "Good evening, ladies and gentlemen, far and near, you are about to hear an interview with the British prime minister Mr. Winston Churchill."

Then the announcer releases the microphone and a man with a midlevel voice is heard, the reporter: "Good evening, Mr. Churchill."

Then Churchill himself, in a very deep voice and with a noticeable foreign accent: "Good evening one and all!"

REPORTER: "I am delighted to welcome you to our studio. And here is my first question: Would you please tell our listeners how from your vantage point you assess the present situation?"

CHURCHILL: "That's not too difficult. I am firmly convinced that the whole schlimazl will soon be over, in another few weeks at most."

REPORTER: "And may one ask the source of this reassuring conviction?"

CHURCHILL (somewhat embarrassed): "Oh well, things are progressing nicely on all fronts. It is fairly obvious that the Germans won't be able to hold out much longer."

REPORTER: "Wonderful! And what is the situation in the area of Bezanika specifically?"

There is a minor interruption. Either it's the sweating and the cold air in the basement, or something has got into Jacob's nose; whatever the cause, reporter, announcer, and Mr. Churchill all have to sneeze at the same time.

REPORTER (the first to recover himself): "Gesundheit, Mr. Prime Minister!"

CHURCHILL (after blowing his nose): "Thanks. But back to your question. In the Bezanika area, things are looking particularly bad for

the Germans. The Russians are having it all their own way, and
Bezanika has been in their hands for some time. Only yesterday they
won an important battle on the River Rudna, if you know where
that is."

REPORTER: "Yes, I'm familiar with that river."

CHURCHILL: "Then you also know where the front is now. I'm
certain it can't last much longer."

REPORTER (delighted): "That will please our listeners very
much, if they don't happen to be Germans. Thank you very much,
Mr. Churchill, for this enlightening conversation."

CHURCHILL: "Don't mention it."

ANNOUNCER (after a brief pause): "That, ladies and gentlemen,
was the promised interview with the British prime minister Mr.
Winston Churchill. Good night."

A fingernail flicks against the bucket, that's how radios are
switched off, and Jacob wipes the sweat from his forehead. A bit thin,
that interview, he thinks, and also a bit above Lina's head, but
unfortunately this will never change. He hasn't the inventive gifts of
a Sholem Aleichem, don't ask too much of a harassed man, that
should be enough for today.

Jacob reappears; the situation proves highly satisfactory not only
in the area of Bezanika but no less so here in the basement. At last
Lina's own ears have heard a radio, strictly forbidden for children,
and she is thrilled. It might have turned out differently, disguising his
voice had been a step onto virgin soil, and in three variations too;
Lina might have icily demanded that he stop this nonsense and turn
on the radio. Jacob would have died of heart failure, the mere
thought of it, but Lina wouldn't dream of saying anything of the kind.
The situation couldn't be better, he sees that at once.

"Did you like that?"

"Oh yes!"

Satisfaction on both sides. Jacob stands in front of her and is
about to suggest they leave — We've had our fun; bed is waiting —
but Lina says, "You don't mean it's all over."

"What else?"

"I'd like to hear some more."

"No, no, that's enough," he says, but without much conviction. A brief verbal skirmish, it's already too late, she would like to hear more, some other time perhaps, anything, can't get enough, all he has to do is turn the radio on again, she'll be happy with anything. Jacob sneezes again, this evening the whole world has to sneeze. As he blows his nose he studies her expression and finds no suspicion reflected in it. That settles it.

"What do you want to hear?"

So Jacob is again sitting on the bucket, in complete silence, now seized by ambition. Ambition in terms of the brass band: he can't get it out of his head, although it has been silent for a good forty years, covered with dust, the instruments all rusty. Jacob is ready to take a chance, so determined is he today.

First there is the flicking, then the buzzing and whistling; the second time it already sounds more convincing, and then the music starts in a rush, with drum and cymbals taking the first bar. Drum and cymbals are followed by a solitary trombone, which needs a few notes to get onto the right track. The tune is uncertain, Jacob tells me, an improvised series of notes, interspersed with a variety of familiar themes but with no particular pattern; the only certainty is that it is a march. Tentatively the feet take over the percussion, supported by the fingers using the bucket, thus leaving the mouth free for the remaining instruments. For one trombone does not a brass band make; it must be relieved by the trumpet, and that in turn by the falsetto of the clarinet, and from time to time a tuba note from the back of the throat. Jacob loses, as one says, all inhibition. The only constraint he submits to — despite his haste his ear has not forgotten a certain rule, strictly observed by his father — is that vowels be used sparingly, if possible avoided altogether, since instruments give voice only in consonants or, to be more precise, only in sounds that can be approximated by consonants and are remotely similar but not identical to them. So his lips don't produce a simple ta-ta-ra-ta or la-li-la; he has to shape sounds not found in any alphabet. The basement reverberates with sounds never yet heard. Maybe too much effort for the sake of a child like Lina, who would be satisfied with less polish, but let us remember that ambition is involved, a self-imposed test, and virtuosity thrives best without compulsion. Soon the key is maintained without difficulty, trumpets and trombones toss phrases back and forth, experiment with antiphony, and almost always bring things to a happy conclusion. The clarinet, too uncomfortably high in pitch, is forced to retreat farther and farther into the background: instead the tuba makes itself heard more often, now and then even venturing a little extra flourish, a run in the lower regions, to escape, when breath runs short, into two or three bars of bucket thumping.

In a word, a piece of musical history is being written, Jacob has brought off a triumph, and Lina can't bear to stay where she is any longer. Without a sound she gets up, all sacred words of honor forgotten, and her legs move irresistibly toward the partition. She must see this thing that sounds so much like Jacob and yet so different, that can speak with various voices, sneeze like he does, and make such strange noises. Just one look, even at the cost of the discovery of a breach of confidence; there's no resisting her legs, which have a will of their own. Actually such great caution isn't necessary; the racket made by that thing drowns out all else. Nevertheless she moves stealthily, as far as the narrow passage, just as the trombone is finishing a masterly solo and making way for the trumpet. Lina cautiously pokes her head around the corner, invisible to Jacob. He is not only sitting sideways, he is also keeping his eyes firmly closed, a sign of extreme physical and mental concentration, the world forgotten as he rends the air according to rules known only to himself. No, Jacob isn't aware that for a few seconds he is sitting there totally exposed. Later, Lina's cryptic allusions will rouse his suspicions, and only much later will she tell him to his face what actually happened down there in that basement. For the time being, a brief glance and a few seconds' surprise are enough for her; she set out for India and has discovered America. The purpose of this expedition was to find out what the thing looked like, and now she knows: it looks exactly like Jacob. There remains only one question: one day she will ask him whether he has another radio besides this one. Presumably not; where could he keep it hidden if not here? Lina knows something that no one else knows. Quietly she returns to her place; her pleasure in listening has not been diminished, only mixed with a few thoughts that are of no concern to anyone but her.

Then the march comes to an end, but not the performance. When Jacob emerges, exhausted and relieved and with a parched mouth, Lina clamors for an encore: all good things come in threes, now especially. This proves to him that she had not become suspicious, and such was her intention. If this march went well, he thinks, nothing can go wrong now.

"But this will be the very last," says Jacob.

He goes back to his post, the next broadcast already in mind, and flicks. Lina is in luck, Jacob soon finds the station where fairy tales are being told by a kindly uncle who says: "For all the children listening to us, your fairy-tale uncle will tell you the story of the sick princess."

He has a voice similar to Winston Churchill's, just as deep, only a little softer and, of course, without a foreign accent.

"Do you know that one?" Jacob asks as Jacob.

"No. But how can there be a fairy-tale uncle on the radio?"

"What do you mean, how? There is, that's all."

"But you said radio was forbidden for children. And fairy tales are only for children, aren't they?"

"True. But what I meant was that it's forbidden here in the ghetto. Where there's no ghetto, children are allowed to listen. And there are radios everywhere. Right?"

"Right."

The fairy-tale uncle, a bit put out by the interruption but fair enough to look for the reasons in himself, takes off his jacket and puts it under him, since the bucket is hard and sharp edged and the fairy tale one of the longer ones — provided, that is, he can remember how it all goes. My God, how long ago that was, he has to think, now of all times. Fairy tales were not his father's responsibility but his mother's. You used to lie in bed and wait and wait for her to be finished with her housework and come to you, and you almost always fell asleep while you were waiting. But sometimes she did sit down beside you, slip her warm hand under the cover onto your chest, and tell you stories. About Jaromir the robber with the three eyes, who always had to sleep on the cold ground because there was no bed long enough for him; about Raschka the cat that wouldn't catch mice but only birds until one day it saw a bat; about Lake Schapun into which Dvoyre the witch made all the children cry so many tears that it rose and rose and overflowed its banks and Dvoyre drowned miserably in it; and sometimes about the sick princess.

"When's it going to start?" Lina asks.

"The tale of the sick princess," the fairy-tale uncle begins.

About the good old king who had a vast country and a gloriously beautiful palace and a daughter as well, the old story, and how he got a terrible scare. Because, you see, he loved her more than anything in the world, his princess. He loved her so much that, whenever she fell and tears came into her eyes, he had to cry himself. And the scare came when one morning she didn't want to get out of bed and looked really sick. Then the most expensive doctor in all the land was summoned to make her well quickly and happy again. But the doctor tapped and listened to her from head to toe and then said in great perplexity: "I'm terribly sorry, Mr. King, I can't find anything. Your daughter must be suffering from a disease I have never come across during my entire lifetime."

Now the good old king was even more scared, so he went to see the princess himself and asked her what on earth was the matter. And she told him she wanted a cloud: once she had that, she would be well again immediately. "But a real one!" she said. What a shock that was, for, as anyone can imagine, it is far from easy to get hold of a real cloud, even for a king. All day long he was so worried that he couldn't rule, and that evening he had letters sent out to all the clever men in his kingdom ordering them to drop everything and come forthwith to the royal palace.

Next morning they were all assembled, the doctors and the ministers, the stargazers and the weathermen, and the king stood up on his throne so that everyone in the hall could hear him properly and shouted: "Si—lence!" Instantly you could have heard a pin drop, and the king announced: "To the one among you wise men who brings my daughter a cloud from the sky I will give as much gold and silver as can be heaped onto the biggest wagon in all the land!" When the clever men heard that, they started then and there to study, to ponder, to scheme and to calculate. For they all wanted that heap of gold and silver, who wouldn't? One especially smart fellow even began building a tower that was to reach up to the clouds, the idea being that, when the tower was finished, he would climb up, grab a cloud, and then cash in the reward. But before the tower was even halfway up, it fell down. And none of the others had any luck either; not one of the wise men could get the princess the cloud she so badly wanted. She grew thinner and sicker, thinner and thinner, since from sheer misery she never touched a morsel, not even matzo with butter.

One fine day the garden boy, who the princess sometimes used to play with outdoors before she got sick, looked into the palace to see whether any of the vases needed flowers. So it came about that he saw her lying in her bed, under a silken coverlet, pale as snow. All through the last few days he had been puzzling over why she never came out into the garden anymore. And that is why he asked her, "What is the matter, little princess? Why don't you come out into the sunshine anymore?" And so she told him, too, that she was sick and wouldn't get well again until someone brought her a cloud. The garden boy thought for a bit, then exclaimed, "But that's quite easy, little princess!" "Is it?" the princess asked in surprise. "Is it quite easy? All the wise men in the land have been racking their brains in vain, and you claim that it's quite easy?" "Yes," the garden boy said, "you just have to tell me what a cloud is made of." That would have almost made the princess laugh if she hadn't been so weak. She replied, "What silly questions you ask! Everybody knows that clouds are made of cotton!" "I see, and will you also tell me how big a cloud is?" "You don't even know *that?*" she said in surprise. "A cloud is as big as my pillow. You can see that for yourself if you'll just pull the curtain aside and look up at the sky." Whereupon the garden boy went to the window, looked up at the sky, and exclaimed, "You're right! Just as big as your pillow!" Then he went off and soon returned, bringing the princess a piece of cotton as big as her pillow.

I needn't bother with the rest. Everyone can easily imagine how the princess's eyes lit up and her lips turned red and she got well again, how the good old king rejoiced, how the garden boy didn't want the promised reward but preferred to marry the princess, and they lived happily ever after. That's Jacob's story.

It is probably the same evening, or possibly one before or one after; lovely, gentle Rosa is lying beside Mischa listening to the battle of the Rudna. Mischa is telling her in a soft voice, but he is not whispering; there is a big difference between talking softly and whispering, and you may well ask, Why isn't he whispering? And you may ask, Why is the cupboard no longer in the middle of the room but standing quite normally against the wall, and Why is the curtain covering the window again instead of dividing the room into two halves? What has happened to the screen? you may wonder, and above all, Why is Rosa suddenly lying there naked although the light is still on, why is she no longer embarrassed? Then please be good enough to glance at the other bed, you will find it empty, and all those questions will boil down to one: Where is the deaf and dumb Isaak Fayngold of the sharp ears?

I don't know the answer any better than Mischa does, let alone Rosa. A week ago Fayngold left early in the morning to go to work, as he did every day, and has not been heard of since. The first evening it didn't seem too serious; Mischa thought he might have gone to visit a friend, that they got to talking and Fayngold suddenly noticed that it was past eight o'clock and too late to go home, so he had just lain down on the floor and spent the night there. "What do you mean, got to talking?" Rosa asked suspiciously. "He's deaf and dumb, isn't he?" "What makes you think deaf and dumb people can't talk to each other?" Mischa answered quick as a flash. "Do you think they're condemned to keep everything that's going around in their heads to themselves? They can communicate every bit as well as you and I, only in sign language, that's all."

But the second evening Fayngold didn't come home either, or the third, so on the fourth day Mischa went to see the only person with whom, as far as he knew, Fayngold was friendly, Hersch Praschker, who worked with Fayngold in the cleanup detail, clearing the streets of garbage and of the bodies of those who had died of starvation. But Praschker had no idea either. "I meant to go and look in at his place tomorrow," he said, "and find out why he wasn't turning up for work. They're sure to come for him; they've already got his name down." "When was the last time he came to work?" "Tuesday." "And Wednesday morning he left home as usual."

He never arrived, never returned home; perhaps he escaped or died or was in an accident or was arrested off the street. Death or accident seems unlikely since he was never found; inquiries established this. A planned escape seems unlikely; none of his things are missing from the cupboard, not even the photograph of his grandson; he would never have left that behind, he guarded it like a treasure. So all that really remains is an arrest off the street. Why, is a mystery, for Fayngold has always been a reliable and law-abiding person, but we all know the saying, where there's a will there's a way. And all this makes it clear why Mischa is telling the story of the battle of the Rudna in a soft voice and not whispering.

Rosa is lying beside him for the second night in a row, something that has never happened before. Old Mr. Frankfurter, who, as a man of the theater, is not known to be partial to ultrastrict morals, has uttered a word of warning: "Very well, children, you love each other, that's understandable. But don't go overboard right away." Because of that and because of Rosa's reserve, the number of nights they spend together remains within modest limits. Mischa has had to persuade her each time almost as if it were the first, with one or two exceptions. And now the very next night again. Rosa imagines it must be something like this when one is married, but, frankly, she doesn't feel all that comfortable about it. This has nothing to do with Mischa, as if he were suddenly different from before, less inhibited, perhaps, or more demanding; Mischa's stock has not dropped by a single point, for she regards him with no less love than on the first day. Or let's say, the fifth. The reason for this, unaccountable though it may sound to some, is Isaak Fayngold; in some strange way she has become accustomed to him. But how can one become accustomed to a person who is only a distraction, deaf and dumb though he may be? In such a situation, in which privacy is taken for granted, how can one? One can, and one can't; we will try to get to the bottom of this.

In the first place, it was in this room that Rosa first made love, in Fayngold's presence; he was there from the very first instant, and keeping him in ignorance was a constant ingredient of all their caresses. In the second place, Fayngold's bed is not just an empty bed: no, Fayngold isn't lying in it, which makes a considerable difference. Each time she looks behind the screen, now superfluous and hence removed, she is reminded of his grim fate — uncertain, true, but the longer she broods over it, only uncertain as to the manner of death. And in the third and final place, when Mischa told her that Fayngold had disappeared, her face showed dismay, as expected, but after a while not nearly as much dismay, and she caught herself thinking: At last. That wasn't directed at Fayngold, she wished him only the best; it simply had to do with herself and Mischa and implied: alone at last, at last undisturbed, at last a little nook for the two of us. That's what she caught herself thinking, and it bothered her quite a bit; she was ashamed of such thoughts, yet kept on thinking: At last. Then she thought too, Just as well Mischa doesn't know what selfish notions are being hatched in my head. And she also thought, Regardless of what happened to Fayngold, it's over and done with now, and the thoughts we keep to ourselves can't have any effect on people's lives.

But they did have an effect; it wasn't that simple. For several days she gave Mischa reasons why she couldn't go with him to his room, and he went off disappointed. Until yesterday, when she couldn't or wouldn't find any more reasons. "And why aren't you coming today?" he asked her. "But I am!" and then he said it: "At last!" They went to his room. Mischa had already rearranged it, now that Fayngold's absence could be regarded as permanent. The cupboard stood, as noted before, against the wall, the curtain hung in front of the window. Rosa stopped short in the middle of the room and first had to get used to it, having never seen it like this. Of course she noticed Fayngold's neatly made bed, sensing right away that there would be a problem about that. "What's that box there?" she asked.

"His things. In case someone comes for them," Mischa replied. And that immediately set the mood.

At some point they lay down, but for a long time without speaking or moving and without joy. In the same way that everything else was different that evening, the light was still on. Mischa lay on his side and she on her back because the bed was too narrow for both to lie on their backs. With a glance at Fayngold's smooth bed he asked: "What do you think, couldn't we —?"

"Oh no, please!" she broke in nervously.

"All right then."

He turned out the light, slid his arm under her head — that's how it usually began — and tried to kiss her, but she turned aside. Until he asked: "What's the matter with you?"

"Nothing."

He pondered for a while what *nothing* might mean, then said: "But you didn't really know him at all, and even if you did, what can we do about it?"

Again he tried to kiss her, and this time she let him, but only just. He soon noticed that there was nothing doing, so he closed his eyes, tomorrow is another day, and fell asleep. That was the only thing that was as usual: he is always the first to fall asleep.

In the middle of the night she woke him up; he wasn't annoyed, he hoped she had finally changed her mind, and one is glad to be woken up for that.

"I have to tell you something, Mischa," she whispered.

"Yes?"

Completely misinterpreting the ensuing silence, he drew her to him, and as he brushed his lips over her face he noticed that it was wet and salty, from the eyes down. That shook him to the core because he was used to her seldom laughing and never crying; not even when her only friend had to board that train six months ago was she able to cry, although for days she didn't utter a word. And now suddenly her face was wet, it was enough to shake anyone, but she hadn't sobbed or moaned, it must have happened quite silently; he wouldn't even have woken up if she hadn't woken him. And besides, it seemed to be more or less over, to judge by her voice.

"I have a request, I'm sure you'll find it strange."

"Tell me."

"I'd like the room put back the way it was before."

"What do you mean — the way it was before?"

"I'd like the cupboard back in the middle. And the curtain."

"But why? Fayngold isn't there anymore."

"I'd like it that way," she said.

He really did find it strange — first strange, then childish, then silly, then plain ridiculous. Then he remembered having heard or read something about the unfathomable moods of women and that it is advisable to nip them in the bud. The whole change that she wanted would have taken him no more than ten minutes, but he said: "Only if you can give me a sensible reason."

"I'd like it that way," she said.

And that wasn't a sensible reason, not by any standards, and he steadfastly refused. He told her that, although it was to her credit to take Fayngold's disappearance so much to heart in spite of hardly knowing him, only his breathing and snoring, in the ghetto many people one knew just as little disappear every day, after all, and if one were to make such a fuss about every single one of those, it would be unbearable. And she accused him of being an uncouth, insensitive clot. Their first quarrel was under way and, if it hadn't been for the eight-o'clock curfew, she would undoubtedly have got up, dressed, and said good-bye. But as it was she merely turned her back to him to make him realize how much she despised him.

The next day — today, that is — he went to meet her right outside the factory because at her home, in the presence of her parents, a reconciliation would have been much more difficult. It was difficult enough anyway, not for any lack of goodwill but because they had no experience in ending quarrels. Finally they both admitted that they hadn't behaved all that well, a kiss in a doorway, and each could breathe more freely again. They dropped by her home to let them know where she would be spending the night. Mr. Frankfurter did not seem enthusiastic; he could not know that last night had been practically a washout. Mischa heard Mrs. Frankfurter murmuring to her husband, "Let them be."

So on to his room. Both did all in their power to be nice to each other, showing their best sides after the quarrel, but one could sense that a little more time would have to pass before everything was back to normal.

Mischa told her about the battle of the Rudna, or rather, since we have returned to the present, Mischa tells her about the battle of the Rudna in a low voice, and finally finishes it, as heard today from Jacob, the latest news, so to speak, from the ether. Rosa melts with bliss, she knows where the Rudna flows and how much progress since Bezanika this battle represents, and she's half-inclined to start making new plans. But Mischa isn't interested in plans, not at the moment, they won't run away as this second night might, and he turns out the light to devote himself to Rosa. There is to be no more talk of victories; last night was practically a washout. The Rudna and Fayngold and words spoken in anger are forgotten; the two come closer together in the old familiar way, insofar as individual volition is in control. But it does not hold unlimited sway; they catch themselves making comparisons: That's how it is now, really no different from before. For a while they lie side by side looking at each other. And perhaps they are even conscious of there being no third person's breathing from the other half of the room to disturb them. Let's come right out with it: the attempt to make up for a lost night turns out rather woefully, even though they would never admit it, even though they pretend to be as content as young lovers.

We will leave them now, with some regret but in the hope that more carefree times will return; we are at liberty to hope this. Let us stop a moment to listen to Mischa, riding the wave of restored harmony, asking with a smile something he would have done better not to ask: "Do you still want me to divide the room again with the cupboard and the curtain?" He says this with a smile, not doubting for a moment that Rosa sees things differently now, that in reply she'll say something about silly moods, that she didn't know what got into her yesterday, and that the whole tiresome incident would best be forgotten.

And, just before we leave, let us hear Rosa say, "Yes, please."

Jacob has to hear with his own ears how distorted his stories become when they are passed on.

Jacob is on his way to the attic to see Lina; not that it's bedtime, but he has to do more with her than just to make sure she washes properly, brushes her teeth, and goes to bed at the right time. At the freight yard we were sent home two hours early; there was nothing left to be unloaded, and the sentries didn't feel like watching over idlers, so they told us to shove off. A few particularly bold theorists speculate that there is more than mere laziness behind this order:

perhaps the sentries are trying to be friends; after all they could just as easily have kept us there another two hours, standing in line. But they sent us home. Perhaps this is a subtle indication that a new era is knocking at the door. Anyway, the two hours will be well spent with Lina, Jacob thinks. As he places his hand on the door handle he realizes that she is not alone. He hears Rafael's voice asking, "What's it all about, then?"

"About a princess," says Lina.

"Does she get kidnapped?"

"What makes you think that?"

"Of course she does. I know all that. She's kidnapped by a robber. He wants a lot of ransom money for her, but the prince kills him and sets her free. And afterward they get married."

"What nonsense you talk," Lina retorts. "That's a whole other story. Do you think there's only one story about a princess?"

"All right then, tell it!"

"Aren't we going to wait for Siegfried?"

"He won't come."

Jacob can hear them waiting and the attic window being opened. Rafael shouts, "Siegfried!"

Then he says Siegfried is nowhere in sight, and shortly afterward Lina screams at Rafael to stop that nonsense. What nonsense she means isn't clear, but he doesn't seem to be stopping right away. Then he asks, "Who told you the story anyway?"

"Uncle Jacob."

That gives an eavesdropper pause for thought. Jacob has never told her a fairy tale about a princess, he would be bound to remember that. It must have been the fairy-tale uncle, and without a tremor in her voice she turns two separate people into one man. That gives pause for thought; perhaps it was even Jacob who played the march music and asked the questions and gave the answers. Or it was a hasty slip of the tongue on Lina's part, or — and this would be best — she had resorted to a white lie so as not to reveal the existence of the radio. That remains to be seen; they will have to discuss it later.

"He won't be coming now, so you might as well start," says Rafael.

And that's what happens. Lina clears her throat, Jacob pricks up his ears; he has never heard what his stories sound like when they are passed on.

"Once upon a time there was a king, a good old king, and he had a daughter, that was the princess," Lina began.

"What was the king called?"

Lina is evidently trying to remember whether any names were mentioned at all. For Rafael this takes too long, and he says, "Surely you must at least know what he was called?"

"His name was Benjamin," Lina recalls. "And the princess was called Magdalena."

"*What* was he called? Benjamin? Do you know who's called Benjamin? My uncle in Tarnopol, he's called Benjamin. But never a king."

"I don't care if you believe it or not, but the king in this fairy tale was called Benjamin."

"Oh, all right!" says Rafi generously, not about to spoil things for the sake of a name. Jacob is almost sure that he is standing there with folded arms in a patronizing manner.

Lina continues, but more hurriedly than at first, as if she had lost the thread, as if expecting further objections: "One day the princess got sick. The doctor couldn't find anything because he didn't know what her disease was, but she wouldn't eat any more bread, and she wouldn't drink either. So the king went to her himself, he loved her so much, you see — I forgot that part. And he asked her what was the matter. Then she told him she wouldn't get well again till someone brought her a bunch of cotton as big as her pillow. And then the old king —"

But that's as far as she gets, Rafael has had enough; he has tried hard and listened patiently, but too much is too much, his credulity can be stretched, but it has limits.

"What kind of a disease is your Magdalena supposed to have had?"

"You just heard."

"And I'm telling you, there is no such disease! Not in the whole world!"

"How do you know?"

"If at least she had measles, or whooping cough, or typhoid," Rafael protests. "You know what the princess really had? A fart in her head!"

He laughs, much louder than Jacob, but Lina can find nothing funny about his explanation. "Do you want to go on hearing the story or don't you?" she asks.

"I don't," says Rafael, still amused; the best jokes are always one's own. "Because she had a fart in her head. Because the whole story is a load of nonsense. First about the king, in the whole world you'll never find a king called Benjamin. And then princesses never eat bread, only cake. And the biggest nonsense of all is that disease. Or have you seriously ever heard of a person getting sick from not having any cotton?"

Lina seems to be impressed by Rafael's reasoning; at least she is silent, without tears, Jacob hopes. And he doesn't alter his opinion; she is a clever girl, anyone can make mistakes. The excitement in the basement may have been responsible for the misunderstanding, or such flights of fancy are simply beyond a child of Lina's age. Jacob's hand is on the door handle again; you should intervene, console and explain, they might — God forbid — come to blows. You could go in quite innocently, Hello Lina, hello Rafael, nice of you to come and see her, how's your mother? Then the conversation will automatically turn to the argument, which will be recounted by both parties, Calm down, children; let's hear you each in turn. Then you will undoubtedly come up with conciliatory words that will make what is unclear appear in a fresh light, Not a reason in the world, children, to be angry with each other; things actually look thus and so. And in the end it'll all be settled to everyone's satisfaction. So Jacob is about to plunge into the fray when he hears Rafael's peaceable voice: "If your uncle happens to tell you another story, ask him to think up something better than that nonsense. That princess just had a huge fart in her head."

Jacob never gets to intervene; the door opens and, with his usual luck with doors, it opens outward and provides a hiding place. Rafael is off to more rewarding pastimes; no doubt he is going to look for Siegfried and report. He can be heard running down the stairs and whistling, he is whistling "Oranges and Lemons," and he goes on whistling as Lina shouts the meager remainder of the story after him: "But she did have that disease! And the garden boy got her the cotton! And that made her well again, and they got married!"

She has said everything, although to closed ears; down on the ground floor the little tune dies away, the front door clicks shut, and up in the attic a long, disappointed tongue is stuck out, and the attic door is slammed, with Jacob outside the door as at the beginning. Doubts arise as to whether the two bonus hours will be well spent with Lina after this. He tells me that although it was quite amusing, listening to those two children, he suddenly lost all desire to go in; he suddenly felt worn out. He would rather keep the two hours for himself after all. And he asks whether he is boring me with such details, if so I only have to tell him.

I tell him, "No."

Jacob goes for a walk with his two hours; there are other places to relax besides cramped rooms or with children one has grown fond of. He still feels the urge to take a stroll, despite the searchlight and the military office. To take a stroll in a little town from which in your whole life you have never been farther away than a week; the sunshine is pleasant on your path, as pleasant as the memories that are after all the true reason for your having left the house, memories to which every second street builds a bridge, as we know. Around one corner, then another, and there you are in front of the building where

it was so often decided how good your next winter would be, for here
lived none other than Aaron Ehrlicher, the potato merchant. Much
depended on the prices set by him: the price of potato pancakes and
with that the volume of business. Ehrlicher could never be persuaded to bargain, so-and-so much and not a penny less, if you think
that's too high, Mr. Heym, you're welcome to look around to see
whether you can get potatoes cheaper somewhere else. If you do,
please be kind enough to let me know, I'd like to buy there too.
Never, ever did he consent to bargain, and once Jacob said to him,
"Mr. Ehrlicher, you don't deal in potatoes, you just sell potatoes."
Only in fun, of course, but Ehrlicher didn't burst out laughing. And it
was hard to tell whether he was a poor soul, a humble tradesman, like
yourself, or a businessman of a higher category. His wife used to wear
a fine, brown fur piece, and his children were plump and round and
stuck-up, yet his office smelled moldy; it was small and shabby and
consisted of a table, a chair, and blank walls. He would gesture at all
this with a sigh and ask, "How can I afford to reduce my prices?"

Now there are strangers living there, you turn the page of Aaron
Ehrlicher and walk on, two free hours are a long time, head for
Libauer-Gasse and stop in front of Number 38. There is no building
you walk to as often as this one, when you're out for a stroll, none that
you stand outside for so long, and there are good reasons for this. The
fact that you even go into the dark inner courtyard . . . it all has its
reasons; suspicious eyes inspect you through the windows, what is a
stranger doing in their courtyard, but you aren't that much of a
stranger here.

On the third floor, behind the door on the left of the corridor, is
where, to put it grandly, you gambled away or won your life's happiness: at the crucial moment you couldn't make up your mind, and to
this day you don't know how good or bad that was. Josefa Litwin
asked you point-blank what your intentions were, and you couldn't
think of anything better to do than cast your eyes down and stammer
that you needed a bit more time to think about it.

A magnificent woman, if eyes are any judge. You saw her for the

first time in the train and instantly you thought, Boyoboy! She was
wearing a green velvet dress with a white lace collar, and a hat the
size of an open umbrella. And she was at most in her mid-thirties and
thus exactly right for the forty-year-old you were then, right as far as
age was concerned. But there in the compartment you never
dreamed that sitting opposite you was the greatest problem of your
next few years. You just gaped at her, so you tell me, like a young
idiot; she may not even have noticed. Coincidence or not, when you
got off the train together and there was no porter in sight, she asked
whether you would mind carrying her heavy suitcase, she lived only a
few streets further on, at Number 38 Libauer-Gasse. But she didn't
ask as if you were a man of inferior position, although even then you
wouldn't have refused; she was helpless and smiled and asked you a
favor in her capacity as a weak woman. In your capacity as a gentleman. Delighted you said: "What a question!" Snatched up her suitcase as if you were afraid a porter might yet turn up and hurried after
her as far as Number 38, as far as her own front door. There you set
down the suitcase, and for a few seconds you smiled at each other in
embarrassment. Then she thanked you nicely and said good-bye.
And you stood there thinking, Too bad.

A few weeks later, and that was certainly a coincidence, she
appeared in your shop one afternoon accompanied by a man. You
recognized her at once, and quite unjustifiably felt annoyed about
the man, but then you were pleased because she recognized you too.
You didn't exchange a word, and the two of them had lemonade and
raspberry ice cream. You observed them and couldn't make out their
relationship, and why should you?

But when she came back the very next day, this time alone, you
knew that was no coincidence. For the first time you were glad your
shop was empty; apart from her, there was no other customer in the
place — and the very next day! You sat down beside her, you chatted
and introduced yourselves; she was the widow of a watchmaker who
had been dead four years. It goes without saying that you didn't allow
her to pay for her ice cream; she was to consider herself your guest,

today and as often as she liked. The man yesterday was mentioned as a casual acquaintance, he was no reason for you not to meet often, and there was no other reason either. So the next day in the shop, once again in the shop, then in another restaurant, in a neutral location so to speak, an innocent little dance. Then soon in your flat. Meanwhile, you had found out about her modest but by no means straitened circumstances, and that she had no children. Finally at Number 38 too. A cup of tea and some little homemade cakes, in the air a hint of delicate, flowery perfume; you spoke of mutual attraction, from the first moment really, and then another cup of tea, and there were more cakes in the kitchen.

That was an evening such as no poet ever described, my God, and a night, my God, ah well. What can one say, this story isn't about Jacob and Josefa, soon this page must be turned too. Just this: four whole years were the result, four years of living together as man and wife, though they never actually moved in together, though one subject was always avoided: rabbi or civil ceremony. Most carefully by Jacob, probably. There was ample opportunity to explore one another, Josefa's glitter wasn't always gold, some less precious metals were worked in with it. Sometimes Jacob found her domineering, sometimes too talkative, sometimes an indifferent housewife, and she in turn found the occasional flaw in him, without any of this immediately leading to a breakup. Quite the contrary, they got along very nicely together, and Jacob was beginning to think that things could go on like this indefinitely. But when she suddenly — what am I saying, suddenly! — suggested it might be better if she moved in with him and she could help in the shop, he was afraid he would become his own employee, and he replied, "We'll discuss that later."

Very well, later, Josefa was in no hurry, or so it seemed. Until, as noted, that particular evening came along, the one at Number 38 Libauer-Gasse, when Jacob gambled away or won his life's happiness, who knows? He arrived as usual and, as usual, took off his shoes and put his feet up on the sofa. Josefa stood at the window with her back to him.

"What's the matter with you today?" Jacob asked her. "No tea?"

Josefa didn't turn around at once, but soon. With a forbidding expression she sat down, not beside him on the sofa but in the armchair opposite.

"Jacob Heym, I have to talk to you."

"Go ahead," he said, prepared for quite a lot but not for what came now.

"Do you know Avrom Minsch?"

"Should I know him?"

"Avrom Minsch is the man I came into your shop with on that very first day, if you happen to remember."

"I remember all right. You told me at the time that he was a casual acquaintance."

"This morning Avrom Minsch asked me to marry him."

"And what did you tell him?"

"Jacob, this is serious! It's time you made up your mind!"

"Who, me?"

"Stop trying to be funny, Jacob. I'm now thirty-eight. I can't go on living like this forever. He plans to join his brother in America, and he asked me whether I would go with him as his wife."

What was Jacob supposed to answer? He didn't care for a pistol being held to his head, even less for the fact that Avrom Minsch had been kept a secret from him until this minute. No one proposes marriage to a casual acquaintance; for this purpose one must be more than slightly acquainted with her, and for four years he had imagined that Josefa and he knew each other inside out. The fact that Josefa was now offering him first refusal, as it were, could not dispel Jacob's disappointment, far from it. Silently he put on his shoes again, carefully avoided meeting her eyes until he reached the door, then by the open door said awkwardly, "I need some time to think about it."

One thinks about it and thinks about it, and to this very day is still thinking about it; even two bonus hours aren't long enough. A helpful person opens his window and calls softly across the courtyard, "Hey there!"

Jacob is startled and sees the moon coming up over the roof. He asks: "What is it?"

"You don't live here, do you?"

"No."

"It's way past seven."

"Thanks."

Jacob pulls himself together, not stopping as he walks home, while further memory-fraught buildings are ignored: it's already way past seven.

Lina is already in bed, and he has to explain why he is so late coming home from work: because there was much more to be loaded than usual. She chats away, not about personal worries such as fairy tales or tiresomely suspicious neighbors' sons, and Jacob can't very well ask. She knows how strenuous the days at the freight yard are, and now this extra work, he mustn't stay too long, just give her a quick kiss and go down to his room, love is entirely mutual.

Jacob leaves her, with a conscience that could be clearer. On the stairs he plans to make it up to Lina, tomorrow or quite soon. At his own table, meanwhile, as he is about to start on his supper of bread and malt coffee, he is not dissatisfied with the day just past, all in all: at the freight yard the Jews had been modest in their demands, the battle of the Rudna was still having its effects; then the bonus of two nostalgic hours, a diverting little fairy tale at the attic door, a less diverting Aaron Ehrlicher, but then Josefa. Josefa still there, between the few mouthfuls, between the sips, you simply can't get rid of the woman, what would have become of us two charmers if at Number 38 I had . . . ? Impossible to say, yet the question asked a thousand times over almost answers itself: a life halfway between heaven and hell, in other words, a perfectly ordinary life. How could it have turned out differently, and in what way, from those four familiar years? Years filled with variety, quarrels and misunderstandings, with moodiness, good times and some measure of contentment. And with a secret not discovered till the very last day. You simply can't get this woman out of your head, until there's a knock at the door.

There is a knock, and Jacob is tempted to call out immediately: "Come in, Kowalski!" That is to say, not exactly tempted, he merely assumes, but then he no longer assumes because it had been past seven over an hour ago, so it must be well past eight now, and even Kowalski isn't that crazy. Jacob calls out: "Come in!"

Professor Kirschbaum is honoring Jacob at his supper, he trusts he's not disturbing him, no not at all, won't he please be seated, to what do we owe this rare pleasure?

Kirschbaum sits down, delays the start of the conversation with many and diverse looks, and succeeds in gaining Jacob's concerned attention, except that Jacob doesn't know for what.

"Can you not imagine why I have come to see you, Mr. Heym?"

His first thought: "Is it about Lina? Is she worse again?"

"I am not here about Lina. To come straight to the point: I am here to speak to you about your radio set."

What a disappointment, what a shock, for a few hours the monster had been blissfully forgotten: now the battle of the Rudna will have to be dug up again. For your fellow citizens you are no longer a human being but the owner of the radio, the two being mutually exclusive, as has been clear for some time, and here it comes again. The right to the normal conversations of the old days has been forfeited. About the weather, or back pain, for which Kirschbaum would be an ideal conversation partner, or gossip about mutual acquaintances. There is no talk of important nothings when you're around — you with your treasure are too good for that.

"You also want to hear the news," says Jacob, more as a statement. Now he has Kirschbaum on his back too; never mind, one more or less.

"I do not wish to hear any news," Kirschbaum says, however. "I am here to express my disapproval. I should have done so long ago."

"Disapproval?"

"I do not know, my dear Mr. Heym, what motives led you to spread the information in question. But I find it difficult to imagine that you have given proper consideration to the danger to which you are thereby exposing us."

Not news but disapproval, the ideas people have! No question, Kirschbaum is a very strange man. Do you, Professor, have to ruin my evening, my hard-earned free time? Do you have to make holier-than-thou speeches about matters over which my conscience was already struggling when for you my radio was an object hidden under seven seals? Do you have to tell *me?* Instead of patting me on the back and saying, Well done Mr. Heym, carry on, there is no medicine people need as much as hope. Or rather, not coming at all, for we learned long ago not to expect a pat on the back, yet here you come knocking at my door, damn you, and interfering and trying to teach me how to survive. And to top it all off I have to look interested because your concern is a thoroughly worthy one, because someday I may need you again for Lina, and I must also provide you with some good reasons for my action, although I can think of nothing that concerns you less. Just so that, after lengthy explanations, your learned lips are able to say: I see, yes of course, I understand.

"I need not tell you where we are living, my dear Mr. Heym," says Kirschbaum.

"No, you need not," says Jacob.

"And yet it seems to me essential. What would happen, for example, if this information were to come to the ears of the German gestapo? Have you thought of that?"

"Yes."

"I find that impossible to believe. Otherwise you would have acted differently."

"I see," says Jacob. "Would I."

Jacob gets up to take a walk, not the first one today, past table and bed and cupboard and Kirschbaum; his fury, since it cannot be put into words, has moved into his legs. But not all his fury, the room is too small for that; there remains for his voice an unmistakable residue that momentarily nettles Kirschbaum. When Jacob says, "Have you ever once seen their eyes when they beg me for news?

No? And do you know how badly they need some good news? Do you know that?"

"I can well imagine. Furthermore, I do not doubt that you are motivated by the best intentions. Nevertheless, I must —"

"Oh, you make me sick with your 'nevertheless'! Isn't it enough for you that we have almost nothing to eat, that in winter one in five of us freezes to death, that every day half a street gets taken away in transports? All that still isn't enough? And when I try to make use of the very last possibility that keeps them from just lying down and dying — with words, do you understand? I try to do that with words! Because that's all I have! — then you come and tell me it's prohibited!"

Oddly enough it is at this moment that Jacob thinks of a cigarette, so he tells me, of an untipped Juno. What Kirschbaum is thinking of is anybody's guess: whatever it is, he reaches into the pocket of his worn double-breasted suit and, hard though it is to believe, at this very moment pulls out a packet of cigarettes. And matches, and asks Jacob, with surprising politeness considering that barely concluded tirade: "Care for one?"

A question, that's how civilized people behave, a tactful example perhaps, a good one, perhaps also a sign of some slight doubts arising, or neither. Silently they smoke and smooth their furrowed brows, whatever the explanation.

The greedily inhaled smoke not only creates a sense of well-being, it also tends to make a person more amenable. Let me tell you: as he smokes Jacob undergoes a change of mood, or something of the kind. Because a noble donor is sitting, intimidated, opposite him. Kirschbaum is helplessly twisting the cigarette between his thin fingers, scarcely daring to glance up, let alone open his mouth for anything but the next pull. Because uncontrolled outbursts are bound to follow: You make me sick with your "nevertheless." Or: Isn't that enough for you? And he had only come to have a talk with his neighbor: after all, a radio like that isn't private property in this town, like a chair or a shirt. He has come not to accuse but to discuss an important matter in quiet debate, and now this. Then you come and tell me it's prohibited. Kirschbaum did not leave, an indication of goodwill or excessive fear. He stayed, put his hand in his pocket like a magician, and fulfilled secret wishes, so surely he is entitled to a few neighborly words.

"Of course I'm aware that the Russians won't arrive any more quickly," Jacob says halfway through his cigarette. "And even if I tell people a thousand times, the Russians won't alter their route. But I would like to draw your attention to one further detail. Since the news has been passed around in the ghetto, I haven't heard of a single suicide. Have you?"

At that Kirschbaum looks astonished and says: "You're right!"

"And before that there were many, nobody knows that better than you. I can remember your being called on many occasions, and usually it was too late."

"Why didn't I notice that?" Kirschbaum asks.

On one of the following days there is a sensation: a car drives through our little town, the only passenger car in our long story. A sensation, yes, but nothing to rouse hopes, not even in the most imaginative among those bold theorists: one is inclined to say, quite the contrary. It drives purposefully, unerringly; the exact route must have been studied in advance on a map of the town. The car is black; the streets empty as it proceeds. In the back sit two men in civilian clothes; behind the steering wheel, a well-pressed uniform. The only ones who are of any importance are the two in the back. That is to say, they're not all that important either; in fact, the whole car isn't important, in spite of its SS pennant, neither does it matter where it comes from or where it's going or whom it is conveying. Or just a little important, shall we say, or not entirely unimportant in terms of the consequences.

The names of the two men are Preuss and Meyer. I know what

they are talking about; I don't know what they are thinking about, although that is no insoluble riddle. I can tell you their ranks, if pressed, even a rough outline of their careers, hence also their names. Later, when it comes to explaining, I shall unfortunately have to intervene clumsily and directly in the action to make sure no gap remains. The explanation will provide a stopgap, but that will come later; first the gap must be visible in its entirety.

The car stops beside Siegfried and Rafael, who, as usual, are hanging around in the street, at the curb, the only heroes far and wide who are not hiding. All the other Jews, neither blind nor crippled, are standing behind their windows or in sheltering corridors, trembling for two crazy children and for the as-yet-uncertain harm the German car can be expected to cause here. But many of those in the know will be thinking that the harm is not all that uncertain, since after all the car is not stopping at random: it is stopping outside Jacob Heym's building.

Preuss and Meyer get out of the car, on a special mission. Preuss is rather tall, with brown hair, slim, good-looking, maybe a bit on the soft side; Meyer, as described to me, a head shorter, beefy, at first sight fiercely determined. Presumably a carefully chosen combination: what one man lacks, the other has, and vice versa, thus complementing each other nicely. They enter the building.

"Do you know which apartment?" Preuss asks.

"One floor up," says Meyer. "The names are probably on the doors."

One floor up, Jacob lives two floors up, yet they walk up only one floor, as far as Kirschbaum's door. After knocking politely they wait patiently outside the door, until a woman's voice, whose tone betrays that visitors are highly unwelcome, asks, "Who is it?"

"Open up, please."

Although this is not a very plausible reason for opening, a key is fumblingly inserted in the lock, then turned, and the door opens, first just a crack, then with no further hesitation. Quite unnecessarily, Meyer places his foot on the threshold. Facing them is Elisa

Kirschbaum, old and severe, with well-concealed fear. Her much-
mended apron does not deceive: Preuss and Meyer are not being
scrutinized by some nonentity; the way she holds her head is enough
to tell them that they are being scrutinized by a masterful woman.
The fear is well concealed, the contempt not; a cool look into the
faces of two tiresome visitors, then a glance at Meyer's foot making its
crudely superfluous statement on the threshold. Meyer is doing his
best to control himself.

"Yes?"

"Good morning," says Preuss politely; perhaps he has no choice
under such scrutiny. "We wish to speak to Professor Kirschbaum."

"He is not in."

"Then we'll wait," says Preuss firmly. He walks past her through
the door, and at last Meyer can detach his unyielding foot from its
position. He follows Preuss. They look around the room: What's all
this talk, they don't seem so badly off here, sideboard with knick-
knacks, sofa and two armchairs, a bit shabby, true, but still, bookcase
crammed with books, like in the movies, a fancy ceiling light, almost
a chandelier, these people are living in the lap of luxury here. Maybe
only this fellow Kirschbaum, supposed to have been some kind of an
authority, special rations and all that. They're certainly smart, these
kikes, always managing to wriggle through and making themselves at
home everywhere.

Meyer flops onto the sofa, but not Preuss, because Elisa
Kirschbaum is still standing by the door with the air of a person
awaiting an explanation.

"Are you Professor Kirschbaum's wife?" asks Preuss.

"I am his sister."

"You won't mind if I have a seat." Preuss also sits down, in an
armchair, crosses his legs, plenty of time, Elisa Kirschbaum remains
standing. But eventually she has to ask, "Kindly tell me what this is
about."

"None of your bloody business," says Meyer. He can't remain
silent any longer; what's going on here already seems weird enough to

him, farce, pure farce, but he wants no part of it. In response to an insolent question he means to give more than an answer, he needs to straighten out the world a bit, or else where will it all end.

Well, Elisa Kirschbaum is hardly in a position to call the maid and tell her to show this boor the way out; her arsenal is as empty as can be. But at least she can punish Meyer by ignoring him, turning to Preuss and demanding frostily, "Would you please tell this gentleman that he is not in his own home and that I am not accustomed to such behavior?"

Meyer is ready to explode, is about to jump up, burst forth, cry out, but Preuss gives him an official look, special mission, then says, "You are absolutely right. Please accept our apologies."

"You were going to tell me why you are here."

"I think I would prefer to tell that to Professor Kirschbaum personally. Do you know when he will be back?"

"No. Not later than eight o'clock."

She sits down in the vacant armchair, very upright, and places her hands in her lap. They wait. I feel safe in saying that Kirschbaum arrives after about half an hour; the time is passed with trivialities. For example, Meyer lights a cigar and throws the match on the floor; Elisa Kirschbaum picks it up, brings him an ashtray, and opens the window. Meyer is a shade disconcerted.

Or: Preuss gets up after drumming a minute or two on the table; he is interested in the bookcase. Sliding open the glass panel, he tilts his head to one side, reads the titles on the spines, then picks out a book, leafs through it, then another, leafs through that one, all this for several minutes, then puts them back in their proper places.

"They are all medical books, every one of them," says Elisa Kirschbaum.

"So I see."

"We have a permit for them," she says. And, since Preuss continues to study more titles: "Perhaps you wish to see it?"

"No, thank you."

He finds one that appeals to him especially, sits down, and has found something to occupy him. *Forensic Medicine.*

Or: suddenly Meyer jumps up, dashes to a door, flings it open, looks into an empty kitchen, is reassured, sits down.

"You never know," he explains to Preuss, who goes on reading.

Or: again Meyer gets up, this time without haste, goes to the window, looks down. He sees two women dragging two children away from the car into the building opposite, sees in that building a face behind almost every windowpane; the uniform is standing beside the car, bored.

"May be a while yet," Meyer calls, then sits down again. As I said, half an hour.

Or: Elisa Kirschbaum goes into the kitchen, where she is heard moving about, and returns with a tray. Two supper plates, two cups, knives, forks, teaspoons, two linen napkins. She sets the table. Preuss hardly looks up from his book, whereas Meyer feels things are getting out of hand. Preuss hardly looks up from his book and says: "Let her be."

After about half an hour the professor arrives. He can be heard trying to insert his key in the lock, but there is another key in it, on the inside. Meyer stubs out his cigar, in the ashtray. Preuss puts the book down on the table, between the plates. Elisa Kirschbaum opens the door.

Alarmed, the professor pauses in the doorway, no use pretending, though he is not totally unprepared: the car down there outside the building. He would have hoped, of course, that it had something to do with Heym — that is to say, not hoped but assumed; he had merely hoped that it had nothing to do with himself. In vain. Preuss stands up.

"We have visitors," says Elisa Kirschbaum. She picks up *Forensic Medicine* from the table, puts it back in the bookcase, slides the panel shut. With a cloth taken from her apron pocket she wipes away any possible finger marks.

"Professor Kirschbaum?" Preuss asks at last.

"Yes?"

"My name is Preuss." Then a look toward Meyer.

"I'm Meyer," growls Meyer.

They abstain from shaking hands. Preuss asks, "Do you know Hardtloff?"

"You mean the head of the gestapo?"

"I mean Sturmbannführer Hardtloff. He requests your presence."

"He requests my presence?"

Now Elisa Kirschbaum has to struggle to remain calm, as, incidentally, Meyer does too: requests his presence, the whole tone here, what a farce. Preuss says: "Yes. He had a heart attack this morning."

The professor sits down, looks helplessly at his sister, who is now standing as stiffly as if turned to stone: Hardtloff had a heart attack this morning.

"I don't quite understand."

"He wishes you to examine him," said Preuss. "Although I can imagine that you feel no particular grief at the sufferings of the Sturmbannführer. You have no cause for alarm."

"But . . ."

"What do you mean, but?" Meyer asks.

More glances toward the sister: his entire life she has removed all unpleasant situations from his path; with her cool head, her clear vision, her keen mind, she has kept every annoyance from him, hence one last look in her direction.

"Dis-leur que tu n'en as plus l'habitude," she says.

"What's she saying?" Meyer asks Preuss and also stands up to his full height.

"Please, you must realize," says the professor. "What you are asking of me is out of the question. Under no circumstances could I as a doctor take the responsibility, after so many years, my . . . After all, it's four years since I treated a patient."

Preuss remains admirably calm and places a soothing hand on the shoulder of the belligerent Meyer: special mission. Then he steps up to the professor, too close for comfort. His eyes express reproach, but not coldly, let alone angrily — compassionately rather, as if wishing to recall an impetuous person to his senses before it is too late. "I am almost afraid, Professor, that you have misunderstood me," he says. "We are not here to plead with you. Please don't make things difficult for us."

"But I just told you . . ."

"Do you need to take anything with you?" Preuss asks firmly.

With that the professor finally grasps that he need not look for further excuses; these two are not motivated by any desire to test their powers of persuasion. The relative courtesy of this man Preuss is his personal mark and does not entitle one to anything. So the professor must forget all the ifs and buts and strive to emulate his sister, to be as aloof and dignified as she. At least this much, at least now, all his life he has admired her for this, admired more than feared; some people say she is rather odd. He is not going to offer two German creatures the spectacle of collapse, did he need to take anything with him was the question, he is not going to fall on his knees before them — look at the way Elisa stands there! That cannot be imitated at first shot, but normal, everyday gestures can be found, an impassive expression as if nothing out of the ordinary has occurred: a dignitary has been taken ill, he has been asked to have a look at him, run-of-the-mill stuff.

"Do we understand each other correctly?" Preuss asks.

The professor gets up. Below the bookcase are doors; he opens one and looks for his brown leather doctor's bag.

"It's in the cupboard," says Elisa Kirschbaum.

He takes the bag out of the cupboard, opens it, checks the contents, then holds it out to Preuss, who doesn't bother to look inside.

"Medical equipment."

"Good enough."

Elisa Kirschbaum opens the cupboard again: a scarf, she holds it out to her brother.

"I won't need it. It's warm outside," he says.

"You will need it," says Elisa Kirschbaum. "You don't know how chilly it gets after eight."

He stuffs the scarf in his pocket, Meyer opens the door, the parting is at hand.

"Good-bye, Elisa."

"Good-bye."

That's what a parting looks like.

Then, outside the building, they get into the car, no doubt according to a preplanned seating arrangement: Preuss and the professor in the back, Meyer in front beside the uniform. Elisa is standing at the window, the whole street is standing at windows, but only the one is open. The car makes a U-turn, driving over the low curb; a pale blue cloud hangs in the air for a few seconds. At the end of the street the car turns left, heading for Hardtloff.

Preuss snaps open a silver cigarette case and asks, "Care for one?"

"No, thanks," says Kirschbaum.

Meyer shakes his head without turning around and casts a sidelong glance at the uniform to see what it thinks of this farce; the uniform merely grins while looking straight ahead. Preuss observes the two in the rearview mirror, but Kirschbaum doesn't; he sits there as if reluctant to waste a single movement.

"Why don't you put your bag on the floor?" Preuss asks. "We've still got quite a long way to go."

"About how long?"

"Oh, about half an hour."

Kirschbaum keeps his bag on his knees.

They reach the ghetto gate, they stop. Meyer winds down the window. A sentry sticks his helmet in and asks, "Who's that old codger you've got in there?"

"Don't tell me you don't know him!" cries Meyer. "Why, that's the famous professor Kirschbaum!"

Preuss shows the sentry a permit and says, very formally, "Open the gate. We're in a hurry."

"Right away — no harm meant," says the sentry, giving a hand signal to another sentry, who releases the barrier and pushes open the gate.

They drive on, now in the free part of town; the street scene changes. Pedestrians not wearing yellow stars will catch Kirschbaum's eye, shops displaying goods, not exactly overcrowded but with customers going in and out, and, above all, trees lining the streets, I imagine. The Imperial in the market square is showing a German film. From time to time a car in the opposite direction, a streetcar, soldiers in dress uniform with a girl on each arm. Kirschbaum looks on with moderate interest; the sights cannot tell him much, cannot evoke memories, as they would with Jacob, for instance, for this is not his town.

"Come to think of it, you must actually be quite glad to get your hands on a new patient again, at long last," says Preuss.

"May I know how you came to choose me?"

"That wasn't difficult. Hardtloff's personal physician had done all he could and asked for a specialist to be brought in. But try and find a specialist these days! We looked through the lists of inhabitants and came across your name. Hardtloff's doctor knows you."

"He knows me?"

"Not personally, of course. Only by name."

They reach the better-class residential areas; the buildings are lower, stand apart with more green and more trees. Kirschbaum opens his leather bag, takes out a little glass tube, unscrews the cap, and shakes two tablets into his palm. A questioning look from Preuss.

"For heartburn," Kirschbaum explains. "Care for some too?"

"No."

Kirschbaum swallows the tablets, screws the cap back on, into the bag again, resumes his former posture.

"Feeling better now?" asks Preuss after a short interval.

"The tablets don't work that fast." They drive out of town, another barrier, and continue more or less through open country: Hardtloff has picked himself a secluded spot. Birch woods on either side. "Naturally you will be driven back again, after everything has been taken care of," Preuss says.

Now Kirschbaum does put the bag down on the floor. All through the drive it has been on his knees; but so close to their destination, down on the floor. With a deep breath he leans back.

"If you would let me have a cigarette now?"

Preuss gives him one, and lights it. We might point again to Meyer's exaggerated display of bafflement. Kirschbaum suffers a mild coughing fit, soon recovers, and throws a half-smoked cigarette out of the window.

"On the other hand, I can in a way understand your misgivings," says Preuss, taking up what seems to have been a long-lost thread of conversation.

"I no longer have any misgivings," Kirschbaum says.

"Oh, but you do, I can tell from looking at you! Your situation isn't exactly enviable, I can see that. If you succeed in saving the Sturmbannführer's life, you won't be very popular with your own people, I imagine. And if you don't succeed —"

Preuss breaks off his pithy analysis, the rest would be tactless, as well as superfluous. He has said enough for Kirschbaum to grasp the value ascribed to Hardtloff's survival. For the first time during the drive, Meyer turns around. His expression makes it plain that he, too, knows how Preuss would have continued; above all it conveys his opinion of that continuation. With this in mind, so to speak, he turns around for a moment. Kirschbaum ignores him; he seems sufficiently preoccupied with himself. Preuss attempts one or two more trivial remarks, but Kirschbaum no longer responds.

They arrive at the Hardtloff villa. A driveway through an overgrown park, then around a circular flower bed containing a dried-up ornamental fish pond, all somewhat neglected, but magnificently laid out, quite magnificently.

"We're here," says Preuss to the still absentminded Kirschbaum, and gets out.

Hurrying down the flight of steps comes Hardtloff's personal physician, a bald-headed little man in shiny boots and unbuttoned tunic, looking as unkempt as the garden. His haste indicates worry or fear, presumably fear; he bears the responsibility here — for Hardtloff's health and, as we have heard, for today's bold experiment. While still on the higher steps he calls out: "He's worse again! What took you so long?"

"We had to wait; he wasn't at home," said Preuss.

"Hurry, hurry!"

There being no movement inside the car, Preuss opens the door on Kirschbaum's side and says again: "We're here. Will you get out, please."

But Kirschbaum just sits there, as if still a long way from sorting out his thoughts; he doesn't even turn his head toward Preuss. Delayed rebelliousness or a professor's proverbial absentmindedness: the worst possible moment to have chosen, whichever it is. Impatience sets in. Meyer would have no problem deciding what should be done.

Preuss grips the professor by the arm and says in a low voice: "Don't be difficult now," punctilious to the last, and pulls him out with gentle force.

Kirschbaum's exit from the car proceeds in a surprising manner: sliding unhurriedly toward Preuss, who is too surprised to hold him up, Kirschbaum falls out of the car onto the neglected ground.

"What's going on?"

Hardtloff's doctor pushes his way between the two, bends down over the Jewish patient, and with no effort arrives at the unequivocal result of his examination.

"The man is dead!"

It's not news to Preuss, not by this time. Preuss takes the leather bag out of the car. The usual brown leather doctor's bag. "Do you need to take anything with you?" "Medical equipment." "Good enough." Perhaps it was he who had given Kirschbaum the idea.

Preuss opens the bag, finds the little tube among the contents. He hands it to the doctor.

"For heartburn," says Preuss.

"Idiot," says the doctor.

Now for the promised explanation.

Superfluous, really, but I imagine that some people will ask suspiciously how I can account for what happened in that car. Hardly via Kirschbaum, so where was my informant sitting? And from the questioner's point of view the question is perfectly legitimate.

I could, of course, reply that it's not up to me to explain, I am telling a story I don't understand myself. I might say that I know from witnesses that Kirschbaum got into the car, that I managed to find out that by the end of the trip he was dead; the part in between can only have happened in such and such a way, anything else being inconceivable. But I would be lying, for the part in between could very well have happened differently, I would even say that it is far more likely to have happened differently. And herein, I suppose, lies the real reason for my explanation.

So: some time after the war I made a trip to our ghetto, on my first holiday. My few friends had advised against it, the trip would merely ruin the whole of my next year, memories were one thing, living something else. I told them they were right, and went. Jacob's room, the military office, Kurländischer Damm, Mischa's room, the basement: I took my time looking at them all, measuring, examining, or just looking. I also went to Jacob's shop, where a shoemaker had moved in temporarily: "Until I find something better," he told me.

It seemed to me that mixed with the smell of leather there was also a scorched smell, but the shoemaker didn't think so. On the next

to last day of my holiday, I wondered as I was packing whether I had
forgotten anything; I would probably never return to this town,
and this was the last chance for anything I had overlooked. All I
could think of was Kirschbaum's journey by car, but I didn't see how I
could check on that; besides, I didn't consider it essential to the story
for whose sake I had come. Even so, I went that afternoon to the
Russian kommandatura, probably out of boredom, or perhaps because I couldn't find a restaurant open.

The duty officer was a woman of about forty, with the rank of a
lieutenant. I told her that I had lived in the ghetto, that before the
war my father and Kirschbaum had been close friends and so I was
interested in Kirschbaum's fate. I made a proper Red Cross action out
of it. Then I explained the connection between Kirschbaum and
Hardtloff: all I knew was that Kirschbaum had entered the car,
beyond that nothing, which was the truth. The two men who came
for him were, I thought, called Preuss and Meyer or something like
that. And I went on to say that, even if she couldn't tell me what had
happened to the professor, maybe she could at least tell me something about those two men, which might provide a starting point. She
made a note of the names and asked me to come back in two hours.

Two hours later I learned that, a few days before the Red Army
marched in, Meyer was killed, by partisans, during a night raid.

"And the other man?" I asked.

"I have his German address here," she replied.

Just as I was about to reach for the slip of paper, she gave me a
worried look and said, "You wouldn't be planning anything foolish,
would you?"

"No, of course not — what an idea!" I said.

She handed me the paper. I looked at the address and said,
"That's a bit of luck. I'm also living in Berlin now."

"You didn't leave Germany?" she asked in surprise. "Why was
that?"

"I don't really know," I answered truthfully. "It just happened
that way."

Preuss was living in Schöneberg, which is part of West Berlin. Nice wife and two children, the wife had only one arm. I went out there on Sunday afternoon. When I rang the bell the door was opened by a tall, brown-haired, good-looking man, a bit on the soft side, scarcely older than myself.

"Yes?" he asked.

"Are you Mr. Preuss?"

"Yes?"

"I'm sorry to bother you," I said. "Might I talk to you for a few minutes?"

"Come in," he replied, then led me into the living room and sent the children out after a few complications. On the wall hung a reproduction of Dürer's *Hands* and a photograph of a little girl in mourning crepe.

He asked me to sit down.

I began by telling him my name, which obviously caught his attention, although he couldn't make too much of it. But he could with my question, which was whether I had been correctly informed that he had worked for Hardtloff. I could observe him turning pale before he asked in a low voice, "Why have you come?"

"I'm here on account of a story," I said. "To be more precise, on account of a gap in that story that you may be able to fill."

He got up, started rummaging in a cupboard, soon found what he was looking for, and placed a piece of paper on the table in front of me. It was his certificate of denazification, duly stamped and signed.

"You don't need to show me that," I said.

However, he left the paper lying in front of me until I had finished reading it; then he picked it up, folded it, and locked it away again.

"Can I offer you something?" he asked.

"No, thank you."

"A cup of tea, perhaps?"

"No, thank you."

He called out, "Ingrid!" His wife came in, and it was obvious that she still wasn't used to having only one arm.

"This is my wife," he said.

I stood up, and we shook hands.

"Would you mind running down to Sebald's and fetching the syphon of beer? He promised me two liters for the weekend," he told her.

After she had left the room I said, "Do you remember a Professor Kirschbaum?"

"Oh yes," he replied at once. "Very well indeed."

"You went to pick him up, didn't you, because he was to examine Hardtloff? You and someone called Meyer?"

"That's correct. Meyer caught it some time later."

"I know. But what happened to Kirschbaum? Was he shot, after Hardtloff died?"

"What makes you think that? The two never met."

I looked at Preuss in surprise and asked: "Did he refuse to examine him?"

"I suppose you could call it that," he answered. "He took poison in the car. As we were driving, right before our eyes."

"Poison?" I asked, and he noticed that I didn't believe him.

"I can prove it to you," he said. "You need only ask Letzerich, he'll confirm every word."

"Who is Letzerich?"

"He was the driver. He was there the whole time. I'm sorry I haven't got his address; all I know is that he was from Cologne. But it should be possible somehow or other to get hold of his address."

I asked him to describe this drive to me in more detail; the result has been told. It took quite a while; at some point his wife brought us the beer, I drank a glass, it tasted horrible. I hardly interrupted him because he was giving me the details without prompting. He attached special importance to the fact that Kirschbaum had offered the tablets to him too. "And I really do sometimes suffer from heartburn, quite often in fact. Just imagine if I had taken one of them!"

"It was a blatant attempt at murder," I said.

He continued his story, driving out of town, the last part of the trip, the last cigarette, Meyer's meaningful looks, until they reached the villa, until Hardtloff's doctor came, until Kirschbaum lay dead on the ground in front of him. How he suddenly grasped what had really happened, how he took the little bag out of the car, the glass tube, handing it to the doctor, how the doctor had said, "Idiot."

For quite some time we were silent; he must have assumed that I was profoundly shaken, but actually I was wondering what else I could ask him. He had told the story well, graphically and omitting nothing, and I felt there were enough convincing reasons for him to have remembered that drive so well.

Finally he felt an irresistible urge to confide to me his present thoughts about those ill-fated times, to talk to a sensible person and get the whole rotten business off his chest. But I really hadn't come to listen to that. I said I had stayed much too long anyway, I still had a few things to do, as no doubt he did too, so I got up and thanked him for his cooperation.

"And remember the name, in case you want to double-check," he said. "Egon Letzerich. Cologne."

In the corridor we met his wife, who was just taking the children to the bathroom. They were already in their pajama bottoms, naked from the waist up.

"Come on now, what do you say?" Preuss asked them.

Both put out their hands simultaneously, curtsied and bowed, and said: "Good night, Uncle."

"Good night," I said.

All three disappeared into the bathroom. Preuss insisted on accompanying me out of the building. In case the front door was already locked.

The front door was still open. Preuss walked ahead of me into the street, took a deep breath, flung out his arms, and said, "May is almost here again!"

I had the impression that he was slightly drunk; after all, he had consumed two liters of tepid beer, minus one glass.

"Ah yes," I said, "can you tell me anything more about his sister?"

"Kirschbaum's sister? We never had anything to do with her. I only saw her that one time. Is there any more to tell?"

As I was finally leaving he said, "Would you answer a question for me too?"

"Of course," I replied.

He hesitated a moment before asking, "How did you find out my address?"

"From the British secret service," I said. Then I really did leave.

Hardtloff is dead, died of a weak heart. The news has come all the way to us here at the freight yard. It must have happened last night. When we left the yard yesterday after work, the flag was hanging limply at its normal spot on the redbrick building, but this morning when we turned up for work it was fluttering gaily at half-mast, so it happened sometime in between. Of course the flag in itself is only a vague clue, betraying merely that someone high up has passed on, without giving any name. The name was supplied by a sentry while he was talking to another sentry: at some point during the morning Roman Schtamm overheard the revealing conversation. He approached a stack of crates, with nothing reprehensible in mind, and the two sentries were standing behind it discussing Hardtloff's death. It was a fluke. Roman took a little longer than usual over the lifting of the crate, only managing to complete the job when the two sentries changed the subject.

By this time every one of us knows for whom the flag is flying at half-mast, Roman having seen no reason to keep it to himself. It can be said that we bear the news with composure; it will scarcely mean any change for us. If there is ever to be any, it won't be as a result of Hardtloff's death; nevertheless, worse things can be imagined. Only Jacob regrets that it was Roman Schtamm and not he who overheard the sentries' conversation: the Sturmbannführer's misfortune would have yielded an excellent radio report. Not only because of the content: it would have been the first report that didn't have to be accepted in good faith. Everyone would have had a chance to verify its truth, with his own eyes and without effort — the confirmation has been flying from the flagpole since early this morning. To tell them now that one had heard about Hardtloff's death on the early morning news would be pretty senseless, what's past is past, a radio has its pride, it doesn't come limping in the wake of events.

When the Whistle blows punctually for soup time, Jacob finally abandons this pleasant train of thought. The little cart with the tin bowls is pulled over, and we form the customary impeccable line.

Someone behind Jacob asks softly, "Were you listening again last night?"

"Yes," says Jacob.

"Did they say anything about Hardtloff?"

"Don't be daft! Do you imagine they're concerned with such trivial stuff?"

Someone in front of Jacob asks, "What stations do you listen to?"

"Whatever's available," says Jacob. "Moscow, London, Switzerland, depends on the weather too."

"Never any German stations?"

"What for?"

"Do you sometimes listen to music too?"

"Not very often," says Jacob. "Only when I'm waiting for the news. I'm not keeping the radio for entertainment, you know."

"I'd give anything to hear some music again. Any music," says someone in front of the man in front of Jacob.

The cauldrons of soup are a long time coming, yet the line is as straight as an arrow, word of honor. The men automatically continue to correct any irregularities, even the almost imperceptible ones, but that doesn't bring on the cauldrons this time. Instead the window in the gable of the brick building opens, a hand commands silence, a voice calls out from above sounding like the irate Almighty in person: "Ten-minute break! No lunch today!"

The cart with its bowls is pushed away again, the hungry line loses its neatness and spreads out over the yard. Unused spoons are returned to pockets, a few oaths, curses, and angry looks, The Russians will show you bastards.

Kowalski comes up to me and asks, "No food for us because Hardtloff is dead?"

"Obviously," I say.

"If you ask me," says Kowalski, "it's worth it."

He wasn't exactly rewarded with gales of laughter; no midday meal, that really hurts, like a blow to the stomach. But Kowalski in his kind way attempts another modest joke: "Just imagine if every time one of us kicks the bucket the Germans get nothing to eat — what a fine starvation that would be!"

No response.

As Jacob walks to the spot he has chosen for those ten minutes he is followed by a faithful little bevy of Jews. Kowalski drops back to join them before Jacob actually misses him. Jacob knows they are behind him; the meal has been canceled so a word from him will have to do instead. He goes to an empty railcar where they can all find a place to sit down, a thoughtfulness that has long become a habit. Jacob doesn't feel quite comfortable: he had intended to rest a bit on yesterday's laurels, on the liberation of the little town of Tobolin. With our enthusiastic approval, Major Karthäuser had set his name with a flourish to the document of surrender, the fortress had fallen; but that was yesterday. No one could have foreseen the desperate need of the following day. Jacob sits unprepared in the midst of his flock.

Suddenly, so I am told, as they are sitting there looking at him, for he is expected to start his report right away, he is struck by a wicked thought that drives out Tobolin and all other victories. Suddenly he realizes that two pieces of news have reached the freight yard today, although only one of them was immediately grasped: Hardtloff. The other, the bad one, has been ignored, although it has been in the air, clear and unmistakable: the only thing needed was the effort. "The news isn't that good at all, I'm sorry to say," Jacob announces gravely.

"What news do you mean?"

"That Hardtloff is dead."

"Did you care about him?" comes a mocking voice.

"Not about him," says Jacob, "but about Kirschbaum."

Reluctantly they must agree, it's not easy, a convincing correlation that most of them understand without any further explanation. The way things are, a Jewish doctor is not likely to survive his Aryan patient for long, in this particular case not at all. "Who's Kirschbaum?" someone asks; it's impossible to know everyone. It is explained to him: a leading light, at one time a famous heart specialist, here Jacob's neighbor, was picked up and taken away to cure Hardtloff. Now belatedly a quiet grieving for the professor; the ten minutes pass without questions or reports of successes. Jacob could have wished for a different distraction. He feels an urge to dispense some sort of consolation, one can't let them sit there hungry like that. The old story about the secret German plans that fell into Russian hands in the fortress of Tobolin flashes across his mind. But the Whistle preserves him from this folly by putting an end in the usual way to the midday meal that today was so singularly lacking in flavor.

Thus in spite of Hardtloff's death the day passes dismally, and continues to do so. In the midst of work a tank wagon appears, drawn by two scrawny horses; the sight is familiar, as is the rattling that can be heard a long way off. On an average it turns up once every three months, less often in summer, somewhat more often in winter, when the ground is frozen, but always on a Monday. Its visit has to do with the little German hut with the heart in the door: for three months the hut can manage without it, but no longer than that, or it will overflow.

The wagon is driven by a farmer from somewhere in the surrounding countryside; no one knows how he came by this honor. We can't stand him. On his first visit the Germans forbade him to talk to any of us, and he strictly obeys this rule. At first, long before Jacob's radio, we tried to coax a word out of him, we didn't know ourselves what kind of a word, any tiny detail from the outside. There would have been no danger, but he would sit there with compressed lips, not saying a word and squinting over at the distant sentries. He probably feared for his head or his manure. Or he is anti-Semitic, or quite simply an idiot.

He stops his wagon behind the outhouse. A German comes out of the brick building and walks in among the men, who all pretend to be terribly busy as soon as the hateful rattling is heard. The job for which four men are now to be picked is no easier than lugging crates; afterward you stink to high heaven and can't wash till you get home.

"You, you, you, and you," says the German.

Schmidt, Jacob, and two strangers grit their teeth as they walk behind the outhouse and begin the filthy job. They take the two shovels and the two buckets hanging from the side of the wagon, and Jacob and the lawyer lift the cover off the pit. They proceed to shovel the muck into the buckets, which the other two empty into the tank. Schmidt's disgusted expression doesn't help matters. It'll take about three hours, and at halftime they switch, shovels for buckets.

"Have you ever done this before?" asks Schmidt.

"Twice."

"I never have."

The farmer is seated on the wagon with his back to them. He takes a little parcel out of his pocket, waxed paper, unwraps it, bread and bacon. The sun low, the world well forgotten, he enjoys his noon or evening meal, Jacob's eyes fill with tears.

The older of the two bucket carriers begs the farmer for a mouthful, with a muttered explanation as to what happened to his lunch, just a little piece of bread, we won't even mention bacon. The farmer seems undecided; as Jacob shovels he observes the farmer's oafish eyes raking the yard for watchers, of whom none is interested in the proceedings behind the outhouse.

"Don't be scared," says our man. "You don't have to speak to us. Just drop a piece of bread, you know, by mistake. No one can blame you for that. I'll pick it up so no one'll notice. . . . Do you hear? No one, not even you, will notice it!"

"Could you eat in this stench?" Schmidt asks.

"Yes," says Jacob.

The farmer puts his hand in his pocket again, brings out the waxed paper, carefully wraps up what's left of the bread and bacon, and stows it away. Either he has had enough, or he really has lost his appetite. Just an ample gulp from his canteen, and he wipes his mouth with his dirty sleeve.

"Asshole" is what he has to hear, but not even this filthy epithet makes him come alive.

Shortly before it's time to switch, Schmidt slows down noticeably in his shoveling. Finally he stops entirely, claiming that he can't go on, that everything is turning before his eyes, black spots. Sweating, he leans against the back wall of the outhouse.

"It's because you haven't had any food," says Jacob.

That's no help to Schmidt; big drops of sweat run down his face; he tries to throw up, but nothing comes. Jacob fills a bucket in his place, the carriers are forced to wait, not a long-term solution.

"You have to keep going," Jacob says.

"That's easy for you to say," gasps Schmidt, leaning back and very pale.

"Either you keep going now, or you might as well just lie down and die," says Jacob.

This appeals even less to Lawyer Schmidt. He picks up his shovel again and on unsteady legs starts filling the waiting bucket. He groans; it looks like a desperate effort doomed, one fears, to failure. The shovel pokes around on the surface, not going as deep as it should, so that it is pulled out of the muck only half full, more work for Jacob.

"By the way, I've heard something from your Mr. Churchill," says Jacob, in an undertone so that the farmer can't understand anything no matter how hard he tries.

"From Winston Churchill?" says Schmidt, weakly yet with audible interest.

"He has a cold."

"Is it serious?"

"No, no, just an ordinary cold. He sneezed through half the interview."

"A whole interview?"

"A short one."

"And what did he say?"

Jacob indicates that this is not a suitable place for a chat: those sentries over there, at the moment they are concerned with other things, but in three hours one of them is sure to come over and check, and by that time the pit must be empty. So a report only if it can be camouflaged with work. Schmidt sees the point, his grip on the shovel grows firmer by necessity, the drops on his forehead remain the same, What did Churchill say?

Jacob tells him; the cellar conversation between the reporter and the British prime minister is still in his memory, although no longer quite so fresh. The situation on the eastern front, without naming any towns, in any case desperate for the Germans, those were his own words, a great colorful bouquet of good prospects. And Mr. Churchill can well afford an opinion, wouldn't you say, from his vantage point? Of course, there are still some problems here and there — I ask you, in what kind of a war does everything go without a hitch?

And there are also differences between Schmidt and Lina, considerable ones, that must be taken into account. You aren't sitting with a little girl in a dusky basement, for fun, as it were, or for love; you are standing in the sunshine with the highly educated Schmidt, every word must be weighed, in three hours the pit must be empty of muck.

On the morning of this day, which has been earmarked for the advance on the district town of Pry — the Russians won't quite reach it but will come a good deal closer to it, Jacob has decided — on the morning of this promising day Mischa while on his way to work notices an agitated little group standing in the street. They point first in one direction and then another, two of them are talking excitedly, the others are listening in dismay. Mischa is not going to walk past without finding out what's going on. Then he hears the name of a street, Franziskaner; Mischa grabs the man nearest him by the arm, pulls him out of the hubbub, and insists he tell him for heaven's sake what's happening in Franziskaner-Strasse. He is quickly told, A disaster has overtaken it, the people living in that street are being lined up in rows of three. A house-to-house search is under way, they have just got as far as Number 10, in a few hours there won't be a soul left living there, off to camp or God knows where. "And the Russians are said to have already taken Tobolin," the man says.

Mischa dashes off. The fate of Franziskaner-Strasse affects him more than in a general way, for that street is a very special one: Rosa lives in it. The man said they had just reached Number 10, which means only a few minutes ago, normally by this hour Rosa is already at the factory. Mischa blames himself for not having simply made her stay with him every night, especially last night. He will go to her factory, the sentry at the gate won't let him in, but he can hang about close by. Until they come off work, Mischa himself will be a sentry, because Rosa must be prevented from going home. He hopes to God he won't have to spend the entire day watching an empty factory; if Rosa left home on time, she must be in there, that's his only hope. Mischa runs, why so fast, he doesn't know himself, Rosa won't be coming off work for a long time, he runs.

Outside the building, a gray brick garment factory, the world looks quite normal. Mischa stands on the opposite side of the street; no one else is about. He is prepared for a long day, but it proves to be much shorter than expected. A Jewish girl emerges from the factory, and Mischa wonders why she is coming out during working hours; she strolls aimlessly across the roadway, past him. Mischa stands there hesitating until she has almost reached the next corner, then follows her. She soon notices it, coquettishly turns her head, once, then again; a blue-eyed, broad-shouldered young man is, after all, a rarity in the ghetto, and in broad daylight at that. She slows down at once, she has no objection to being overtaken, and that finally happens too; just past the corner he is standing beside her.

"Excuse me," says Mischa. "Do you work in that factory?"

"Yes," she says with a smile.

"Do you happen to know whether Rosa Frankfurter is still in there?"

She considers this for a few seconds before saying: "You're Mischa, aren't you?"

"Yes," he replies. "Is she inside?"

"She left a few minutes ago. She was told she could go home today."

"How many is that, a few minutes?" his voice already shrill. "How many, exactly?"

"Ten, maybe," she answers, surprised at his sudden agitation.

Again he rushes off, feverishly calculating that he can make it if ten minutes is correct. From here to Franziskaner-Strasse would take Rosa almost half an hour, more if she's not hurrying, and she's not likely to be. They told her she could go home, without giving any reason, the bastards, so there's no need to hurry. All at once Mischa turns on his heel, dashes back the same way, an oversight must be corrected, an unforgivable one. The girl is slowly coming toward him and smiles again.

"Did they send you home too?" he calls out while still some distance away.

"Yes."

"Don't go home! Hide somewhere!"

He hears her calling after him: "But why?"

"Because Franziskaner-Strasse is being deported!"

"But I don't live there, I live in Sagorsker-Strasse!"

This awkward exchange costs him far too much time. So Sagorsker-Strasse too. He has told her all he knows; she can draw her own conclusions and save her life or not. If she's smart, she'll stand outside the factory and tell each of the women being sent home, "Don't go home, hide somewhere, never mind where you live!" All this is going through his head long after he has started running again, to catch up with Rosa, and that Franziskaner- and Sagorsker-Strasse don't even meet: between them is Blumenbinder-Gasse, which doesn't have many houses, mostly open storage places that are not being used these days, except for a few. And beyond each new corner he looks for Rosa. Maybe she isn't even taking the shortest route, maybe she's going for a stroll in this nice weather and wants to make the most of the unexpected free day. If she is really taking her time, he can't fail to reach Franziskaner-Strasse ahead of her, and he could occupy one end and intercept her. But only one end, Franziskaner-Strasse has two ends, which of those ends do you propose to occupy, and at this hour you won't find anyone to help you at any price. For a moment, a new glimmer of hope flares up: Mischa is banking on Rosa's instinct for self-preservation. Regardless of which end she appears at, she will see what's happening to her street. Perhaps she'll turn around then, run to his building, stay hidden in the courtyard, and wait until he arrives in the evening with the key. But Mischa doesn't rely too heavily on that, he knows her too well, his crazy Rosa won't be able to banish her love for her father and mother from her head, all that useless girlish stuff. The best she'll be able to manage at that sight will be a hesitation, then she'll burst into tears and run straight into her doom, to where her parents are, who can well do without her, and all this won't help a soul.

All calculations come to an end when at last he sees her in a long, straight street. In Argentinische-Allee, whose linden trees have been carefully chopped down, close to the ground, resulting in a wide, clear vista. The street is virtually empty; he recognizes her rust-colored dress when it is still only a dot, then her blue headscarf, her walk — slow, as he had foreseen. What luck, Mischa thinks.

Within a short distance of her he stops running and follows her quietly for a few steps. Rosa is looking at the fine old gables in this once-prosperous merchants' area; Rosa is out for a stroll. His last thoughts before making himself known are that his behavior must seem perfectly natural: he happens to be on his way to her home because he has heard that the factory has given her the day off. Nothing about great anxiety, not a word about the fate of Franziskaner-Strasse, that would only remind her of her love for her parents.

He intends to put his hands over her eyes from behind and in a disguised voice ask her to guess who it is; that would be a harmless enough way to begin. He notices that his hands are sticky with sweat, his face too; he wipes it dry with his sleeve and says with forced casualness, "Fancy meeting you here!"

She quickly turns around, startled at first, then smiles, the prettiest girls smile at Mischa. "What are you doing here?" she asks.

"And what are you doing here?"

"I'm on my way home," she says. "Just imagine, I was at the factory less than an hour and I was allowed to leave!"

"Why?"

"No idea. They simply told me I could go home. A few others too, but not everyone."

"The same thing happened to me," Mischa says.

"Have you got the day off too? The whole day?"

"Yes."

"Wonderful!"

She links her arm through his; a solitary passer-by looks in wonderment at young love.

"We'll go to my room," says Mischa.

"But how do you happen to be here of all places?"

"Because I wanted to fetch you from the factory. When they gave me the day off, I thought maybe they'd let you off today too."

"You're a clever one."

"But you had just left. A girl told me so, a cute-looking girl with red hair."

"That was Larissa," she says.

They go to his place, in no hurry, for the direction doesn't worry him, Franziskaner-Strasse being off to the left. Rosa tells him about Larissa, that she had sometimes spoken to Larissa about Mischa, Rosa hopes he doesn't mind, they sew at the same table, and the day is long. Larissa is still water that runs deep, one mustn't be deceived by her dreamy eyes. For instance, she also has a boyfriend, his name is Neidorf, Josef, she calls him Jossele, he works in a tool factory, Mischa wouldn't know him. They live in the same building, Larissa has a mother and two grown-up brothers, and a funny thing happened with the two brothers. They once gave Josef Neidorf a beating when they caught him with their sister in the attic, doing what, do you suppose? Necking and kissing, of course, but Larissa let them have it all right. Meanwhile they've calmed down; they realize she is no longer a child; Jossele is sometimes even allowed to visit her at home, just for a chat of course. And abruptly, in the midst of her flow of talk, Rosa stops and asks: "Why on earth would they suddenly give us a whole day off?"

"How should I know?"

"But there must be a reason."

He shrugs, he had hoped she wouldn't bring up the subject. He can't give her an answer, but she's right, it is strange.

"I wonder if it has anything to do with the Russians," she says.

"With the Russians?"

"I mean, if they feel that the game is up and they want to try and make themselves popular while there's still time," says Rosa. "Don't you see? Thinking ahead."

"Maybe," says Mischa, having no better explanation to offer.

So on they stroll toward his place, Rosa chattering away as never before, out of sheer lightheartedness. Mischa lets her chatter on without interruption; she has much more to talk about than just

Larissa: Klara and Annette and above all Nina are having affairs, and what affairs! Furthermore, her father is at last beginning to have some tentative thoughts about the future. Two evenings ago he placed a curious piece of paper on the table, says Ròsa. On it, divided into three groups, were theatrical roles corresponding to his ideas of what he hopes one day to perform, God willing; the theater management has denied them to him long enough. Rosa doesn't know the details, she doesn't understand enough about the theater for that, but there were at least twenty.

At the front door an unpleasant thought strikes Mischa: no work means no midday meal today. He asks Rosa whether she happens to have her ration card with her. Sorry, she's left it at home; wouldn't you know it, he thinks. Should she quickly go and get it; No, she shouldn't. He gives her the key, he'll follow in a few minutes, and goes off with his own ration card.

In the shop Mischa is the only customer; normally after work there's never less than a half-hour wait.

"So early?" asks Rosenek the well nourished. His scales are suspected of inaccuracy, always in the same direction, only they could have provided him with that potbelly. Although he tries to hide the little monster with an outsize overall, overall and Rosenek cannot deceive: no overall, no matter how big, can hide those pudgy cheeks.

"They've given us the day off," says Mischa.

"Day off? What does that mean?"

"A day off."

Mischa puts his food coupons down on the counter in front of Rosenek, all of them.

"It's only Tuesday," says Rosenek in surprise, as a reminder.

"Never mind."

"Well, it's up to you."

From a floury drawer behind him Rosenek takes out a round loaf that doesn't smell of bread like in the old days, puts it on the counter, groans as he cuts it in two with a serrated knife, then places one half on the famous scales, the deceitful brass weights ranged like organ pipes.

"Please weigh properly," Mischa says.

"What's that supposed to mean? I always weigh properly!"

Mischa is not about to engage in hairsplitting, which will lead nowhere, so he says: "Be sure to weigh properly. I have a guest."

"A guest? What does that mean?"

"A guest."

Rosenek discovers his heart and gives Mischa the other half of the loaf, the alleged half, without placing it on the scales. Two pocketfuls of potatoes come next, Mischa having nothing else to carry them in, then a small bag of ground dried peas, some sausage, more so in appearance than in essence, and a little package of malt coffee.

"The coupons also say something about fat," Mischa says.

"So they do! Do they also say where I'm supposed to get it from?"

"Mr. Rosenek," says Mischa.

Rosenek looks at him as if faced with the most difficult decision of his life, You'll be the death of me yet, my boy. "Do you need the coffee?" Rosenek asks.

"Not that badly."

Rosenek persists for a while longer in his long-suffering pose, finally picks up the little package of coffee from the counter, and goes off into an adjoining room. He returns bearing a piece of waxed paper. At first sight it appears to be nothing but a folded piece of paper, but then it is clear that there is something wrapped in it. Fat. To judge by his expression, Rosenek has cut it out of his own belly.

"Because it's you," says Rosenek. "But for heaven's sake don't tell anyone!"

"What do you take me for?"

Mischa arrives upstairs with his spoils. Rosa marvels at what he has brought; she has opened the window wide.

"Otherwise the sun will think no one's home and will go away again, Mother says," she says.

Mischa puts Rosenek's largesse away in the cupboard and empties his pockets of the earth from the potatoes. Rosa calls him to the window: he doesn't like the sound of her voice. Leaning out beside her, he sees a gray procession approaching, still too distant to make out details. So far the only sound is of the dogs barking, intermittently and unnecessarily since no one is getting out of line.

"Which street is it today?" Rosa asks.

"I don't know."

He pulls her away from the window and shuts it, but he can't prevent her remaining behind the windowpane and waiting for the procession to pass by. "Let me look," Rosa says. "Maybe there'll be people we know."

"Are you hungry?" he asks. "Shall we make ourselves something?"

"Not now."

He saves himself the trouble of further offers, knowing that her answer to any suggestion from him would be "Not now." Only force could separate her from the window — quite silly, really, because she has no idea whom she will see in the procession, but she fancies that in such situations she mustn't hide her head in the sand. A kind of rule of the game for Rosa: that's how she is. The simplest would be to grab her, throw her on the bed, and start kissing her as if obeying an uncontrollable impulse. Mischa takes his first step in this direction, but at the second his courage deserts him; Rosa knows him too well and would immediately see through his ruse. He has no choice but to leave her standing there until the terrible sight: there is no way she can be spared that.

He sits down on the bed and tries to look composed, a total waste of time since Rosa continues to look fixedly out of the window. Her forehead leans against the glass so she can obtain the earliest possible view of the transport. A little patch of mist forms on the pane; she is breathing through her mouth, as excited people do.

"Come on over here!" he says.

Why did those idiots have to pick his street of all streets? There are enough others. Mischa feels an urge to get up and go out into the corridor, or at least into Fayngold's half of the room, which, needless to say, had resumed its former appearance the day after Rosa's intervention. What in the world will she do? The yapping of the dogs becomes louder; when it subsides for a moment they can hear the sound of the people's feet on the pavement, even a single voice calling out: "Step lively now, step lively!"

"Mischa," Rosa says softly.

"Mischa!" she screams seconds later. "Mischa, Mischa, Mischa, it's our street!"

He is standing behind her now; the thought that her parents must be in that transport doesn't seem to have occurred to her yet. In a whisper she counts off the names of neighbors whom she recognizes; each of them is carrying something, a bag, a suitcase, a bundle of whatever was worth taking along. Mischa has time to look for her parents; he discovers them before she does, Felix Frankfurter with his inevitable scarf wound about his neck. His walk somehow expresses confidence; his wife, a head shorter, is walking beside him. She looks up at their window; Mischa had never been a secret.

Rosa is still counting off names; her mother's upward glances give Mischa the push he needs. He grips Rosa tightly in his arms and carries her away from the window, intending to put her down on the bed and keep her there by force. But nothing comes of that; on the way they fall to the floor because Rosa is struggling. He lets her hit him and scratch him and pull his hair while he just keeps his arms gripped tightly around her waist; they lie on the floor for an eternity. She screams for him to let her go, maybe twenty times she screams nothing but the words "Let me go!" Until they can hear no more barking, no more footsteps; her blows become weaker and finally cease. Cautiously he lets go of her, ready to grab her again the next instant. But she lies there without moving, with her eyes closed, breathing heavily, as if after some great exertion. There is a knock at the door, and a woman from the building asks whether she can help; she thought she heard someone screaming.

"No, no, it's quite all right," says Mischa through the closed door. "Thank you."

He gets up and opens the window, otherwise the sun will think no one's home and will go away again, so we've been told. The street is silent and empty. He looks out for a long time, and when he turns around Rosa is still lying on the floor, her position unchanged.

"Come on, get up."

She gets up — not, it seems to him, because he has told her to. So far not a tear has been shed. She sits down on the bed; he dare not speak to her.

"Your neck is bleeding," she says.

He goes over to her, squats down in front of her, and tries to look into her eyes, but she looks past him.

"That's why you came to fetch me," she says. "You knew."

He is shocked at the reproach in her words. He wishes he could explain that there was no time to warn her parents, but at the moment she won't accept any reasons.

"Did you actually see them?" he asks.

"You wouldn't let me," she says, and at last begins to cry.

He says he didn't see them either, not even right at the end of the transport, maybe they sensed the danger in time and found a safe place to go. He knows how ridiculous this is; after three words he realizes the futility of lying, but he finishes his sentences like an automaton.

"I'm sure you'll see them again," he adds. "Jacob said —"

"You're lying!" she screams. "You're all lying! You talk and talk and nothing ever changes!"

She jumps up and tries to run out of the room, but Mischa manages to catch her just as she flings open the door. In the corridor the woman straightens up, from keyhole level. "Are you sure I can't help?" she asks.

"For God's sake, no!" Mischa screams; now he is screaming too.

Offended, the woman withdraws; most likely her desire to help has been quenched forever, at least as far as this screaming maniac is concerned. However, the appearance of a third person has brought Rosa to her senses again, it seems; she goes back into the room without Mischa having to force her. He closes the door. Dreading her silence, he sets to work immediately to take renewed possession of Fayngold's fallow half of the room: the cupboard against the wall, precisely covering the big square of still-clean wallpaper, the curtain down from the ceiling and in front of the window again. For Rosa is going to be living here now; that much at least is clear.

Have you been hearing anything recently about the deportations?" Mischa asks.

"No, I haven't," Jacob replies.

"They've not only evacuated Franziskaner-Strasse. They're in Sagorsker-Strasse too and —"

"I know," says Jacob.

They walk on for a bit without speaking, on their way home from the freight yard, having shaken Kowalski at the last corner. He had held back with his questions in Mischa's presence.

Since that day, five men have failed to show up at the yard, maybe even more; one only misses the five one knows personally. Jacob had thought there were six, having included Mischa among them because he didn't show up for work that day. Luckily that was a mistake.

"How are things going with Rosa?" Jacob asks.

"How should they go?"

"Are you managing with food?"

"Splendidly!"

"But she can't go and get any more ration cards, can she?"

"Don't I know it!"

"Couldn't someone in the building help out? I have the same

problem with Lina. Kirschbaum always used to let me have something for her."

"I can no longer believe this will end well," says Mischa. "They're combing street after street now."

Jacob seems to hear a veiled reproach in his voice.

"Maybe," says Jacob. "But think for yourself. The Germans are in a state of panic. The transports are the best proof that the Russians must already be really close! Seen in that light, they're actually a good sign."

"Some good sign! Try explaining that to Rosa."

On one of her deadly boring and tear-filled afternoons, Rosa leaves the room, although Mischa has strictly forbidden her to do so. Actually he would have liked to lock her in, regardless of her protests; the only reason he hasn't is that the toilet is in the courtyard.

She has no fixed destination; all she wants to do is stretch her legs after a whole week of prison. The dangers Mischa is always talking about seem to her exaggerated. In his room she is no safer than anywhere else, it can be this building's turn any day. And who is there to recognize her? There is hardly anyone left whom she knows, and the street patrols don't show up until the evening, about curfew time. None of that really matters to her anyway, and besides, Mischa needn't find out about the walk she's taking, she won't stay away long.

Later when, as it happens, he arrives home long before her, it doesn't necessarily have to be the truth when she tells him that she happened to have the key to her old home with her, and that, without really intending to, she found herself in Franziskaner-Strasse, her feet having taken that route by force of habit, she says.

The street seems eerily empty to her; people also avoid walking through it, as if it had been smitten by the plague. Rosa looks into deserted ground-floor rooms, into rooms of people she had spoken to only the other day. Through one window she notices a boy, about fourteen years old. He is kneeling in front of an open cupboard and hurriedly stuffing whatever he can lay hands on into a rucksack — dishes, bed linen, trousers, a wooden box without checking its contents for usefulness. Rosa stands stock-still as she watches him, the sole living creature apart from herself. The cupboard appears to be completely empty, but the rucksack is not yet full; the boy straightens up and carefully surveys the room. Then he sees the wide eyes outside the window; at first he gets a shock, then he also sees the yellow star on Rosa's chest, and a conspiratorial grin spreads over his face. He probably takes her for a harmless competitor.

Rosa hurries on, wondering whether someone like that has meanwhile been in her home too: she can't think of any other word, a looter. While she feels no rage, mere tolerance is not enough. What bothers her is the thought that behind the walls there exists a second, secret life, at first sight not discernible, slowly wiping out all traces.

She quietly opens her front door and listens with a beating heart. She wishes she had Mischa with her, perhaps he could have been persuaded to come, but now she happens to be here without him. One can never be sure, but after a lengthy silence she assumes that there is no one else in the building. She walks quickly up the two flights and looks through the keyhole before unlocking the door. Then she is standing in the room, which looks very tidy. The dust hasn't had much time to settle; the four chairs are standing neatly around the table, which is covered with a yellow cloth, a tassel at each corner. The tap is dripping. So far no one with a rucksack has been here, Rosa can see that right away, also that her parents must have left without haste. The first thing she looks for is some kind of a message: this only occurs to her when she remembers that her mother never went out for a second without leaving a message. But this time she had broken with her old habit, evidently; this time there is no scribbled note, which anyway could say no more than "I don't know where to, I don't know for how long."

Then Rosa looks again, this time no longer for a message, simply looks around. Mischa tells me she is a sentimental little thing and wanted to get some idea of what her parents had taken with them. Probably she wept buckets as she did so. The brown-and-white-checked shopping bag is missing, as is the black cardboard suitcase, nothing else in the way of containers. Since Rosa knows exactly what had been in the room, she would have been able at the end of her search to draw up a list of what her parents had taken along. Including the album of photos and reviews, the book about Felix Frankfurter's true life.

Her own things lie untouched, among them the ration card, part of which has already expired. Rosa puts it in her pocket; otherwise there are no objects to which she feels especially attached. She forces herself to think in practical terms. A briefcase has been left behind; into it she stuffs her other dress, underwear and stockings, finally her winter coat, wondering as she does so how she can manage to think as far ahead as next winter. With the coat in it, the briefcase won't close. Rosa considers wearing it, but then she would have to unpick the yellow stars from her dress and sew them on the coat. So she crams it as best she can into the briefcase, which she then ties up with the belt from her coat. If she should run into that boy in the street, he will be envious of her rich booty.

Rosa firmly turns off the tap; she is finished here. As she goes she leaves the key in the door, for the boy or anyone else, as if to draw a line under her past.

"I'll give you ten guesses," Mischa says to me, "but you'll never guess where she went next."

Rosa goes to see Jacob, whom she doesn't know, except from Mischa's accounts, though from them quite well. Since Bezanika they have never spent an evening together without talking about him, about his radio, his courage, about the Russian successes at the front. At the time, when the first rejoicing over the news reports had subsided, Rosa had asked why this Jacob person had waited until now before beginning to pass on reports; after all, they had been living in the ghetto for three years, and if he was keeping a radio hidden he must have had it from the very beginning.

"Most likely the Germans were advancing all the time until just recently. Was he supposed to tell us that things were getting worse and worse every day?" Mischa answered, and that sounded convincing.

So here she is standing outside his door, not, so she tries to persuade herself, out of any desire for revenge or personal resentment. No doubt he is nice and kind and well meaning, but those reports, day by day more encouraging, and then the empty room in Franziskaner-Strasse, the whole neighborhood in fact — she's going to ask him how one can be reconciled with the other. She's going to put it to him, is it permissible to raise such hopes in their situation, don't start telling me about the radio, that can report what it likes, all he had to do was take a look around.

Rosa knocks several times, with no result. Why hadn't it occurred to her earlier that Jacob must come home at about the same time as Mischa? The waiting saps her confidence; by the time she confronts him her head will feel hollow. There is still time for her to leave and get back to their room before Mischa and avoid the argument that is bound to arise if she doesn't. The longer she waits, the more clearly she has to admit to herself that she has come with the vaguest of intentions. Jacob will persist in citing his radio, regardless of what she blames him for. She had hoped to survive these times intact; now things have turned out differently, and that, when one gets right down to it, is her whole reason. "She plays faster than she thinks," her father once said after a game of checkers; her father. The thought crosses Rosa's mind that Jacob may be spreading news other than what he hears on his radio.

Suddenly Lina is standing at the end of the corridor, just back from the street and Rafael. She sees a young woman with a bulging briefcase outside a certain door, and she approaches, full of curiosity. They eye each other for a few moments, neither of them suspicious. Lina asks: "Are you looking for Uncle Jacob?"

"Yes."

"He should be here soon. Wouldn't you rather wait inside?"

"Do you live here, then?" Rosa asks.

For an answer, Lina takes the key from behind the doorframe, unlocks the door, and gestures invitingly and a little proudly. Rosa enters with some hesitation, a chair is promptly pulled out for her, she has fallen into the hands of an attentive hostess. Lina sits down too, and they continue to look at each other, approvingly.

"You're Lina, aren't you?" says Rosa.

"How do you know my name?"

"From Mischa. You're good friends, I hear."

"Of course. And now I know who you are."

"Do tell me!"

"You're Rosa. Right?"

They exchange whatever information they have about each other. Lina, incidentally, is still cross with Mischa because the whole time she was ill in bed he didn't come to see her once, just sent his love via Jacob. Rosa looks around surreptitiously — not that she expects the radio to be standing there in full view to regale every chance guest.

"What do you want to see Uncle Jacob about?" Lina asks, any other topic having soon been exhausted.

"Let's wait till he's here."

"Have you brought a message from Mischa?"

"No."

"It's all right to tell me. He has no secrets from me."

But Rosa refuses to budge; she smiles and says nothing. Now Lina tries a roundabout approach.

"Have you ever been here before?" she asks.

"No, never."

"I mean, lots of people have been coming here lately, and you know what they want?" Lina pauses, to give Rosa a chance to appreciate this special proof of trust, before divulging: "They want to hear the news. Is that why you're here too?"

Rosa's smile vanishes: she certainly hasn't come for that reason; on the contrary, rather. She already regrets having come at all, has regretted it increasingly from the first moment. She feels she is in the wrong place with her despair; here everything is being done honestly and in good faith. She wonders what she would do if Jacob were to come in now and tell her that the transport with her parents on its way to such and such a place had met up with the liberators. And she dare not give an answer, nor to the second question either: whether she has been deceiving herself all along as to the real reason for her coming. She doesn't exclude the possibility.

"Well?" says Lina. "Is that why you're here too?"

"No," says Rosa.

"But you've heard about it?"

"About what?"

"That everything's going to change soon?"

"Yes."

"So why aren't you glad?"

Rosa sits up straight; the threshold has been reached where one either turns around or speaks the truth, but what is the truth, apart from her misgivings? "Because I don't believe it," she says.

"You don't believe what Uncle Jacob has been saying?" Lina asks, in a tone implying that she must have misheard.

"No, I don't."

"Do you think he's fibbing?"

Rosa likes the word and wouldn't have thought of it in this context. She would quite like to discuss nice things with this nice child. On no account continue in the direction already taken; how could she have done that, with a child? Without any conclusive reasons to offer, she is suddenly convinced that she has made a mistake that, she hopes, will have no bad effects. She can't just calmly get up and leave. So she sits there forlornly, waiting — now no longer for Jacob — but for some convenient opportunity to bring to an end a visit that she now perceives to be wrong. But that opportunity is moving further and further away. After her first shock, Lina becomes almost alarmingly worked up, for her uncle is most certainly not a liar. But Rosa didn't say that, Yes, that's exactly what you said, how can anyone say such a thing? Since she heard for herself on his radio that the Russians will soon be here, with her own ears, what do you say to that? A man with a very deep voice told that to another man, she can't remember his name but she remembers his voice exactly, word for word he said that the whole schlimazl would soon be over, in another few weeks at most. Does Rosa think that man has been fibbing too, what has got into Rosa anyway, to accuse her uncle of telling lies? Just wait till he comes home, *he'd* give her the right answer!

Before she has got it all off her chest in a torrent of verbal indignation, Lina suddenly breaks off and stares past Rosa, with a startled look. Rosa turns her head toward the door: Jacob is standing there, stony faced; no one has noticed the door opening.

Rosa gets up. Regardless of how much or how little he may have heard, she feels he has seen through her, such is the dismay in his eyes. With lowered head she goes to the door, no chance now for a breezy departure; she has put her foot in it. Jacob takes half a step aside for her, but back she must go to the chair for the briefcase lying forgotten on the floor. The whole length of the corridor Rosa doesn't dare look back. But on reaching the stairs she does: Jacob is still standing there motionless, watching her go. Soon the little girl will tell him what he no doubt already knows.

Let us stay with Rosa. She comes out into the street, in the early dusk, where the next unpleasantness is waiting. What meets her eyes is wild excitement, Jews fleeing into hallways, yet again. At first Rosa can't make out why. Then she sees a car approaching, a small, dark green van with a man in uniform standing on the running board. Without thinking, Rosa dashes the few yards back into Jacob's building, caught up in the panic. She leans against the wall and keeps her eyes closed, then opens them when she hears hurrying footsteps. An old man, gasping for breath, stops beside her, also coming in from the street.

"What do they want?" he asks.

Rosa shrugs her shoulders. The van will drive on and soon be forgotten; the scene with Mischa awaits her. The man assumes that it is a matter for the highest authorities, otherwise they would come on foot, as apparently happens every few days. To their horror there is a screeching of brakes; the frightened old man clutches Rosa's arm so tight that it hurts.

Two men in uniform come into the very hallway they are standing in, leather straps under their chins. The old man clings desperately to Rosa's arm. Outside, the engine has been left running. At first the Germans think they are alone in the semidarkness, but when they have almost reached the stairs one of them says, "Look!"

They turn toward the two figures against the wall. Rosa seems to interest them more than the man does, but maybe she is just imagining it. They come a few steps closer, then one of them shakes his head and says: "No, no."

The other one tells them, "Get out of here!"

Then the Germans walk up the stairs, the clatter of their boots alarming the whole building. A door is slammed. Agitated voices sound confusedly from everywhere, though it would have been better to stay calm. A child is crying.

"Come on!" whispers the old man.

Rosa follows him. In the doorway he hesitates, afraid of the van, but they must pass it if they are to obey the German's order.

"Go on, get going!" says Rosa.

They hurry straight across the road, toward the building opposite where the door is already being opened for them from the inside. The old man sits down exhausted on the bottom stair, groaning as if he had run around the entire block and massaging his chest over his heart. Rosa sees three other men and a woman in the hallway, which is even darker than the first one; she doesn't know any of them. She looks toward the door, which is of metal; a fourth man, fairly young, is peering out through the keyhole and reports for the benefit of all.

"Nothing yet," he says.

"Who are they looking for over there?" the woman asks the old man.

"How would I know?" he says, continuing to massage his left chest.

"Does someone special live there?" asks a bald-headed man.

At first he receives no reply; they are all on their way home from work and strangers in this street, until Rosa says softly, "They've come for Jacob Heym."

Who is Jacob Heym, which Jacob Heym? The scout at the keyhole straightens up and asks, "Jacob Heym? Is he the one with the radio?"

"Yes."

"Nice mess," he says, without much sympathy, it seems to Rosa. "It was bound to come out sooner or later."

At that the old man on the stairs flies into a rage, much to Rosa's surprise; he had appeared to be fully occupied with his fear and his heart. Now his veins are swelling. "Why did he have to be found out, you young pip-squeak? Eh? Why? I can tell you why he was found out. Because somebody ratted on him! That's why! Or do you imagine it happened all by itself?"

The embarrassed pip-squeak submits to this dressing-down without protest. He bends over again to the keyhole and says after a short pause, "Still nothing."

The old man summons Rosa to him with a movement of his head and, when she is standing in front of him, moves slightly to one side, so she sits down beside him.

"Do you know him?" he asks.

"Who?"

"That Jacob Heym?"

"No."

"Then how do you know he lives there?"

"From friends."

"They're still inside," the pip-squeak reports. The old man ponders for a few moments in silence, then says in the direction of the door, "When they bring him out, let me know. I'd like to see what he looks like," a remark that, right at this moment, Rosa finds in poor taste; then she doesn't.

"He has taken a great risk," says the old man admiringly, now back again to Rosa, who nods. And wonders what she will tell Mischa now. Let him scold her all he likes about her visit to her old home, she couldn't keep that a secret even if she wanted to; the telltale briefcase and ration card would be enough without any confession on her part. But she would rather not mention Jacob; she doesn't dare face Mischa with that, especially after what's happening now. And, bitter as it is, she runs no risk if she doesn't mention her encounter with Jacob: Jacob will be in no position to tell Mischa she's lying.

"Perhaps he isn't even at home," says the old man.

"He is at home," Rosa says without thinking.

The old man looks at her in surprise, a question already in his eyes, but before he can voice it the pip-squeak calls from the door, "You were wrong — they're bringing out a woman!"

Let us permit ourselves a closer look and go out into the street. The woman being led away is Elisa Kirschbaum. She is being made to pay for her brother's incompetence, for the fact that, contrary to expectations, he was unable to cure the Sturmbannführer: it has taken them long enough to think of that.

For some time now, people living in the building have been afraid that events might take such a turn; anyone can put two and two together. Someone had mentioned the hitherto unknown expression "clan liability" in conversation. The very evening of the day the flag at the freight yard was flying at half-mast, Jacob had gone to see Elisa Kirschbaum. He had put it to her that it might be better for her to go into hiding with friends she undoubtedly had, at least for the time being, until it became clear whether the threatened reprisals would actually be carried out. For, however painful it might be, they had to assume the worst for her brother, and if by some miracle he should, in spite of everything, return unharmed, Jacob promised to let her know at once. But she wanted none of all that and told Jacob, "It's very kind of you, my dear Mr. Heym. But let that be my worry." As if she still held a trump card that nobody suspected.

Now she is walking ahead of the two Germans, briskly so there can be no excuse for pushing or touching her. And briskly also, as Jacob behind the window suspects, so as not to offer any spectacle to the street, which, although apparently deserted, is full of hidden eyes. The display of concentrated power being exuded by the two men behind her appears excessive for so frail a prisoner. Elisa Kirschbaum stops behind the van without looking around at her escorts. One of them lets down the tailgate, on the inside of which is a narrow step. Just as she is about to put her foot on it the van moves forward, and Elisa Kirschbaum steps into a void and falls onto the street. The van is merely making a U-turn so it can wait on the other side of the street; the driver has already stuck his head out of the window in preparation.

Jacob's vantage point is not near enough for him to make out the expressions of the participants. People living closer by report later that the Germans had grinned as if at an oft-repeated practical joke. Elisa Kirschbaum gets up immediately, with surprising agility; she is on her feet again, waiting, before the van has completed its turn, for which it has to stop and back up twice. Then she climbs in; it is rather high for her, and in spite of all her efforts she is given a shove. The two Germans also climb into the back, the tailgate is pulled up, Elisa Kirschbaum has finally disappeared behind the dark green tarpaulin. The van drives off, and after a safe interval many of the front doors open. The narrow sidewalks gradually fill up again with people, some silent, some debating, most of them on their way home from work, as we already know, and strangers to this street.

Meanwhile, according to the radio the Red Army has advanced to the outskirts of the district town of Pry. Pry is not to be compared with Bezanika; anyone can visualize Pry, no one has to ask where in the world Pry is. Pry is exactly eighty-seven miles away from us; most of the local inhabitants know the little town from occasional visits. A few have even lived there and were moved here after the outbreak of the war, for due to its fortunate population structure Pry has no ghetto of its own.

The position of the Russians becomes the subject of an argument. Kowalski has a quarrel with his three roommates, whose names I don't know. Now, as both the easygoing Jacob and I have good reason to know, it is the simplest thing in the world to disagree with Kowalski, but in this particular case one is inclined to agree with him. The issue is no trivial one: what is involved is that this one man, for simplicity's sake let us call him Abraham, this Abraham claims that the Russians have already passed through Pry on their way to Mieloworno. Someone at his factory, let us assume the brickyard, has said so. Kowalski, on the other hand, swears up and down that they haven't even reached Pry. But Abraham sees no reason whatever to believe Kowalski more than his fellow worker.

"Who's working at the freight yard?" Kowalski asks angrily. "You or me? Who hears everything firsthand? You or me?"

For Abraham this is no valid proof, presumably because his version sounds so much better than Kowalski's. Anyone can make a mistake, he says. Nor will he accept the logical objection that whatever this mysterious fellow worker at the brickyard claims to know must, in some way or other, originate with Jacob.

"Or are you suggesting there is another radio?"

"How should I know?" says Abraham.

It might not matter to Kowalski — let Abraham think what he likes, let him be taken in like a naive child by crude rumors — except that somehow he feels partially responsible for the truth. For the radio is, in a way, also his radio, given his long-standing friendship with Jacob, as strong today as it ever was; during the power failure the radio had actually come within an ace of landing in his room. So he patiently explains the long route that every news item has to take from Jacob's mouth to the factory, via so many people, the dangers it is exposed to along the way, dangers of mutilation and enhancement. How everyone adds something to it, turns something good into something better, which means the news finally arrives, as it turns out, in such shape that even its own creator doesn't recognize it.

"Anyway, the Russians are on their way to Mieloworno," Abraham says stubbornly. "Maybe you got it wrong, or he got it wrong. You'd better ask him again tomorrow."

Kowalski doesn't ask Jacob tomorrow; excuses for a leisurely chat with Jacob are scarce enough, so Kowalski goes to Jacob then and there.

He finds him in the worst possible shape: weary, apathetic, taciturn. Half an hour ago they took Elisa Kirschbaum away.

"Am I intruding?" Kowalski asks, conjuring a smile that, as soon as he has peered into Jacob's face, he feels is all wrong.

"It's you," says Jacob. After closing the door behind Kowalski, he lies down fully dressed on the bed, where he obviously was already lying before the knock at the door. He clasps his hands behind his head and stares at the ceiling. Kowalski wonders what has suddenly got into him. Only a little while ago, on their way back from the freight yard, he seemed quite cheerful, if the word *cheerful* may be used in these times at all.

"Has something happened?" asks Kowalski.

Happened or not happened: Jacob feels a strange new weakness, alarmingly sudden. Before, on his way down from the attic, where he had gone with Lina, he had had to hold on to the banister. He has tried to account for this new condition with that perpetual hunger, but that could explain only the trembling of his knees, scarcely the origin of that other weakness, equally tormenting, his sense of discouragement. This is what he is now attempting to analyze while staring at the ceiling, trying to dissuade himself from minimizing it; it is too massive and weighty for that. The incident with Elisa Kirschbaum was probably only a small component; it had unquestionably shaken Jacob, but it would be too much to describe it as the experience that robbed Jacob of his courage from one minute to the next. Certainly of greater impact was Rosa's visit, having to hear Lina defending him with lies, with his own weapons, although even that visit should not be held wholly responsible, for Jacob's dwindling powers either. It is a number of things coming together from all sides — mainly, perhaps, just contemplating the situation all around. More and more often someone takes you aside and says, Jacob, Jacob, I can no longer believe this will end well, and by the time you have offered one person some modest consolation by way of the very latest news, there are already six other people waiting to tell you the same thing. According to the radio, the Russians are exerting pressure on Pry; God alone knows who they are really exerting pressure on, or who is exerting pressure on them. According to the radio, one should soon be able to see the first artillery flashes in the distance, but day after day all you ever see is the same scene, that repulsive desolation. You will gradually have to consider some withdrawal tactics, for in your enthusiasm you have allowed the advance to proceed at a speed that unfortunately won't stand up to grim reality.

And Kowalski stands around idly, waiting in vain for an inviting look.

"Do you want me to go away again?" he asks after an appropriate interval, and sits down.

Jacob remembers that he has a visitor; he abandons the ceiling and says, "Sorry, I'm not feeling too good."

"Has something happened?"

"Yes and no," says Jacob. "They've just taken Kirschbaum's sister away. But apart from that, I'm beginning to feel my age."

"Kirschbaum's sister? After all this time?"

"Yes, just imagine."

Jacob gets up; his ears buzz with suspicious signals, and these are combined with giddiness and nausea. All he needs now is to become seriously ill. From quite far away he hears Kowalski saying, "Are you all right?"

He quickly sits down at the table; fortunately he begins to feel

better. He thinks of Lina and what is to become of her and that it's
preferable to stay well. And when he finally looks at Kowalski he is
reminded of a little cardboard sign, a little white sign with green
lettering: CLOSED TEMPORARILY DUE TO ILLNESS. He got it from
Leyb Pachman when he bought the shop from him, together with a
lot of other stuff in the inventory. Only once did he ever use it, during
all those twenty years spent over potato pancakes, ice cream, and
comparatively minor worries, only once did the little sign hang on the
shop door. And it wasn't even a proper illness, Jacob having the
constitution of an ox: while trying to repair a stuck blind he had fallen
off the ladder and broken a leg. The best health in the world is of no
help there. That had been long before Josefa Litwin's time; she
could have been very useful as a nurse, but he was looked after by a
wizened old witch from the building across the courtyard. For money,
of course, since he had no one else. But as for looking after him, all
she did was push the table with his meals close enough for him to
feed himself, occasionally empty the ashtray and air the room, and in
the mornings straighten the bed. Beyond that, all she did was say,
"And if there's anything else you need, Reb Heym, just call me. I'll
leave my window open." Jacob took her up on this once or twice, but
either she had closed her window or she was as hard of hearing as an
old mule. And every second or third evening Kowalski would drop in
with a small bottle and express his sympathy for Jacob having to lie
there with his leg in a splint, unable to move. Would sit there until
the bottle was empty, neither of them being great conversationalists.
Jacob thanked God that the fracture healed without complications. A
few days longer, and the boredom would have killed him. And
shortly after that he threw the blameless little sign into the stove,
watching with grim enjoyment as it was consumed by the flames.
The threat had such a lasting effect that to this day he has never again
had to be confined to bed.

"Are you sure you don't want me to leave?" asks Kowalski, at the
end of his patience and interrupting Jacob's thoughts.

"Don't go," says Jacob.

Kowalski looks at him with raised eyebrows. He has a feeling that Jacob intends to tell him something, most likely nothing good to judge by the past few minutes and the sluggish introduction. Yet all he had in mind was a completely innocent visit, for on his way here he decided not to bother about a confirmation regarding Pry, an error being out of the question — that fellow Abraham must have been hoodwinked by a busybody. He merely wanted to drop by and say hello and talk a bit about the old days and the days to come, with whom else if not with his only old friend, if he doesn't come to you, you come to him.

"What do you think, Kowalski, how much can a person endure?"

So he wants to philosophize, Kowalski must be thinking. He waits for a clarification of the question, for it to be narrowed down in one direction or another, but Jacob appears to have asked it in quite a general sense. "Well?" he says. "What do you think?"

"If you put it like that," Kowalski replies, "a lot. An awful lot."

"But there is a limit."

"Of course. . . ."

"I'm sorry," says Jacob, "but I have now reached that limit. Perhaps someone else could have gone on longer, but I simply can't."

"What can't you?"

"I can't go on," says Jacob.

Kowalski lets him take his time. He doesn't know that Jacob is preparing an unconditional surrender, the worst of all admissions. He sees only Jacob's gaunt face, propped on his hands, maybe a bit paler than usual, possibly a bit more weary, but it's still the face of that same Jacob he knows better than anyone else. He is worried, because such attacks of melancholy are completely foreign to Jacob; he can be grouchy and quarrelsome at times, but that's different. He's never been known to moan; moaning is what all the others do, whereas Jacob has been something of a spiritual comforter. Quite often, whether consciously or not, Kowalski went to him for his own weaknesses to be exorcised. Even before the days of the radio, actually even before the days of the ghetto. At the end of a particularly foul day, after standing from early morning to late evening behind the shop window, watching in vain for customers, or when some enormous bill arrived and he hadn't the slightest idea out of which pocket it was to be paid: where did he go that evening? To Jacob's shop, but not because his schnapps tasted any better. It was the same schnapps as anywhere else, besides being illegal because it was served without a license. He went there because afterward the world looked just a bit rosier, because Jacob could say something like "Chin up" or "Things are going to be all right," with just a bit more conviction than other people. But also because among his scanty acquaintances, only Jacob made the effort to say such things. Kowalski lets him take his time.

Now Jacob starts to speak: judging by appearances, to Kowalski, there being no one else in the room; judging by the words, to a larger audience, that is to say just thinking out loud, into the room, with a wistfulness in his low voice and that new tone of resignation, the last of an extravagant diversity of messages to everyone. That, if their vanishing strength permits it, they shouldn't be angry with him: the fact is, he doesn't have a radio, he has never possessed one. Furthermore, he doesn't know where the Russians are; maybe they will come tomorrow, maybe they will never come, they are in Pry or in Tobolin or in Kiev or in Poltawa or still farther away, maybe by this time they have suffered a crushing defeat, he doesn't even know that much. The only thing he can say with certainty is that some numbers of days ago they were fighting at Bezanika. How can he be so sure? That's a whole separate story, no longer of interest to anyone, but at least that is the truth. And he can well imagine how devastating this confession must sound to their ears, so once again his plea for forbearance; he had only acted for the best, but his plans went awry.

Then there is a long silence in the room as if a king had abdicated. Jacob tries in vain to discover some emotion in Kowalski's face, but Kowalski looks straight through him and sits there like a pillar of salt. Needless to say, Jacob feels pangs of conscience the moment he comes to the end of his speech. Not because of the message itself, which is overdue and could no longer be delayed, but couldn't he have conveyed it more gently, perhaps tucked in with a Russian retreat, instead of shifting the whole load all at once onto other shoulders, shoulders no broader than his own? Was he sure Kowalski was the right man in whose presence the curtain had to be rung down, Kowalski of all people? If he had heard it from a stranger, or from someone not that close to Jacob, he would undoubtedly have taken it for an error or spiteful slander. After a night filled with doubts he would have said to you, "Do you know what those idiots are telling each other? That you haven't got a radio!" "That's true," the answer would then have been, which would also have hurt him but perhaps less so because during the previous night he would have at least considered the possibility. And it could somehow have been arranged like that, exactly like that; it was Kowalski's bad luck that he turned up this very evening.

"You're not saying anything?" says Jacob.

"What can I say."

From unfathomable depths Kowalski brings his smile to the surface; without this smile he would not be Kowalski. He looks at Jacob again. Although his eyes smile less than his mouth, they still do not proclaim the end of all hope. They have more of a sly look, as if this time too, as always, they could see beyond appearances.

"What can I say, Jacob? I do understand you, I understand you very well. You know, I'm what you might call the opposite of a hero, you've known me long enough. If I'd had a radio here, I don't suppose a single soul would ever have heard a word. Or more likely still, fear would have simply made me throw it in the fire, I have no illusions about that. To keep an entire ghetto supplied with news! I would never have gone that far — you never know who else is listening. If I have ever in my life understood anybody, I can understand you now."

Jacob could not have expected such a flight of fancy; cunning old Kowalski has surpassed himself, has even made his calculations where there was nothing to calculate. How are you going to convince him that at least now you are telling the truth? All you can do is suggest that he ransack every nook and cranny in this room and the basement. But to protest with upturned palms — "When did I ever lie to you?" — that you can no longer do. And if you actually do urge him to search the place and tell him that whatever radios you find here, Kowalski, you can keep, he will give you a knowing wink and respond with something like, "Let's not play games, Jacob. Haven't we known each other for forty years?" He will intimate that any attempt at hide-and-seek is a waste of time. The impossible can never be proved. Jacob, alarmed, says: "You don't believe me?"

"Believe, disbelieve, what's the difference?" says Kowalski in a low voice and more absently than expected, in a tone similar to Jacob's just now in his little speech to all. That's all he says for the time being, as his fingers drum a measured theme on the table, his head tilted back, sunk in private thoughts.

Jacob considers further ways of justifying himself. It means a lot to him that he be judged with leniency, and for that the reasons for his actions must be known, as well as the reasons for the sudden cessation. But these are still not entirely clear to himself; and because of this, and because he realizes that not only his standing but Kowalski's, too, is at stake in all this, he says nothing and saves his request for extenuating circumstances for some later date.

This is followed by the sobering thought that his own standing is not at stake at all; no one in the ghetto is less important than he, without a radio. The only people who matter are his recipients, Kowalski among a great many others. And they couldn't care less about excuses, however plausible; they have other worries, and not minor ones either — they want to know, for instance, what is going to happen now after Pry.

Kowalski stops his drumming and brooding, gets up, and places a friendly hand on Jacob's shoulder. "Don't worry, old man," he says. "You're safe with me. I won't ask you anymore."

He goes to the door, reviving his smile. Before opening the door he turns around once more and actually winks with both eyes.

"And I'm not angry with you."

And leaves.

Next morning, after the most sleepless night for a long time, Jacob is on his way to work. Before stepping out into the street he had furtively pressed down the handle of Kirschbaum's door, for whatever reason, but the door was locked. Horowitz, his neighbor, caught him at the unrevealing keyhole and asked: "Are you looking for something in particular?"

Of course Jacob hadn't been looking for anything in particular, just looking, human curiosity, and with a vague explanation to Horowitz he left. Then there had been that iridescent patch in front of the building, on the road, where the small German van had stood yesterday. A few drops of oil had seeped from it and were now gleaming in thin streaks on the dwindling remains of a reservoir deposited there by Siegfried and Rafael, first by way of their rolled-up shorts, then, when their sources had dried up, with the aid of a bucket of water. They had set to work immediately after Elisa Kirschbaum's departure, for with so little motor traffic such opportunities were few and far between. Jacob had still been at the window observing them with Lina, who was disgusted at the boys' indecency.

But back to Jacob on his way to work: from a distance he can already see a fair-sized crowd at a street corner, right in front of the building where Kowalski lives. Jacob's first thought is that Kowalski must be at the center of the crowd; his best friend will have come out into the street and, true to his nature, been unable to keep his mouth shut. Either, in thinking it over last night, he has come to the conclusion that he has after all been told the truth, or, as is more likely with Kowalski, he still doesn't believe it but outwardly pretends to do so, for true friendship means sticking together. Has come out of the building and has lost no time in scaring the Jews to death with his dire news, since he must at all costs be the first; whether on the road to hell or to paradise, Kowalski always in the lead. Has thereby cut off all one's paths of retreat — not that, after giving it much thought, one meant to take any such path, but what business was that of Kowalski's?

Jacob feels inclined to turn back, he tells me, and to make a short detour; it's going to be hard enough anyway, they'll give him a grueling time at the yard. Let Kowalski cope with this on his own, that's his problem, this is a good opportunity to stay out of it. Now Jacob notices, while still some way off, that those people are hardly speaking, yet surely they should be agitated after the presumed revelation. As he approaches he sees that most of them are standing in shocked silence. Some are looking up at an open window that, at first sight, does not seem to have anything unusual about it, being merely empty and open. Jacob is not quite sure whether it is Kowalski's window or the one next to it. But on closer inspection he does see what is unusual: a short piece of rope, fastened to the transom and no longer than a finger, hence unnoticed until now.

Jacob, forcing his way through the crowd, dashes into the building. He tries to take two stairs at a time but manages only the first two; luckily Kowalski lives only one floor up. The door is open, like the window, so there is a draft. Kowalski's three neighbors, one of whom we arbitrarily called Abraham, are not at home. Only Kowalski is at home, and two complete strangers are in the room, the first passersby to have seen him hanging. They have cut him down and laid him on the bed; now they are standing about helplessly, not knowing what to do next. One of them asks Jacob, "Did you know him?"

"What?" Jacob asks, standing by the bed.

"I said, did you know him?"

"Yes," says Jacob.

When after a while he turns around, he is alone; they have closed the door. Jacob walks to the window and looks out into the street:

nothing left of the crowd, only people walking past. He tries to shut the window, but it jams: first he has to remove the rope with its double knot from the transom. Then he draws the curtain shut; in the subdued light, Kowalski's face seems easier to bear. He pulls up a chair, not wanting to sit on the bed, and sits down for an indefinite period. I say indefinite because later he is unable to tell me anything about how long he stayed there.

The sight of a dead person is far from unfamiliar to Jacob; it is not uncommon to have to step over somebody, a victim of starvation, lying on the sidewalk and not yet removed by the cleanup squad. But Kowalski is not just somebody, dear God, no he isn't. Kowalski is Kowalski. A confession has resulted in his death, a confession, moreover, that he pretended not to believe. You crazy fool, why didn't you stay on last night? We would have had a calm discussion about everything and scraped up that little bit of courage needed to go on living. Haven't we scraped up enough together, rightfully or wrongfully? If it works, no one asks how it was done. Why did you have to behave like a poker player on your last evening? We could have helped each other, but only you knew what was going on inside both of us, you hid from your friend Jacob Heym, you showed me a false face, yet we could have gone on living, Kowalski, we could have managed.

By profession a barber, had some money stashed away, as we know, intending to change his life one day but would probably have gone on being a barber; was equipped with various questionable attributes, was suspicious, quirky, awkward, garrulous, too clever for his own good, but all in all, in hindsight, suddenly endearing. Once rescued Jacob from a horrendous situation, from a German outhouse, subscribed to the *Völkischer Kurier* for the advertisements, could sometimes put away seven large potato pancakes at a sitting but couldn't tolerate ice cream, would rather borrow than pay back, wanted to seem calculating but wasn't like that at all, except once.

As is to be expected, self-reproaches are whirling around in Jacob's head: that he had Kowalski on his conscience, that he with his petty fatigue was to blame for Kowalski's resorting to the rope, once you start something you have to see it through, you have to estimate your strength in advance. Here I interrupted Jacob and told him, "You're talking nonsense. You didn't overestimate your strength because you had no way of knowing that it would go on so long." And I told him, "The point is not that you're to blame for Kowalski's death but that he has to thank you for having stayed alive up to that day." "Yes, I know," was Jacob's response, "but none of that helps."

Finally Jacob gets up. He pulls the curtain aside again and, when he goes, leaves the door wide open so that one of the neighbors returning from work will see what has happened and do what's necessary. It is far too late to go to the freight yard; he can hardly tell the sentry at the gate that he was delayed on the way, and there'll definitely be no midday meal for him today. Jacob goes home, his only hope being that Kowalski kept his reasons to himself, that for once he held his tongue. For Jacob has rediscovered his radio.

No matter how often Jacob rediscovers, reports, invents battles and circulates them, there is one thing he cannot prevent: inexorably the story approaches its infamous ending. Or rather, it has two endings; actually, of course, only one, the one experienced by Jacob and the rest of us, but for me it also has another ending. Without wishing to boast, I know an ending that could make a person turn pale with envy; not exactly a happy one, somewhat at Jacob's expense, yet incomparably more satisfactory than the real ending. I devised it over the years. I said to myself, What a terrible pity for such a beautiful story to peter out so miserably. Find a halfway satisfactory ending for it, one that will hold water; a decent ending allows many a weakness to be forgotten. Besides, they all deserved a better ending, not only Jacob, and that will be your justification, in case you need one. That's what I told myself, and so I spared no effort — successfully, if you ask me. But then I was beset by misgivings as to its veracity; by comparison it simply sounded too good, and I asked myself whether attaching a peacock's magnificent tail to some miserable animal, merely out of love, has any hope of success, whether that wouldn't be just creating a monster. Then it seemed to me a weak comparison, but I never could make up my mind. And now here I am with the two endings, not knowing which one to tell, mine or the ugly one. Until it occurs to me to get both off my chest, not because I lack decisiveness but merely because I think that this way we will both have our say. On the one hand the story that is independent of me and, on the other, myself with all the effort I would like not to have made in vain.

So, first the ending that never happened.

Kowalski is allowed to celebrate his resurrection; he completely ignores transom and rope, Jacob having foregone his confession. The evening in question they chat about irrelevant things, although Jacob has something else on his mind. However, Kowalski needn't be aware of that. Only later, when he is alone again, does Jacob realize that it is beyond his dwindling strength to carry on with the radio lies, especially with no end in sight. Nevertheless, the true state of affairs must not come to light. Jacob imagines the consequences this would have: he might have to fear, for example, that the series of suicides, which for some time has mercifully been at a standstill, would flare up again and increase by leaps and bounds.

The following nights — which, of course, are now free because he need not reproach himself with Kowalski's death — Jacob spends trying to come up with a final credible lie. Its purpose is to explain why the radio has stopped playing; he has to get rid of this worst of all torments, but the lie simply won't come to him. It is proving harder to find than all the others.

I imagine for a moment that Jacob hits upon the obvious idea of announcing that the radio has been stolen from him. A lot of things are stolen in the ghetto, why not a radio too? Objects of less value and

usefulness have gone missing. I imagine an entire ghetto hunting for
the unscrupulous thief. People eye each other suspiciously; visits are
now made only to camouflage inspections. In the evening each person listens at the door of his neighbor — perhaps he has just tuned in
to the BBC, perhaps he is this contemptible person — hasn't there
always been a strange look in his eyes that your inner voice warned
you about? Only one thing is a mystery: what advantage does the
thief derive from his crime? None at all; even now he won't find out
any more than he would have heard anyway from Jacob or one of the
intermediaries. Just that the rest of us are left groping in the dark:
what sense is there in that? How else can one explain his motives
than by a thoroughly evil disposition? I go on to imagine that the
search for the thief assumes alarming proportions, that a sort of illegal
committee is formed that combs through the ghetto building by
building after work. And let us assume that, among the several
thousand inhabitants, there is one other person like Felix Frankfurter, just one, who also keeps a radio hidden and, unlike Frankfurter,
has not destroyed it.

I am well aware that this one person would present a problem for
the whole story; for either, like Frankfurter, he was always too scared
to listen, or he did listen and must therefore know that Jacob's daily
reports were a tissue of lies, except for the battle of Bezanika. And all
this time said nothing. However unlikely either of these two possibilities may be, let us accept one or the other of them for the next
three sentences, since that person is a mere figment of my imagination, an ephemeral fancy. During the search the radio is discovered at
his place; he is killed by the enraged searchers, a fine fancy one might
say, or he isn't killed, it's of no consequence. The radio is taken to
Jacob, the rightful owner: just the thought of his face is worth the
whole idea. Now things resume their normal course, Jacob listens
and reports, and for days the talk continues to be of the outrageous
incident, how any person can behave so despicably, for no good
reason.

But enough of that. Jacob doesn't come up with the idea of the theft, neither in the actual ending, which surprises me, nor in mine. In mine, no matter how hard he tries he can't rid himself of the radio, so he decides to rid himself of the Jews. He stops receiving visitors, simply doesn't open the door; at the freight yard he goes off by himself to eat his midday soup near the Germans' brick building, where he can't be asked anything. And as soon as work is over he vanishes like a ghost, even taking the long way around so as to dodge those lying in wait for him. Now and again he does get waylaid, in spite of all his precautions, and he is asked what has suddenly got into him, why he's stopped telling them anything.

"There's no news," he says then. "Don't worry, if there is any I'll tell you."

Or, to even greater effect, he'll say, "It's getting too dangerous for me, I don't want to run any risk so close to the end. Do me a favor and stop asking me."

This doesn't make him exactly popular; there are only a few who feel for him in his situation, and yesterday's great man rapidly declines in prestige. He's called a coward and a bastard, also because he stubbornly refuses to hand over the radio to someone else, someone with more guts. Soon glances come his way that could scare a person; words are whispered behind his back that are better not heard, but Jacob sticks to his guns. Let them look upon him as the wicked one, he would feel exactly the same in their place, never mind if they take every opportunity of letting him know the taste of contempt: anything is better than telling them the truth.

Not that he has been entirely deserted by well-wishers. I would think that Kowalski and Mischa remain faithful. Mischa goes on carrying crates with him, and Kowalski says sometimes, although less often than before, "Well, what's new, old man? Surely you can give *me* a little hint? No one else needs to know about it."

Jacob always refuses, even if it means losing his oldest friend. He doesn't lose him; Kowalski proves to be a tenacious friend.

One day Mischa says, "Jacob, I hate to tell you this, but they're talking about taking away your radio."

"Taking it away?"

"Yes," says Mischa gravely. "By force."

Jacob looks across to the others. So there are one or two among them who are prepared to resort to intimidation; Jacob doesn't want to know who it is.

"Can't you stop them?" he asks.

"How?" asks Mischa. "I'd be glad to. But can you tell me how?"

"Tell them I've hidden it so well that they'll never find it," says Jacob.

"I'll tell them," says Mischa.

At home Jacob strictly forbids Lina to be in his room when he is not there. As a precaution he no longer leaves the key in the hole in the wall behind the doorframe, not for Lina and not for anybody. As far as possible she is to remain in her attic and stay put. To offset her boredom he lets her take the book about Africa upstairs; she can use it to learn to read, which will do her more good than hanging around doing nothing.

The next few days prove to be a strenuous test of Jacob's sorely tried nerves. Twiddling his thumbs, he has to sit still and wait, for liberators and intruders, in both cases uncertain whether they will come or not. Mischa tells him he has no idea whether the opposition has changed its mind; ever since his loyalty to Jacob has been noticed, in spite of all that has happened, ever since he has offered his services as a go-between, he has been excluded from the deliberations. Moreover, something of the general contempt has rubbed off on him too. The same goes for Kowalski.

I have not given any thought to my own attitude in this matter, on whose side I am, whether I am Jacob's friend or enemy. But knowing myself, and considering how much the steady flow of information has meant to me, I would say I am his enemy, one of the worst, in fact. Let us assume that I strongly plead that no one be confused by all this talk, that the sooner his radio is taken away the better. Many people share my view, but there are also some Jews who think differently and want to be heard — those, for example, who right from the start have regarded the radio as a danger. Basically they are delighted with Jacob's change of heart. "What's all the fuss about?" they say. "If the Russians come at all, they'll come, radio or no radio." And others again say, "Let's hold our horses, maybe Heym will come to his senses. We must give him a little more time."

In any event, the break-in does not take place, not in my ending.

These bad days are a test of Jacob's nerves in another respect, too. At some point he has to acknowledge that he has clung to what is by now almost an old habit, that once again he has overestimated his own strength. He was convinced that the wave of hostility, which he obviously had to count on, would not affect him very much, that he could survive it intact. He found encouragement in the thought that he was experienced in such matters, that all his years in the shop had, after all, been little more than a struggle of one against all. That was a facile and mistaken conclusion. What Jacob overlooked was the period after Bezanika during which he had been showered with goodwill, affection, and respect, with every indication that he was indispensable, something to which he had become accustomed with absurd rapidity. And now the exact opposite: after ten days at most, that wave of hostility threatens to engulf him; the cold shoulders become unbearable.

Lina notices changes in Jacob that she cannot account for. Because she obediently heeds his instructions and keeps to her attic, she hears nothing. She merely notices that, whenever Jacob is with her, he sinks into a gloomy abstraction, hardly speaks, doesn't even show the proper surprise when she reads out a whole sentence from the Africa book, unaided. Whenever she sits on his lap she might as well be sitting on a chair. Only a short while ago he would gladly take her on his knees, and now he seems not to notice her at all. When she asks him for a story he says he can't think of any and puts her off till such time as he remembers one.

"Are you angry about something?" Lina asks.

"Angry? Why angry?"

"Because you're acting so strangely."

"Acting strangely, am I?" says Jacob, lacking the strength to avoid an unmerited sharpness in his voice. "Look after your own business and don't bother me."

Lina continues to be mostly alone and has very little to look after — except Jacob, to whom something incomprehensible must have happened.

One important evening in my ending, shortly after the first of the month because that is when the ration cards are always distributed, Jacob knocks on Mischa's door. He has to wait a while before it is cautiously opened. Mischa says in surprise: "Jacob?"

Jacob enters the room. The first thing he says is: "If you really want to hide her you shouldn't leave two cups on the table, you donkey."

"You're right," says Mischa. He goes to the wardrobe and lets Rosa out. Rosa and Jacob stand facing each other wordlessly, until at length Mischa finds the situation embarrassing.

"Do you two know each other?" he asks.

"We once saw each other very briefly," says Jacob.

"Won't you sit down?" Rosa says quickly, with a smile, before Mischa can ask about that once. Jacob sits down and looks for a way to begin, for he hasn't just dropped in: what he has in mind is quite a tall order.

"The reason I'm here," he says, "I want to ask you a favor, and if you say no I'll fully understand. I just couldn't think of anyone else to turn to."

"I'm listening," says Mischa.

"The thing is, these last few days I've been feeling rotten. Physically, I mean. I'm not as young as I was, my heart's starting to act up, so's my back, and my head aches all the time — it's rather sudden and a bit much all at once."

Mischa still can't think what kind of favor it could be and says, "That's bad."

"Well, not that bad really, it'll pass. But until it does, Mischa, I was wondering whether you could take Lina in for a while."

The general awkwardness results in a pause, during which Jacob doesn't look up; probably he's expecting a bit too much of the young man. Two illegal womenfolk in his room; but after all Jacob did say he wouldn't blame him if he refused.

"Well, you know," Mischa says slowly, his intention being quite clear.

"Of course you can bring Lina here," says Rosa, with a reproachful look at Mischa.

"I would never have come to you if you'd been alone," Jacob tells the unhappy Mischa. "But since Miss Frankfurter is here all day, and Lina is always alone too . . ."

"I'm looking forward to having her," says Rosa.

"How about you?"

"He's looking forward to it too," says Rosa.

Mischa gives himself time to rearrange his expression — they all know he isn't exactly happy. "All right," he says, "bring her here."

Relieved, Jacob puts the ration card down on the table; it is intact except for one coupon, so Mischa need no longer fear that Jacob is also demanding full board, free of charge.

"When can I bring her?"

"When did you have in mind?"

"Tomorrow evening?" asks Jacob.

Although Jacob assures him that it is entirely unnecessary, Mischa accompanies him for a few steps out into the street. When Jacob holds out his hand to say good night and Mischa keeps it in his a shade longer than necessary, Jacob detects a vital question in Mischa's blue eyes. Mischa is absolutely right, Jacob concludes, one good turn deserves another, especially when it is sought so modestly.

"You'd like to know what the situation is?" he asks.

"If you don't mind," says Mischa.

Jacob divulges that Pry has meanwhile been taken but that halfway to Mieloworno the Germans have established a fortified line that will be fought over for quite some time, it appears, but which has already been breached at several points, this in turn leaving room for

hope. And he asks Mischa to keep this news to himself, otherwise
there'll only be endless questions at the freight yard, why is one
person told and all the others are not. Mischa promises, no doubt
hoping for further periodic news items. That is how I account for his
tactics.

The following evening Lina moves. Jacob has given her the
same reason he gave Mischa, a separation for only a few days, and
Lina accepts it calmly enough. After all, she is fond of Mischa, it's
almost a secret love, and he is presumably fond of her too, only that
Rosa woman sticks in her gullet because of that visit and those
reproaches — she might have some trouble with her. But Jacob again
assures her on the way to Mischa's that Rosa is very easy to get along
with, helpful and kind, that only last evening she told him she was
looking forward to having Lina. It would be best not to say a word
about that stupid visit the other day.

"You're a big girl now, so don't disgrace me."

After delivering Lina, Jacob goes straight home, ostensibly to lie
down. For a long time he sits in the dark room, brooding over
whether his decision, for the sake of which Lina had to leave, is
justified. He doesn't want to have to reproach himself later, if there is
a later; he has made enough wrong decisions recently. To have the
Russians come almost within sight was a mistake, to discontinue the
radio broadcasts was a mistake, the radio itself was the first and
biggest mistake, it seems to him: too many mistakes for one man. Of
course, he could still undo some of that, go back to his old routine. In
three or four days he could feel better, illnesses of this kind can be
cured at will, then he could bring Lina back, act as though he's had a
change of heart and go on supplying reports, both good and bad, to
the news hungry at the freight yard. But where would that all lead,
Jacob wonders?

After a couple of hours, I imagine, Jacob makes up his mind. He
hangs the cloth in front of the window, turns on the light, then picks
up a knife, takes off his jacket and removes the yellow stars from
front and back. He does this very carefully, even unpicking the little

white threads so they won't betray the infamous places. That done, Jacob puts on the jacket, which now seems strangely denuded. His eyes roam the room for objects that might be useful for his undertaking: the pliers, of course, which he puts in his pocket. Nothing else catches his eye, so he turns out the light and gives a last look out of the window, into the black deserted street. It is long past eight o'clock and curfew time, probably already midnight. In the distance he might, if you like, recognize his searchlight as it ranges duty-obsessed and aimlessly over the roofs.

Since there are no limits to my arbitrary inventions, I say that it is a cold and starry night. Not only does that sound pleasing, it also comes in handy for my ending, as we shall see. Accordingly, Jacob, without his yellow stars and long after eight o'clock, walks along the street, or rather, he slinks along close to the buildings, trying to resemble a shadow; after all, he has no intention of forfeiting his life. One street, and another, and yet another: what they all have in common is that they represent the shortest route to the boundary of the ghetto.

Then the boundary. I have chosen the most favorable spot of all, the old vegetable market, a small cobbled square with barbed wire drawn across it. Previous escape attempts have succeeded or failed almost invariably at this place. To the right, at the very end of the square, is the watchtower, this one without a searchlight. The sentry on top doesn't move while Jacob observes him from a doorway on the far left side. The distance may amount to five hundred feet. Along the whole length of the barbed wire, which surrounds the entire ghetto without a gap, there is no other spot that far from a watchtower. Only here have they left that much space, either for the sake of economy or because of the unimpeded view.

On the tower all is as quiet as on a monument, so that Jacob is already beginning to hope that the sentry has fallen asleep. Jacob looks up at the sky, waiting prudently until one of the few clouds drifts across the inconvenient moon. When the cloud finally does him the favor, Jacob takes the pliers out of his pocket and starts running.

Let us pause briefly at this highly dramatic moment in my ending, to give me a chance to admit that I cannot provide the reason for Jacob's sudden flight. In other words: I don't take the easy way out and declare, "In my ending he just wants to escape, that's all." Obviously I am in a position to offer several reasons, all of which I consider plausible; I just don't know which one to choose. For instance: Jacob has given up all hope of the ghetto being liberated while there are any Jews still left in it and therefore decides to save his own skin. Or: he is fleeing from his own people, from their persecution and hostility, and from their thirst for news too, an attempt to find a refuge from the radio and its consequences. Or a third reason, for Jacob the most creditable one: he has the daring plan of returning to the ghetto some time during the following night; he only wants to get out now so as to obtain some useful information to feed through his radio.

Those would be the chief reasons. None of them to be ruled out, one must admit, but I can't bring myself to commit Jacob to any one of them. So I offer them as a selection; let each reader choose the one that, according to his own experience, he finds the most valid. Maybe some readers will come up with even more plausible ones. I merely wish to remind them that almost anything of importance that has ever happened has had more than one reason.

Under cover of the cloud, Jacob reaches the barbed wire unobserved. He lies flat on the ground; his simple plan is to crawl out under the barrier, which, of course, is easier planned than done, the lowest of the many strands being only four inches above the ground; but that is no more than was expected, hence the precautionary pliers. These are now put to work, rapidly snipping away at the thin wire that can't resist them indefinitely and splits more quickly than expected. But then there is that noise, for the wire is taut, an appalling whine that Jacob imagines capable of rousing a whole town from its sleep. He holds his breath and listens in fear, but everything remains as calm as before. Gradually, however, the light increases, for no cloud lasts forever. The next strand is four inches higher, thus

eight above the ground. Jacob calculates that to crawl under it would
entail some risk to body and clothing; after all, though he has become
terribly thin, he still is a fully grown man. On the other hand, he
would rather not risk breaking the silence by twanging the second
wire, which will be not a jot quieter than the first one, and he can't for
the life of him think of any third option.

Jacob is still lying there undecided, plucking cautiously at that
second strand to see if it can be loosened and the noise thus reduced
as the pliers cut through it, when the decision is taken out of his
hands by a higher authority. I said at the beginning that this ending of
mine is rather at Jacob's expense. A raucous burst from a submachine
gun shatters the night silence: our sentry hasn't been that fast asleep.
And there is nothing more to calculate, and Jacob is dead, all his
endeavors at an end.

But there's more to come; what kind of an ending would this be
anyway? I imagine further that tranquillity is far from returning to the
ghetto. I visualize a revenge for Jacob, this, I have decided, being the
cold and starry night when the Russians arrive. Thus the Red Army
succeeds in surrounding the city in no time at all; the sky is lit up by
flashes from the heavy artillery. Immediately following the salvo
aimed at Jacob, an ear-splitting, thunderous roar starts up, as if inad-
vertently triggered by the unfortunate marksman on the watchtower.
The first ghostly tanks, shells hitting the military office, the watch-
towers in flames, tenacious Germans defending themselves to the last
bullet, or fleeing Germans unable to find any hole to crawl into — dear
God, what a night that would have been. And, behind the windows,
weeping Jews for whom everything has happened so suddenly that
they can only stand there in disbelief, holding each other by the hand,
Jews who would give anything to rejoice yet find themselves unable
to; there'll be a time for that later. I imagine that by dawn the last
battles are over, the ghetto is no longer a ghetto but merely the most
run-down part of town. Anyone can go wherever he likes.

How Mischa thinks that Jacob is sure to be feeling better now;
how he tries to take Lina back to him but doesn't find him in his

room; the taste of the bread given us in ample quantities; what happens to the poor Germans who fall into our hands — all that and more is, to my mind, not important enough to be accorded a place in my ending. Only one thing is important to me.

Some of the Jews leave the ghetto by way of the old vegetable market. There they see a man, not wearing stars, lying on the ground with the pliers still clenched in his right hand, under the barbed wire of which one strand is cut — obviously caught while trying to escape. They turn him over on his back, Who is this poor fellow, they ask, and someone is there who knows Jacob. Preferably Kowalski, but it could also be a neighbor or myself or anyone else from the freight yard, just someone who knows him, except Lina. This person stares in horror at Jacob's face; perhaps he heard the first good news from Jacob the very day he himself was preparing to forego the rest of his life, and he now murmurs words of incomprehension. Someone asks him, "What do you mean, you don't understand? The poor fellow was trying to escape because he didn't know the end was so near. What's so hard to understand about that?"

And, with a lump in his throat, that one person makes the hopeless attempt to explain what will forever remain inexplicable to him.

"But that's Jacob Heym," he says. "Don't you understand? It's Jacob Heym! Why was he trying to escape? He must have gone out of his mind. He knew perfectly well that they were coming. He had a radio. . . ."

That, roughly speaking, is what he says; then, shaking his head, he walks with the others out into freedom, and that, roughly speaking, would be my ending.

But, finally, after the invented ending, here is the pallid and depressing, the true and unimaginative ending that makes one inclined to ask the foolish question: What was the point of it all?

Kowalski is irrevocably dead, and for the time being Jacob goes on living, with no thought of foisting Lina upon strangers, does not strip his jacket of the prescribed stars, leaves the pliers in the drawer (assuming he even owns any), consequently does not tempt any sentry at the old vegetable market, on a cold and starry night, to fire shots capable of setting off such a mighty echo. That day, and we know why, he missed going to work; the friend who hanged himself haunts his mind but must by next morning give way to some hard thinking. Jacob could see with his own eyes what the elimination of the radio can lead to; perhaps not in such extreme form in every case but quite possibly in one or two, and for that reason there will be no change regarding the radio. The grieving for Kowalski, whom suddenly he misses more than he ever wanted him around while he was still alive, must be put aside for now. Instead, the little news factory that feeds its man so laboriously starts working, for tomorrow there will be questions again, as there are every day. Like it or not, life drags on.

So next morning Jacob, tight-lipped, walks past Kowalski's building, his eyes fixed firmly on a safe point at the end of the street. Yet, as we know, any attempt to force oneself not to think of something specific is doomed. Jacob sees him lying there exactly as if he were still standing beside him in the room; once again he unties the remains of the rope from the window, pulls up the chair because he doesn't want to sit on the bed, and as if that were not enough, hears the end or the beginning of a conversation.

"In that building there."

"Number 14?"

"No, 16. The corner building."

"And do they know who?"

"Not really. A name like Kaminski or something."

While still some distance from the freight yard, Jacob realizes that something unusual must have happened: the Jews who have arrived for work are crowding around the entrance because the gate is locked. Why they are not being allowed in is at first a mystery to him;

a mystery also why the first man to notice him points in his direction, says something, and the others turn to look at him. Fifty or sixty men have been waiting for Jacob, myself among them: we are watching the only person who can still, we hope, stand between us and disaster as, looking puzzled, he hesitantly approaches us. We make room for him, forming a narrow lane to allow him to walk right up to the gate and read the notice on it, then tell us that things aren't that bad. Beside me, Lawyer Schmidt shifts his weight from one foot to the other, and I hear him muttering, "Get a move on, can't you?" because Jacob is walking with such maddening slowness and looking at people's faces rather than straight ahead.

Punctual for work, Jacob reaches the locked freight yard gate and reads the notice attached to it. That today, at 1300 hours sharp, we are to assemble in the square in front of the military office, ten pounds of luggage per head, all rooms to be left unlocked and in clean condition, anyone still found in his building after the appointed time . . . , the same applies to the bedridden and the infirm. Further details at 1300 hours at the location indicated.

And now try and give them some more comfort, where to find it is your business, make them believe it's all a bad joke, that actually it's going to be a mystery trip with lots of nice surprises; after all, that's the kind of thing they're waiting for behind your back. Not to worry, brothers, is what they want to hear, just forget about that scrap of paper. Anyone who is curious can, if he likes, go to the military office at one o'clock if he has nothing better to do. Either way, nothing can happen because — of course you don't know this yet, stupidly I forgot to tell you — the Russians are waiting around the corner and will take care that not a hair on the head of a single one of you will be harmed.

Jacob stands so long in front of the sign without moving that one would think he is learning the few lines by heart. Why is he standing there so long? we silently wonder and begin to fear the worst. What will his face look like when he shows it to us again, and what will he say? He'll have to say something. I also notice the first few starting to drift quietly away. With dreadful certainty I know they are right, there is nothing more to hope for here, yet I go on hoping and stay rooted to the spot like most of the others.

A waste of time. After an eternity Jacob turns around, presenting us with two vacant eyes, and at that same moment even the stupidest must recognize that the last hope of salvation is gone. Jacob has no time, he tells me, for any private horror at the course of events, this being pushed aside by the horror of the others who are looking at him like bilked creditors, as if he were someone for whom it was now time to redeem the pledges he had so carelessly distributed. Again he stands for a long time without daring to raise his eyes, and they don't make things any easier for him either, by leaving, say. For the ten pounds of luggage to be selected there is still plenty of time, the rest of their lives so to speak. The narrow lane that had opened for Jacob on his way to the gate has closed up behind him; now he is standing in a tight semicircle — to use Jacob's own words, like an entertainer who has forgotten his lines at the crucial moment.

"Don't you have anything better to do than stand there gaping?" asks a sentry on the other side of the fence.

Only now do we notice him standing a few feet from the gate; he alone knows how long he's been there. In any case he won't have heard much, though everything that matters has already been said. We finally move off, why annoy him unnecessarily, and silently go our separate ways. The sentry shakes his head in amusement at these strange creatures. Jacob is almost grateful to him for the unintentional help.

On reaching home Jacob immediately goes up to the attic, expecting to find Lina still in bed, but she is not even in the room, although the weather is by no means ideal, with only a few patches of blue visible in the sky, but Jacob can imagine that his instructions are not taken too seriously. Her bed has been neatly made, the piece of bread has disappeared from the plate on the chest of drawers. Right after he said good-bye to her this morning she must have got up and hurried off to some project or other that he is never told about. Jacob decides to look for her later and first to pack her things, then his own. When that's done, he can still go and find Lina. He wastes no time wondering whether the notice on the gate applies only to those employed at the freight yard or to all inhabitants of the ghetto. For he has no choice but to take Lina with him; leaving her behind would not mean hoping for an uncertain fate for her, that's pretty obvious.

The maximum luggage allowance proves to be fairly generous, the total of her usable belongings amounting to scarcely more than a handful. Jacob stuffs underwear, stockings, and scarf into his pockets. While he is folding her winter dress, Lina shows up, holding what remains of the bread in her fingers. She is very surprised to see Jacob but is immediately aware of his disapproving look, which she has no trouble interpreting: he won't like her having left the attic against his wishes.

"I just went to the pump. I was thirsty," she explains.

"Never mind," says Jacob.

He finishes folding the dress and gives it to her to hold, then looks around and once again opens the cupboard doors to see whether he has forgotten anything.

"Am I going to stay with you again downstairs?" asks Lina.

"Come along," he says.

They go down to his room. On the stairs they meet Horowitz, the neighbor, who has apparently come up from the basement and is lugging a heavy leather suitcase whose locks fail to keep the lid shut.

"What is your opinion about it?" Horowitz asks.

"Have a guess," Jacob replies.

For the first time he knows with certainty that the proclamation on the freight yard gate applies to the whole ghetto; Horowitz's inane question and the suitcase he is carrying mean that the same notice was posted overnight at every factory entrance.

"Did you happen to hear where they are taking us?"

"No," says Jacob.

He hurries into his room with Lina before he can become involved in any lengthy discussions; the only thing he might like to know is what Horowitz, a single man, hopes to gain by that enormous suitcase — his notice can hardly have mentioned four hundred-weight per person.

When the door is closed behind them, Lina confesses that she can't stand Horowitz. She always gives him a wide berth because he invariably has some admonishment ready for her, such as not to hang about, to say good morning nicely, not to act so fresh, to stop making that noise: there's always something he can think up. Once he even shook her by the arm because she had slid down the banister and landed at his feet.

Jacob says, "Well, fancy that."

After taking Lina's things out of his pockets and putting them on the table, he starts packing. But first he has to choose between suitcase and rucksack; there's plenty of room in either one. Because of its handiness the rucksack wins, for on a journey of uncertain length, when one hand must constantly be available for Lina, a suitcase can become a nuisance.

For quite a while Lina patiently hopes that Jacob will volunteer an explanation for his strange actions, but all he says from time to time is, Hand me that, Hold this, and not a word to satisfy her curiosity. So she has to ask: "Why are you packing all those things?"

"Well, why does anyone pack?"

"I don't know," she says, emphasizing her words with an exaggerated shrug, the kind already known to us, pulling her shoulders up to her ears.

"Then think about it."

"To go on a trip?"

"Clever girl."

"We're going on a trip?" Lina cries, and it sounds a bit like, And you're only telling me now?

"That's right, we're going away," Jacob says.

"Where are we going?"

"I don't know exactly."

"Far away or not so far?"

"Quite far away, I think."

"As far as America?"

"No,"

"As far as China?"

"No."

"As far as Africa?"

Knowing from experience that she is capable of keeping up this game for hours, Jacob says, "Yes, about as far as Africa."

She starts skipping around the room, hardly able to grasp her good fortune, and Jacob doesn't try to stop her — after all, the child has never been on a real trip. The hardest part comes when she suddenly gives him a kiss and asks why he isn't glad too.

"Because I don't like traveling," he answers.

"You'll see what fun it will be!"

As he is finishing up with the rucksack, putting two spoons on top, and is about to fasten it, Lina lays her hand on his arm and says, "You've left out the book."

"What book?"

"The one about Africa."

"Oh yes. Where is it?"

"Under my pillow. I'll run and get it for you!"

Lina hurries out of the room, and Jacob can hear her cheery voice in the corridor and up the stairs: "We're going on a trip! We're going on a trip! . . ." From sheer joy, or to annoy grumpy old Horowitz a bit while under Jacob's protection.

Then we are on our way.

It is very cramped and stuffy in the boxcar. The Jews are squatting or sitting on the floor beside their ten pounds, at least thirty of them, I would think. Sleeping at night, if the journey should take that long, will be a problem, for we can't all lie down at the same time; we'll have to do it in shifts. It is dark, too; the few narrow openings right under the roof let in only a meager light, besides being almost permanently occupied. There is hardly any conversation to be heard; most people look as if they had terribly important and serious matters to reflect upon, yet with the noise of the rumbling wheels it would be possible to talk, if one wanted to, without being overheard, despite the close quarters.

I am sitting on a checked pillowcase containing whatever I'd been able to salvage, and I am bored; beside me a very old woman is weeping, quietly, out of consideration for others. Her tears have long since been used up, yet from time to time she sniffs so violently that it would seem whole torrents were being held back. And her husband, with whom she is sitting on their suitcase, looks around apologetically each time, because no doubt he is embarrassed, because he wants to convey that there's nothing he can do about it.

To my left, where I now switch my attention, Jacob has managed to get hold of a spot by one of the narrow openings, but I can truthfully state that this proximity is pure coincidence. I didn't push my way next to him; I don't go as far as some idiots who make out he is partly to blame for this journey, but I can't deny a feeling of unwarranted resentment toward him because everything I built up on the foundations he supplied has collapsed. I didn't push my way next to him; I don't care who I'm next to: it simply happened that way. Looking between Jacob's legs I can see Lina, who so far I have known only from hearsay; she is sitting on the rucksack. Because of Lina I find myself liking him a little more again. Who else, I think, would have taken on the burden of a child, and that, I think, almost outweighs my disappointment.

I would so much like to be friends with her, by winking or making funny faces, the kind of thing one does, but she takes no notice of me whatever. She is looking dreamily at the floor, her mind doubtless occupied by thoughts that are remote from everyone else's, for she occasionally smiles to herself. Or her lips form soundless words, or she grimaces as if suddenly unsure of herself. I enjoy watching her. On the floor I find a little pebble and flick it against her arm. She comes out of her reverie and gazes around to see who it could have been, in every direction except mine. Then she looks up at Jacob, who is beyond all suspicion as he stands motionless at the little opening, his whole attention absorbed by the passing countryside. She taps his leg.

He looks down and asks, "What is it?"

"Do you remember the fairy tale?" asks Lina.

"Which one?"

"About the sick princess?"

"Yes."

"Is it true?"

It is clear from his expression that he finds it strange for her to be thinking of that just now.

"Of course it's true," he says.

"But Siegfried and Rafi wouldn't believe me."

"Maybe you didn't tell it properly?"

"I told it exactly as you did. But they say there's no such thing in the whole world."

"No such thing as what?"

"That a person can get well again by being given a bunch of cotton."

Jacob bends down and lifts her up to the little window. I stand up too: the wheels make quite a racket, and I'd like to hear how it goes on.

"But it's true, isn't it?" says Lina. "The princess wanted a bunch of cotton as big as a pillow? And when she had it she got well again?"

I see Jacob's mouth widen, and he says, "Not exactly. She wished for a cloud. The point is that she thought clouds are made of cotton, and that's why she was satisfied with the cotton."

Lina looks out for a while, surprised, it seems to me, before asking him: "But aren't clouds made of cotton?"

Between their heads I can make out a bit of sky with a few clouds, and I must admit that there really is an amazing resemblance: they do look like tufts of cotton.

"Then what *are* clouds made of?" Lina asks.

But Jacob promises to give her an answer later, probably partly because she is getting too heavy for him. He sets her down on the rucksack again, then resumes watching the landscape slip past.

This, I think, is my moment. I sit down too, move closer to her, and ask whether she would like me to explain what clouds are made of. Of course she would, and I tell her about rivers and lakes, and about the ocean, about the never-ending cycle of water, about that almost incredible process of evaporation, how water flows invisibly into the sky, in tiny droplets, and forms clouds there, which at some point become as heavy and wet as soaking sponges until they lose the drops again as rain. I tell her about steam too, from locomotives for instance, and from chimneys and all the various kinds of fires. She listens attentively but skeptically; I know that the whole lengthy story cannot be covered in one lesson. And I see Jacob casting a friendly eye on me; perhaps that lesson is responsible for his singling me out, a few days later, to tell me an even crazier story. For there is nothing from my appearance to show that I would be one of the few to survive.

When my knowledge about the formation and composition of clouds is exhausted, I tell Lina not to be shy about asking if there is anything she hasn't understood. But she makes no use of this offer; with her chin cupped in her hands, she takes her time thinking through the whole matter again. After all, she has to come to terms with a very significant mistake: clouds are not made of cotton.

"You don't know what you're letting yourself in for," Jacob whispers in my ear.

"Why?"

"Because you have no idea the kind of questions this child can ask."

I look at her and say, "I'll manage all right."

His eyes tell me, Just wait and see. Then he asks me whether I would like to look out of the opening for a bit.

"Thanks, I would," I say.

I stand up expectantly and look out until darkness falls. I see villages and fields, once even a little town in the distance; at a half-overgrown pond I see a group of soldiers resting among lorries, cannon, and cows. And I see a few sleepy stations with platforms and barriers and railway men's cottages with green window boxes over-flowing with flowers, and I wonder whether these are regulation window boxes because they are attached to each cottage and each one is green. And I see people whose faces I can't make out watching our train pass, but above all I see trees, which I had almost forgotten although I'm still a young fellow, vast numbers of trees. Beeches and alders and birches and willows and pines — my God, look at all those trees, there's no end to them. A tree was responsible for my not becoming a violinist, and under a tree I became a real man: the wild boar came too late to prevent it. And at an unknown tree my wife Hannah was lost to me, and an ordinance tried to deprive me of trees for all time. Some say that trees addle my mind, I go on standing there, and to this day I like sometimes to take a ride on a train passing through a thickly wooded area, best of all a mixed forest. Till I hear Jacob's voice: "Aren't you ever going to get some sleep?"

"Let me stand here a little longer," I say.

"But there's nothing more for you to see," I hear him say.

"Yes, there is."

For I can still see the shadows of trees, and I can't sleep. We are heading for wherever we are heading.

PLUME  **MERIDIAN**

A LOOK AT MODERN HISTORY

☐ **TREBLINKA by Jean-Francois Steiner. With a Preface by Simone de Beauvoir and an Introduction by Terrence Des Pres.** This is the inspiring story of the 600 Jews who revolted against their murders and burned a Nazi death camp to the ground. "*Treblinka* shatters pessimism about human dignity . . . a book that restores our faith in the human spirit."—*Los Angeles Times*
(011248—$13.95)

☐ **DENYING THE HOLOCAUST *The Growing Assault on Truth and Memory.* by Deborah Lipstadt.** This first full-scale history of Holocaust denial shows how—despite tens of thousands of living witnesses and vast amounts of documentary evidence—this irrational idea not only has continued to gain adherents but has become an international movement, with organized chapters, "independent" research centers, and official publications that promote a "revisionist" view of recent history. "Important and impassioned."—*New York Times Book Review*
(272742—$10.95)

☐ **SCHINDLER'S LEGACY *True Stories of the List Survivors.* by Elinor J. Brecher. Foreword by Thomas Keneally, author of *Schindler's List*.** Through the words of the real people whom Oskar Schindler saved and more than 100 personal photographs, we learn the truth of their experiences with Schindler, their incredible day-to-day survival, and their ultimate triumph of rebuilding lives, reclaiming family, and recording their memories for future generations.
(Hardcover 939415—$27.50)
(Paperback 273536—$14.95)

☐ **PASSION AND POLITICS *The Turbulent World of the Arabs.* by Sandra Mackey. With a new Epilogue analyzing the Israeli-PLO accord.** In this knowledgeable portrait, a highly regarded authority explores the history, the cultures, and the personalities behind one of the world's most misunderstood regions. This book makes sense of the often puzzling turbulence of Arab affairs and actions.
(270367—$13.95)

Prices slightly higher in Canada.

Visa and Mastercard holders can order Plume, Meridian, and Dutton books by calling
1-800-253-6476.
They are also available at your local bookstore. Allow 4-6 weeks for delivery.
This offer is subject to change without notice.

PLUME　　　　　　　　　　　　　　　　　 **DUTTON**

ACCLAIMED FICTION

☐ **WOMAN OF THE INNER SEA by Thomas Keneally.** "A delicious coupling of thriller and character study and a remarkable heroine . . . Intense, luminous prose remains ferociously bold, ever roaming into new territory."—*New York Newsday* (271770—$10.95)

☐ **THE CERTIFICATE by Isaac Bashevis Singer Winner of the Nobel Prize for Literature.** In 1922, young David Bendiger, an aspiring writer with neither money nor prospects of success, comes to Warsaw. His only hope is to emigrate to Palestine . . . His only way to obtain the certificate is to marry a woman who will pay all expenses. This necessity plunges him into a sensual, ethical, moral and intellectual maelstrom mingled with comedy and tragedy, absurdity and profundity. (270928—$10.95)

☐ **MESHUGAH by Isaac Bashevis Singer. Winner of the Nobel Prize for Literature.** The time is the early 1950s. The place is New York's Upper West Side. Aaron Greidinger is a Jewish refugee from Poland, scratching out a living as a writer for the Yiddish press and as a radio personality dispensing once-a-week advice. Then, a ghost from his Warsaw past comes into his life. "A contemporary story of love and betrayal with Holocaust overtones . . . a rich, complex tale in the great Singer tradition."—*Newark Star-Ledger* (273846—$10.95)

Prices slightly higher in Canada.

Visa and Mastercard holders can order Plume, Meridian, and Dutton books by calling
1-800-253-6476.
They are also available at your local bookstore. Allow 4-6 weeks for delivery.
This offer is subject to change without notice.

PLF1